THE
UNION
MANIFESTO

BY DAN ESIEKPE

Order this book online at www.trafford.com/07-1531
or email orders@trafford.com

Most Trafford titles are also available at major online book retailers.

Note for Librarians: A cataloguing record for this book is available from Library
and Archives Canada at www.collectionscanada.ca/amicus/index-e.html

Printed in Victoria, BC, Canada.

ISBN: 978-1-4251-3831-8 (sc)
ISBN: 978-1-4251-3832-5 (e)

*We at Trafford believe that it is the responsibility of us all, as both individuals
and corporations, to make choices that are environmentally and socially sound.
You, in turn, are supporting this responsible conduct each time you purchase a
Trafford book, or make use of our publishing services. To find out how you are
helping, please visit www.trafford.com/responsiblepublishing.html*

*Our mission is to efficiently provide the world's finest, most comprehensive
book publishing service, enabling every author to experience success.
To find out how to publish your book, your way, and have it available
worldwide, visit us online at www.trafford.com/10510*

Trafford rev. 6/26/2009

Trafford PUBLISHING www.trafford.com

North America & international
phone: +44 (0)1865 487 395 ♦ local rate: 0845 230 9601
facsimile: +44 (0)1865 481 507 ♦ email: info.uk@trafford.com

The United Kingdom & Europe
phone: +44 (0)1865 487 395 ♦ local rate: 0845 230 9601
facsimile: +44 (0)1865 481 507 ♦ email: info.uk@trafford.com

10 9 8 7 6 5 4 3

To Brother John... for rising up to the challenge...
to "father" us all... when the old man's head rested
on the bosom of earth – so prematurely!

..And to Bridget....for providing the "pillow" and the
"ripening breast" whose "every rise and fall"
made the difference.

Cover Design by Ovie Esiekpe
&
Onori Esiekpe

Chapter 1

THE EVENT WAS billed for nine o'clock, that morning. But the crowd started pouring in as early as 5.00 a.m. By seven o'clock, the sea of heads present at the Bar-Beach in Lagos was indicative of the topicality of the execution.

Yellow painted taxis with black stripes on the sides were making brisk business dropping spectators. They came from afar – from Ojota, Agege and other shanties on the outskirts of Lagos. Others came from the satellite towns of Epe, Ajegunle, Egbeda and of course from nearby Ikoyi and Maroko.

Presently, a white air-conditioned Mercedes-Benz saloon pulled unto the Kerb by the large,expectant crowd. A plump man with a snow-white, beautifully tailored safari suit peered out through the tinted glasses.

Apparently in recognition, a section of the motley crowd roared. The driver of the Benz with a well-starched khaki suit and a very pronounced moustache stepped out, came round and opened the back door with a bow. The plump man at the back stepped out gingerly. A section of the crowd roared again in recognition. The plump man quickened the applause with a wave of the hand as he mingled with the incongruous crowd. The driver followed at a respectable distance with dark sunglasses.

The Atlantic Ocean was particularly violent this Saturday morning. Rumbling and ferocious recurring waves hit the beach with alarming strength. The scene was awesome and at the same time beautiful to witness. Some spectators were momentarily embroiled with the beauty and spectacle of the giant waves. Some were seeing the Bar-Beach for the very first time. Some were even coming to Lagos Island for the first time!

It made no difference. They were there for a more spectacular event greater than the concrete jungle and traffic bottlenecks which to them were the only features Lagos Island could boast of.

The crowd was swelling every other minute now. Ramshackle buses usually based on the Mushin-Ebutte-Ero and the Yaba-Igboshere routes were trying their best at conveying the overflowing spectators.

All over the town, the crowd was surging towards one direction – The Bar-Beach. At the Yaba bus terminus, the crowd was instantly thrown into a frenzy as a bus pulled up. The conductor was thrown aside as the battle to gain entry into the bus assumed an alarming proportion. They were all there. Young,office girls with trendy gowns. Pot-bellied old men with white flowing robes. Dashing students with beautifully labelled jeans trousers. On one jeans pocket was a sticker, which read: "Take Your Time". But nobody was taking his time that morning. A plump woman tried to elbow her way into the bus with her five-year old son. She was earlier heard boasting that she must let her son see the "Saturday Show" on the Bar-Beach.

The CMS bus stop on the Marina was packed full. Most of the passengers there had taken buses from other areas. From Ketu, Egbe, Ikorodu, Igbobi – all of them en-route the spectacle at the Bar-Beach. Those who couldn't wait any longer could be seen trekking to the venue in clusters.

There were also very many ships waiting on the Atlantic that morning. Just before dawn, the skipper of one of the ships, the "MV Kokori" received a note from his look out man. The note was precise: "Tumultuous and incomprehensible crowd on the portside beach"

The skipper thereafter radioed other ships to find out what was amiss. The "River Ogidigbo" which had been on Nigeria's territorial waters for over two months, waiting for berthing space and whose skipper happened to be well-informed on current happenings in the country explained the situation.

By dawn, all the mariners were on the deck, armed with binoculars to feed their eyes on the happenings on the beach. On the other side of the road, opposite the beach, most of the tall buildings had their windows open. Many of the employees in the buildings were also watching the whole proceedings on the beach through their binoculars.

Petched on one of these buildings, a team of radio commentators was running live commentaries on the situation at the beach. Their Outside Broadcast van, relayed all the audio signals via its microwave link to the transmitters at the station and from there unto the millions of listeners all over the country.

The Black Maria pulled to a halt in front of the roaring crowd at the Bar-Beach. There was a brisk surge as the crowd pressed around it.

"Alhaji" peered through the slits at the world outside of the Black Maria, then turned back. "Easy Tobacco", a dark, squirrel-faced convict, shrank back in his seat and pulled his beret over his face.

"It's a big crowd", he half muttered.

"Well, 'Easy Boy'. So this is the last stop ... see you over there".

A flying squad of soldiers cleared the area around the Black Maria. The army officer in charge of the operation surveyed the busy scene and bellowed to the military escort.

"Okay, let's go boys".

"Easy Tobacco" got out first, followed by "Alhaji" and long-faced "Bob-knockout" who missed a step and slid down unto the sandy beach. They were held back and made to stand by the Black Maria for a moment whilst the security detail cleared the way.

Then, the officer bellowed again ... and like sacrificial lambs meant for slaughter – they started walking, without rhythm towards the stakes prepared for them.

A roar of recognition came from the mammoth crowd. The law people closed in around the criminals as they started to move through the mass. Photographers and reporters were yelling questions at them – but they kept moving on.

"This way", the officer yelled, pointing to the stakes as he led them up the steps. " Alhaji" looked at, without seeing the crowd. He was filled with fright and sweat. The smile disappeared from "Black Tobacco's" face. The law people smiled at each other as they secured the convicts to the stakes.

The Firing Squad marched in from nowhere. This was an elite squad, from an elite corps, these soldiers.

"One-two, one-two, left-right, left-right,,,,,"

These were members of a Section of Charlie Company of the elite 7th Amphibious Battalion.

"Left-Right, left-right ... "

Wearing sun-tanned camouflage uniforms, they all wore special jump boots and black berets. On their armband, a frightful insignia showing a crocodile in flight - the special arm insignia of the elite 7th amphibious battalion -was displayed.

The mere sight of this insignia had sent shivers into all enemies of the fatherland in the past. Repeatedly, members of this elite corps had shown their true worth in valour for the fatherland.

The much decorated bunch of fighting machines saved the 21 Marine Commandos from total annihilation, by cutting off the Biafran bridgehead at Ihuo during the Nigerian civil war. Later, they made an amphibious landing on Bonny Island and the Port-Harcourt refinery and successfully held their ground until they were linked and relieved by the infantry boys who moved in through Bori and Ebubu, thereby saving the precious refinery from destruction.

Mid-way in the Nigerian civil war, the 44th brigade of the Nigerian Army was trapped in a massive tactical encirclement in Owerri, Obako, Obinze and the strategic Umu-Uvo on the Imo River. For three months, irregular supplies of food and ammunition came through airdrops – most of them falling into enemy hands.

In the early hours of the 20th of November, the 7th Battalion made a drop on Eziama, a few kilometres from strategically placed junction town of Okpuala. This was a diversionary move to weaken the Biafran defence perimeter and cut off supplies from Aba. The next day other elements of the Battalion seized Obaku, thereby cutting off the Biafran troops from Oguta.

The encircled Federal brigade then made a break -out at the weakest point on the perimeter through Emuakpu and on to Elele and Port Harcourt.

"One-two, one-two, left-right, left-right ..."

After their last successful strikes behind enemy lines in which they blew up airports and fuel dumps and successfully disorganised a garrison at Amufu, the 7th Battalion had been lying low, undergoing specialised training at Ogogoro Village, near Lagos.

The Section marched with steeled muscles and glaring pride towards the stakes

"Left-right, Left-right ... "

With blazing insignias, sun tanned uniforms and harsh unsmiling eyes. Four magazine pouches were tied along with the belt round their waists. There were also water and mess cans and a dungaree knapsack. The A.K.47 assault rifle was held in regulation manner as they marched briskly towards the stakes.

"Left-right, Left...right ... squad – Halt!"

And the squad stopped and banged their feet in unison. The crowd stared in awe and roared in admiration. The convicts shivered. The squad knelt down to firing positions without emotions. These were no weak-hearted soldiers. These were members of the spearhead of the elite 7th Amphibious Battalion.

⌯

Two more orders were barked at high pitch at the squad. Three minutes later, "Alhaji" was no more... "The Knockout" was knocked out by one volley and "Easy Tobacco" didn't live to smoke trouble again.

The crowd milled out noisily. Writing about the executions the next day, a leader writer in the Daily Times said the execution, the first of its kind in Lagos "was a spectacle witnessed by a myriad of heads and colours, all with one common purpose-to be entertained. But the very

9

fact that there were so many people with the same purpose at the execution was not accidental" he argued

He continued his argument "that the crowd came together because of a common object of attention, a common desire and united by witnessing a common event and one expression of a common mood" .

The Leader Writer continued.."The assembly had been tailored into the whims and values of the crowd. The fact of presence in the execution crowd was purposeful, not accidental and particular behaviour shown on that occasion as a member of the crowd emerged out of mutual stimulation......

They say birds of the same feathers flock together. But it was also true that when birds flock together, they become of the same feather" he wrote. "Hence" according to the article "you will find in the execution crowd, the top bureaucrat, who had with one stroke of his pen amassed thousands, the diabolical ritualist, who even was at the execution to look for human blood to make his concotions and the deft and agile fingered hood who even with the massive security around was busy at his trade filching precious pounds from pockets!". These conclusions were considered rash and by many readers of the Daily Times.

The crowd at the execution milled out. Some of them cursed ... "Why did they get themselves caught?" ... Others who were better at defensive projection shouted "good riddance". Yet some too were quiet and extremely sober as they all milled out of the Bar Beach.

One of those was the man in the white suit who came in the super air-conditioned Mercedes-Benz. "Did you see Alhaji?" he whispered to his driver as they entered the vehicle.

"Yes. Too bad ... saw how he sobbed like a kid".

"Well, Joe, it was no time to play the brave section leader .you should know that!".

"It's true. Really bad show"

"That's a very careless way to talk Joe ... and you should know that".

"But boss, they are gone, I mean dead".

"Yes, I know, but they were not of us. They were not in The Union and they had to be taken out..for our own good".

"Does it matter, boss"

"It matters very much. Let's go ... see the chief".

"Alright sir" and Joe sped off, cutting off Victoria Island, unto Onikan and into the heart of Lagos.

The white Mercedes Benz meandered through the busy traffic along the new bridge which linked Victoria Island with Awolowo Road. It came out near the National Museum, through the Tafawa Balewa Square and forked into Brown Street. The vehicle veered unto a side street and came to a halt by a five-storey building.

∞

A rotund security man clad in starched khaki and a fire-service face cap stepped forward and opened the back door.

The man with the white suit at the back of the car stepped out smartly;and walked into the headquarters of Tissio-a nationwide chain of supermarkets and general merchandise.

"The chief is waiting for you upstairs" the security man whispered.

"That's alright. Thank you Tunde"

It is not well known how the Tissio supermarket chain came to be. But many years ago, there were whispers in top Union circles that the venture was worthwhile. And so very early one morning, bull-dozers moved into the site of the present headquarters, which before then was occupied by small union kiosks serving as links in its long chain of operations.

The construction company – UNIKONTRAKT – was of course union- owned. It worked day and night for six months to complete the building.

Next, announcements were made for the Initial Public Offer of the Tissio shares to the public. The shares were all fully subscribed by firms and persons representing Union interests. And Tissio was legally born.

The man in the white suit stepped unto the first floor of the Tissio Supermarket. He looked through the newspaper and magazine stand

and bought a popular edition.

Next he took a lift to the fourth floor. There,he took a service stair-case linking the fourth and fifth floors – strictly reserved for top execu-tives of the Tissio chain.

Mid-way to the first rung he was stopped by a polite looking girl.

"Yes ... can I help you sir"?

"Yes ... you can ... I'm going upstairs ... you know the way around"?

"I think what you need is the lift. It will take you up in no time".

"No. I think what I need is a good stroll up on the stairway.

"O-ho. Then you need a guide so you don't miss your way in our maze of steps".

"Roy ... Roy", she beckoned to a man in service uniform. "Take him up".

As they left she punched one electronic button three times. They marched up in silence without rhythm. The stairway led them to a cen-tral lobby and the adjoining offices were shut off from the rest of the supermarket by a thick,glass wall which had been serving a privacy pur-pose since the store was opened.

Roy led him to one of the doors. He pushed it open and beckoned to someone inside.

"He wants to see The Chief"

"Who ... him"?

"Yes. He is expecting him".

"Okay".

The Chief was busy writing when he entered. It was a big office, with ankle deep rugging and an array of telephones. It was not the presence of the telephones – some of which he knew were microphones for hid-den tape recorders – that made him feel jittery. He always had that feeling when he faced The Chief. Something triggered off a mechanism which in turn triggered off a feeling of constipation and an urgent need to pass urine and stool simultaneously. There was always that wide gap. The Chief, high up on the table there with his imperial telephones and him down on the sofa trying to relax, but not feeling easy.

"Sit down Rocky" he ordered as he looked up momentarily.

"Thank you Chief".

"Now, how did it go"?

"Smooth. Alhaji didn't even know what hit him"

"What about "Bob Knockout", I hear his boys tried to make trouble"?

"Not that I know of... but we can always take care of them".

"Yes I know. Really I got some things for you to do. You see these small timers are spoiling business for us. I want a complete strike at all of them. Shake them up. I am tired of having them mess up things and make the law people inquisitive"

""When should this be"?

"Any time from now. Tell the boys to be on the ready. I'll want a complete knockout for Ajala and his mob, The Mushin Giants and the Shakaras of Ketu. And I'll also want you to carry out that job... I mean that outstanding one we talked about. I've talked to our brothers there. They are expecting experts from here".

"Okay chief".

"Rocky" earned his nickname the hard way. Once in Shagamu when he was a pools agent and operating a hemp peddling chain for the Union, he was arrested by the local police with ten wraps of hemp in his pocket. Before they knew it, he snatched the wraps and swallowed them in one quick move.

He was taken into custody and tortured with fire and judo chaps on his neck. They played tricks with his genitals. But Rocky refused to name the source of his supply. In no time, the legend of Rocky was born. And in no time too, the name Rocky obliterated his real name – Adams Yemoja.

Soon after this, he became a trusted member of the Union and rose rapidly through the ranks. On Christmas day, he was given his first independent assignment – to kill a man who had done wrong to the Union. He did not know the victim but he heard the man was secretly having an affair with the wife of a Union chief. The next man to him in the Union hierarchy relayed the order. He was also briefed – the man was a business man with chains of taxi cabs. Every day at an appointed time, he picked the woman from her stall at Oyingbo market and spent the spare time relaxing in a nearby bar regularly.

Rocky began hanging out around the bar near the market and eventually struck up an acquaintance with the businessman. He was called Papa Dele. Rocky would drop in regularly for drinks and make small conversation with Papa Dele.

On the day Papa Dele was hit, Rocky feigned a punctured tyre and pleaded with Papa Dele to drop him off by a vulcaniser. They moved right into the timber area by the lagoon and packed. Papa Dele went for the flat tire in the boot. He felt a sharp pain in his heart and that was all.

Next morning, the car was found on the expressway with the body wrapped in the boot. And that was the end of Victor Salako, alias Papa Dele.

There were other killings. And then came the political days in which he found better use for his ways and experience. The name Rocky struck fire into political opponents then as victim after victim fell.

There was that politician who was gunning for the Governorship of the North. He had attended a congress in Kaduna when Rocky got the contract. For two days he stalked him until he finally scratched him and his Mercedes-Benz saloon from the face of the earth on the Zaria-Gusau road.

There was also that head- on collision in which Rocky reduced the occupants of a Range Rover to smithereens. For that job, he used a thirty-ton trailer raided from the state ministry of works in Benin.

Rocky had one motto, which had seen him through so many assignments in business. And of course he considered all he did for the Union as business. Nothing more.

"Chief, we'll need things" he said as he got up to go out.

"What and what ... just tell me anything you want".

"Well, logistics ... and we are going down on ammo ..and money".

"O-ho that. You'll see me next week after what we talked about ... yes that reminds me of this man in Onitsha you must see ... next week right ..."?

As he moved out, he could feel the sharp glare of The Chief on his back. Terrible. Why he always felt that way in his presence he couldn't understand. Who knows, he thought, probably The Chief felt like that before him too. Just normal tension between warriors.

Chapter 2

AJANI DAVID

THE CHIEF WAS born and bred in Ajegunle. Not the peaceful Ajegunle of latter years. But the Ajegunle of "Captain Blood", "Captain Dope", "Mighty Dagger". The Ajegunle of "Bola Kaballa" and "Ajani-Koko, The Bloody" – where you needed more than nine lives to survive. It was the Ajegunle where one more corpse at the Boundary bus stop raised no eyebrows.

That was where The Chief grew up and perfected his trade. First as an errand boy for the Captain Blood mob, later as a Danfo conductor, but from the beginning,always a killer.

When he was ten, he stopped school. And to be fair to David Ajani - for that was his real name – his education was stopped by his parents for lack of funds.

It was a time when there were no standard measure for land in Ajegunle. Chief Nanka, Benson Okome and Adidi Okoloba who were the best known land dealers in Ajegunle of those times were not even indigenes. They were not even Yoruba. But it was the simple law of the place: Might is Right. And even justice was then handed down by strong non-natives sitting in customary courts with the gangland customs and traditions of Ajegunle as the abiding laws.

To put some drama into land purchase of those days, the prospective buyer was just made to finish a bottle of locally brewed dry gin, also variously called "Ogogoro","Sapele-Water", "Skian", "Akpavin" etc in Ajegunle.

Then, in that tipsy state, the buyer was taken to the piece of land for sale and asked to throw the empty bottle. Wherever the bottle landed from the point of throw, was what your money was worth. Thus the stronger willed and more resolute drinkers and more physically fit, who could throw the bottle farther gained, according to the laws of Ajegunle.

It was in one of such gangland transactions that David Ajani lost his educational ticket. His father after taking one full bottle of "Ogogoro" was in no state to throw anything. Little David, who saw it all cried and cried for pardon and the refund of his father's then twenty pounds. One of the men cuddled him and teased him: "Grow up strong … you hear me? Don't you grow up like your father … I know you are listening … grow up big – because the world is not for weaklings like your father … C'mon boy … put a smile on your face … I know you'll grow up strong … I see it in your eyes".

And that was how his father lost a fortune saved over a period of ten years working at the Apapa wharf. And that was how an end was put to David's educational pursuit.

Initially, he could not bear the jeers from the neighbourhood children. Every morning as they went to school, they made it a point to call on David to laugh at him for dropping out of school.

But young David was resilient. His attachment to the Captain Blood Mob had given him a new source of pride and a completely new set of values. One afternoon, when the neighbourhood children had returned from school, he called three of them for a football game.

They played a little game and he lured them with a chewing gum into a classroom. Once inside, he picked on the biggest boy and gave him a thorough thrashing. Next, he picked on the other two and laid them flat on the floor. And using newly learnt slangs from the mob he warned:

"Look here ... Lemme warn you guys. Leave me alone, and let me be... Lemme live my life the way I wan it right? And you listen... after today, I aint warning again ... I kill. Heard that?"

Then he brought out a knife and shoved them into an adjoining store-room. He brought out a key and locked them up in the store.

They were almost dead when they were found the next morning.

From then on, David Ajani became a legend. And the teasing stopped.

The primary school near Mba Street was a co-educational one. And while there David Ajani made his mark in many things which made older girls fall for him. He was in primary four when he met Dupe. After school, Dupe would keep him behind to teach him things. And she would make him do some things to her. She would then lie down and enjoy it all. But funny, David didn't even know what it was all about then.

Now David was a bus conductor and Dupe still had a soft spot for him. By now she was a professional prostitute and lived in a famous brothel. But she just liked keeping David as a regular. So everyday David went there after work to do things – but this time he knew what he was doing.

It was one night after a heavy down-pour that he started showing his trait. Dupe had warned that he should always come late when she must have finished her normal tour of business and made some money. So, this night David came late, close to one o'clock and knocked. There was no reply. He knocked again.

Dupe came out followed by a fat man who gnarled at David.

"What's this small thing looking for? He wants you too?

David remained silent. "Come, you had better answer me or I'll give you the thrashing of your life".

"Okay, you asked for it. If you know what's good for you, you'll put on your clothes now and gerrout...Did you hear me? Gerrout. This is my house and I want to sleep".

The fat man went in and came out dressed. "Okay, let me see you off. I'll be back soon Dupe".

That was the last anybody ever saw the fat man alive. They found his body at the Okoya intersection the next morning.

The next night, Dupe shouted about it. How he heard the story in the market and confirmed it. How she knew from the beginning that David was a bad boy. How the fat man was her money bag and how she didn't want to see David again. She shouted and raved that night. But that was all. She did not live to shout again. Her body was also found at the Okoya intersection the next morning.

There was no rain that night. And for once in several weeks Abeokuta was moon-lit. There were only patches of darkness around shrubs and clusters of impending storms.

It was the month of July and it had rained cats and dogs continually for many weeks. But this did not disturb the training programme of the boys at the edge of the town.

From a small detachment of the Army school of electrical and mechanical engineering, the Abeokuta Depot had grown to be a full fledged military training school and other special corps during the civil war. And as the Biafrian resistance increased, more and more young men were drafted and moulded into skilled soldiers from this Depot.

The initial glamour of wearing the respected uniform of the Army had lured many recruits into the Abeokuta depot. But with the beginning of training, the stark realities of military life gradually began to dawn on them.

Normally, life at the Abeokuta Depot started with a military wake-up call at four- thirty in the morning This was followed by hurried orders to "fall in". Next came roll calls and regrouping into squads. Physical training then started immediately at 5 a.m..

But abnormally, life at the depot started with the arrival of RSM "Abori" at the sleeping quarters of the recruits at 3 am. He would order everybody up and at attention and to remain "as you waya" until five thirty when it was the official rising time.

And it would be a very sad day indeed for any recruit to make the mistake of "attempting to fall asleep" or "almost dozing" while RSM Abori was around.

From the very first day, he made it clear to the recruits that the day they enlisted into the army, they lost their rights as citizens of Nigeria. And that henceforth, their bodies and their lives were now properties of the Nigerian Army.

Pointing randomly at their shaven heads on the parade ground, he would bark at them.

"You idiots, you see your skinny heads ?... we call such heads "Abori" here in this depot ... Your "aboris" are symbols of your enslavement to the government ... Quiet there ... stop rubbing your body ... Attention you bloody recruits", he would bark out,in drunken frenzy. "Stand erect with your legs ... they are all government legs ...Look straight ...with your government eyes..you lazy idiots!! ".

It was widely rumoured in the camp that RSM "Abori" never slept in the night. And that every night, he would go to a popular liquor and whore house to get drunk. He would drink through the night; and at ten minutes to three he would leave straight from the bar to wake up his recruits.

The actual torture and death started for the recruits during the period for Physical Training exercises.

"Abori" had earlier warned them that the Abeokuta depot was a filter ... A depot where the army gradually and systematically eliminated materials unfit for military life. For this purpose, he said, the Army allowed for a twenty per cent casualty in every batch of recruits trained at the depot. Death in such cases could come from "unnecessary signs of fatigue", "Lack of physical stamina", "Lack of moral fibre,""accidental discharge" and "Cowardice in simulated enemy situations".

"Aboris'" maxim was that the best thing you can do for a dying soldier was to quicken his death by finishing him off. Thus any recruit who showed "unnecessary signs of fatigue" during cross-country and

Endurance walks was finished off on the spot. For this purpose "Abori" had a heavy iron rod with which he delivered killer blows to the skull.

Any signs of "Lack of moral fibre" during obstacle crossing, "Cowardly comportment" during military drills and "Lack of physical stamina" during field trainings also met similar fates.

Through this elimination process, four hundred recruits brought into the depot in early July were gradually brought down to three hundred and seventy – two weeks later. By the third week seven more were killed through the same way. It became a frantic struggle to live as the death toll continued to rise every other day.

David Ajani was still alive largely because of his criminal nature and his uncanny street wisdom. He had since lost his exaggerated vision of glory and splendour of army life ever since he set foot on the Abeokuta Training Depot. Not that he cared. He had remained alive because he had learnt most of Abori's requirements informally before in his criminal background. But his uncanny mind told him the elimination would soon catch up with him. And he cared. Ajani was angered by the fact that he had to die defenceless. That he should be clobbered in the head, rushed to the hospital, declared dead and a phoney death certificate showing fatigue as being cause of death issued to cover up the criminal acts of people like Abori. He thought about it throughout the day.

Ajani had a refreshing sleep and woke up at half past one that morning. He tip-toed and put on a short and a black shirt he had secured in the afternoon for the purpose he had in mind.

Next he slipped out, through an open window near his double decker bed. The air outside was cool and refreshing. He went down and crawled towards the perimeter of the camp, not by a straight approach, but by a long detour, which avoided the first set of sentries on guard. The sentries had recently been doubled because of the high rate of desertion, which had plagued the camp. Construction work was also going on to install 360 degrees – five-second sweep floodlights, mounted on observation post tripods at the perimeters of the camp. When commissioned, the camp would be desertion proof. And any attempted deserter caught near the perimeter would be shot at sight.

But there were no flood lights that night. Although the camp was moon-lit, Ajani successfully crawled and avoided the guards and slipped out through the barbed wires. Once outside, he moved with speed. Five minutes later, he was scanning the area surrounding the liquor and whorehouse. He looked further down, near a line of hibiscus flowers and saw the army Land Rover he was looking for.

He crept towards it stealthily. He looked round again for personal guards. There were none. He knew there would be no guards. The maniac called Abori didn't even have a batman. Carefully he got up, opened the bonnet and destroyed the distributor cap of the land rover. It was then five minutes past two O'clock. Ajani moved back into the shrubs to wait.

Forty minutes later, RSM Abori staggered drunkenly into the Land Rover. He gave the ignition starter a kick and there was only a dry cough and a dying moan from the Land-Rover engine. He kicked again and again. No way. He staggered down and opened the bonnet. It was then he started feeling a tightening pressure on his throat. He was too drunk to even attempt a fight back as he was violently strangled to death. All he muttered was a slow agonising moan as he slumped unto the waiting cold and stony earth near his Land Rover.

And there was peace and fewer deaths in the training depot thereafter.

"One-two, One-two, left-right, left-right". It was the Armed Forces Medical Services sergeant, marching off a detachment of wounded to see the Medical Officer.

All over the civil war battle front, the casualty rate was appalling. And the deaths and style of death formed a grotesque kaleidoscope on the vast rain forest vegetation.

Some died peacefully as if in deep sleep with a bullet through their hearts. Others were blown to smitherens by land mines and their limbs were only vaguely discernible.

Some others had their heads completely chopped off by mortar attacks and close range bazooka hits. The style of death presented amazing variations, with buttocks chopped off, pelvic regions blown off,
intestines and bowels emptied, limbs screwed off and others burnt all
over.

Some had their hands stretched upwards in apparent submission to
the death they saw coming to them. Others had their eyes closed in apparent relaxation. Yet others too, were wide-eyed, horror stricken, with
limbs doubly stretched, with mouths wide open in snarling grimes and
gritting teeth. They were all there. Short, tall, fat, slim, black, fair – all
of them with mutilated bodies and uniforms. All of them cold and resting on the cold earth, never to rise again.

This was the pathetic picture on the whole of the extended line formation, which marked the primary wall of defence of the 503 infantry
brigade. The extended line, which ran from Alakire, through Ilugbo,
Awka to Udi. There was an advanced Observation Post supported by
a motorised Recce unit of the 22 Tank battalion at Awgu. There were
also spearheads headed for Ekuku, Obubra and Abakaliki.

A secondary wall of defence began at Obudu. It ran through Ogoja,
Obolo Eke, Obolo-Afor and Neneh.

The Biafran attack in December took the primary extended line by
surprise. With the newly captured Nigerian tank "Corporal Nwafor",
blazing the trail and supported by air and long range artillery manned
by Nigerian Army veterans now embedded with the Biafrans, the attack threw the Nigerian defence line out of gear.

For the first time in a very long while, the Biafrans had the initiative
and were throwing everything into the attack. When the attack was finally halted at Ilugbo, the field of battle was a massive heap of decaying
flesh and limbs. The stench and the mass of twisted limbs when viewed
against the horrifying death of men and the serenity of the natural vegetation amounted to an amazing natural contradiction.

The survivors could hardly take in the scene. Some retched at the
sight and others could not recover from the battle shocks. Temperatures
and blood pressures ran abnormally high. All had fevers.

There were others who had bullet injuries but refused to die. Some had dangling limbs sawn off by stacatto bursts from the enemy mortar fire. Others were incredibly alive after bullets had missed very crucial organs. Ajani was one of them.

All of them were now marched to see the M.O. at the medical centre.

Left-right, Left-right, One-two, One-two ... squad – halt.

The medical centre was an old Unimog lorry. This was made available to the Armed Forces Medical Services by the Rural Health and Basic Medical Services Department of the Federal Ministry of Health at the outbreak of the war.

The vehicle was parked near a shrub at the edge of the Operational Headquarters. Nearby stood an old Bedford lorry which served as the medical store and pharmacy. Behind the old Bedford, the West African rain forest vegetation ran in thick undergrowths and trees which sloped towards the rear of the Federal extended line formation. Underneath this massive jungle ran numerous foot- paths and a dusty, snaking laterite road, which served as the supply line.

At strategic points all over the camp, well dressed and polished rear guard troops watched, armed with AK47 assault rifles.

The door of the medical centre creaked open and a stout firm figure in dark sun glasses came out and surveyed the wounded. He held tightly to his strong moustache as the medical orderly saluted smartly.

"Captain" Simon Adamu was fifty-one and still waxing strong. His official rank was Warrant Officer Grade One at Army Headquarters. But he preferred to be called "Captain" and usually demanded all entitlements and respect due to a Captain in the Army as a result of an unconfirmed field promotion in the war front. He had a capacity to impute to himself what he was not, which was incredible. He also had an unlimited capacity for callousness, hatred and vicious retribution and vengeance.

As a medical man, he believed he was a trained doctor – which he was not. And as a soldier he believed he was the army's best field tactician and commander. Adamu had been a lance corporal in the Second

World War, when he served as a kitchen help and a back-up man to a British machine gunner. When the Second World War broke out, Adamu was a gate man to the River Valley Tin Corporation in Bukuru, near Jos.

At the outbreak of the war, he packed his bags and enlisted in the West African Frontier Force which was later merged with British, Indian and New Zealand elements and tagged "Small Army". That war saw Africans in combat alongside whites for the first time. It depicted the height of colourless and inter racial co-existence, which had formed popular topics of debates of that time. African soldiers saw battle in Burma and the swamps of Indo-China. This marked the heroic and gallant struggle of Africans to seize Japanese held grounds in Indo-China. Several of the men who later became top army chieftains – Army chiefs of Staff, Commanding Officers, Adjutants – and later heads of states after the military coups that plagued Africa in the sixties began their careers in gun totting in the jungles of Burma.

But despite his claim to full participation and valiant roles in Burma, Adamu was a weakling who was content with his role as a kitchen help and a back-up man. He consequently had no anxious moments to recall from Burma – except the ones he made up. He showed his lack of incapability in military manoeuvres when as a section leader in the UN Peace Keeping Force in Congo; he flunked and led his boys into a rebel ambush in Katanga.

To make the Burma veterans more useful, a comprehensive retraining scheme was embarked upon after the war. Adamu was made a medical orderly and initially attached to the Igbobi Orthopaedic Hospital as a ward mate. Here he picked few medical tricks and was later transferred to the Armed Forces Medical (Creek) Hospital at Ikoyi, Lagos as an assistant Nurse.

Just before handing over the Army to Nigerian Officers, the British sent Adamu for a three-month course in field dressings and surgical care in Aldershot, England.

Adamu surveyed the wounded again.

"You … yes you…" he chimed into the erstwhile silence, pointing at a full corporal with a case of gangrene. "What is wrong with you"?

"Eh… it's my leg Captain"

"Shurrup. What leg"?

"Captain it's … "

"I say shurrup. You mean you want us to cut the leg … hen? So that you can run away from battle hen"?

"No Captain".

"So what do you want"?

"Treatment Sir".

"That's better corporal, you'll march back to your unit immediately. Your leg will heal in no time",

"Next" Adamu barked.

"So you have fever …? Who told you, you had fever"?

"I don't know captain".

"Do you know what you are? You are a deserter. You are a weakling in army uniform. You'll run back to your trench immediately and if you show your face here again, I'll have you shot for desertion."

"Next!!" he roared.

"What do you say is wrong with you? Shell-shock"?

"Yes", the medical orderly replied.

"There's nothing like shell-shock. That's a term invented by weak-hearted soldiers to camouflage their cowardice … Private! …Private!, come here"

The patient moved two rows and climbed the steps shakily unto the Unimog.

Without warning, Adamu seized the private by the collar and slapped him harshly on both cheeks. He repeated the slaps again and asked: "Private, are you still sick? Talk to me … are you still sick"?

"Eh … Eh.. No Sir …" the private muttered incoherently.

"Okay. That settles it. Run back to your unit".

"Well, Orderly … you'll march the rest back to their units. Those who can come, and need come, should come tomorrow". Adamu then adjusted his sun shade and stroked his moustache as he marched off. But the medical orderly defied the "captain" and administered secret treatments to the wounded before they were marched back to base.

It rained that night. Ajani spent two hours meticulously crawling and avoiding the guards. He circled the darkened huts, which were fortunately not lit to avoid enemy attack. He had squeezed in through an opening in the shrubs and had a good look at the side of the hut. There were no patrolling guards. But on a second look, he saw guards at the front and near a small thicket at the back.

He crawled in closer through the side. In the thick darkness, which followed the rain, Ajani was sure the guards could not see far and he was sure too they must be feeling sleepy after the rain. Fifty yards further he got up and squeezed through an open window. The hut was dimly lit inside by a crude kerosene lamp. In the dim light from the lamp, Ajani could make out a lump on a camp bed to the right. He moved towards it stealthily.

The man stretched, yawned and made to get up. Evidently surprised at the dark mass lounging towards him, Adamu tried to reach for his service pistol – a .45 beretta automatic. But he was too slow. Ajani dived and stabbed repeatedly at his heart. He squealed inaudibly as he died in his own pool of blood.

Ajani rolled the body into two army blankets and covered it with a rain coat and tossed it into a dark corner.

He came out through the window. Ajani looked up and scanned the horizon. There were no guards. Quietly, he went down and crawled into the dark night. Two hours later he was back in his unit.

The scene was a massive rumbling of movement. Cooks and stewards moved lazily across the camp putting their pots and essential utensils together. Seemingly unbothered by the general melee some haggard looking soldiers smoked easily away at the edge of the camp. There was no formal handing over as the Headquarters of the 503 Infantry Brigade moved to their new Forward Operating Base near Ijute. From there the strength of the formation would be boosted by the newly linked 507 and the 27 artillery corps for the final onslaught on Owerri.

Churning up the wet muddy grounds and green cassava farms, Nigerian tanks thundered out of the location in neat formation. The infantry followed closely behind in a convoy of rugged military trucks.

Moving in an opposite direction to the convoy was a large body of refugees. With the changing tide of war, many had seen vaguely the handwriting on the wall and the perils of remaining in Biafra. Some of them escaped into federal lines looking ghostly with malnutrition. Others escaped with their kids strapped to them with their only form of clothing, munching raw leaves for survival. But all of them were resolute on the need to escape from the Biafran enclave. They fled across field and grounds littered with the charred remains of automobiles, tanks and oozing skulls and entrails of dead soldiers. Usually, Nigerian rear units checked the hordes of refugees before they issue relevant passes for identification in rear towns. But with considerable ease, most of the refugees managed to evade this check. There had been rumours of over zealous guards who fired before asking questions and this had made the refugees to hack their way through impenetrable dark jungles to evade the rear guards. Many died from cold and hunger in this attempt.

And still they came. For those who made the extremely perilous escape out of Biafra, there were promises of a settled occupational life in towns long liberated, and which had returned to normalcy with bustling business activity.

Ajani was in the midst of this refugee horde, dressed in tattered clothings, with mud smeared all over him and carrying a battered suit case. After a long detour through the jungle, he emerged on a muddy laterite road, which served as a supply line for Nigerian Forward Operating

Bases . It was almost 7 p.m. when he finally tucked himself into the carefully camouflaged trench under the ticket overlooking the muddy laterite road.

He opened the battered suitcase and brought out a waterproof bag. He extracted a gun butt, barrel, magazines, stock and a cup of grease. Gradually, he oiled and cleaned the parts and tested the firing mechanism of the Cetme automatic he had picked up from the field of battle and kept for this purpose.

Next, he opened a box containing 9mm bullets, and began to load the empty magazine. He had filched these particular shells because they fitted into pistols, machine pistols and the Cetme and Madsen – which with more massive black market sales from Europe were becoming standard Biafran assault weapons.

Ajani also had the Kalashnikov AK47 assault rifle in his tattered suitcase,with sufficient 7.62mm shells for the purpose he had in mind. In the absence of a silencer,Ajani had a crude bamboo pipe padded with mud fitted to the barrel of the AK47 to muffle any sound from the rifle.

Next, he examined the Cetme automatic and the loaded magazines resting in canvas pouches round his waist. He heaved a deep sigh and prepared for the long wait.

It was the month of July and the grounds were chilly cold from continual monsoon rains. Ajani was properly dug into the cold earth surrounded by high shrubs and green vegetation and hemmed in by giant trees and gigantic mangrove tap roots. From this vantage point and under this natural camouflage, Ajani watched the snaking laterite road closely.

It was the last week of July and for the previous three months, soldiers of the 503 infantry brigade had not been paid their allowances. This was not without reason. It would have been suicidal for Pay Masters to have come round when the whole front was grinding under the weight of the Biafran attack and the subsequent general push during the Nigerian counter-offensive. Moreover, the money would have been worthless to the soldiers then anyway.

Ajani had been posted for guard duties at Brigade Headquarters; just before the order to change locations came over the radio. He was patrolling an area to the rear of the Comanding Officer's office when he eavesdropped on a conversation between him and his Second-In-Command about pay boys and paymasters and the morale of the troops. He had eased himself closer to the conversation.

"So, when is the pay master arriving … the boys should need some money now …".

"From what we received, tomorrow or the day after … they have since left Abikpo for our station…" "Well, you'll better inform them of the change in our locations"

. "Alright sir, I'll send a despatch rider immediately".

And that was enough for Ajani. He made up his mind there and then on what should be the destination of the pay mission. When he was relieved two hours later, he rushed immediately into putting his plans into action. Quietly, methodically, independently without arousing even the interest of his best friends in his unit, he started to put finishing touches to his plans about the future.

2nd Lt. Haruna was a jovial man. Every time he met a soldier from the trenches, he puts on his best smile and says "I'm sorry", because as he puts it,

"I can never be a combatant … I know I'm not built to be a soldier".

Haruna had his teacher training education at Gusau. He quit the classroom and joined the groundnut oil mill in Gusau as a Cashier two years later. From Gusau he moved into the Federal Ministry of Finance and was later transferred within the Ministry to the Federal Pay Office in Kaduna. At the outbreak of the Nigerian civil war, he joined the Army Pay and Records Department and quickly rose.

On a good road, it is at most a four hour drive from Abikpo to Emeni – the new Forward Operating Base of the 503 infantry brigade. But on a poorly maintained laterite road in the thick of the rainy season, there was no limit to how long the journey could stretch.

Apart from 2nd Lt. Haruna, there were two other pay assistants in the army Land Rover – both of them corporals. The two corporals were smartly dressed, like Haruna, in smart army trousers and shorts-sleeves, wearing the proud insignia of the Pay and Record corps.

There was hardly anyone of adult age in the major towns affected by the Nigerian civil war who didn't know the dashing Lieutenant of the Army Pay and Records Corps called Haruna. From Lagos through Benin to the war fronts, he was popularly known as "Pay and Roll". When Haruna was on his pay missions, he knew it was time for business. But as soon as pay time was over, it was then time for fun, time to "roll". Since joining the Pay Corps, money had never been his problem. Nobody really knew how they made their money. But it was rumoured that with the ever growing death toll in the fronts, allowances due soldiers who had died were quietly tucked away by pay officers. It was also rumoured that some of them faked robberies and rebel ambushes – only to emerge out of interrogation rich men with their loot.

The army Land Rover moved sluggishly along the Abikpo-Emeni road that evening. The evening was dark – grey with signs of imminent rain. Large bodies of cloud could be seen moving and collecting to form a dark umbrella over the whole area.

The road suddenly skewed downwards, running into a gauntlet of pot holes and marshy terrain. On the flanks, strong monsoon winds blew violently shaking the dense forest. Giant oil bean trees shook and swayed violently as the monsoon torrent swept the landscape. The Land Rover slugged on, hemmed in on both sides by thick shrubs and forests. The trees were almost bending and blocking the passage as they curved under the force of strong torrential winds, which had made prostrate many trees and plants.

Without warning, the sky opened and poured down strains of strong windy, torrential rains, which bent the trees and ran through the forest in lightning downpours. This was followed by a violent gale, which shook the shrubs ferociously. The Land Rover trudged on grudgingly. It negotiated a sharp snaking curve on the road and held course firmly as the road led down sharply.

Ajani watched the Land Rover led by two motor cycle escorts slide down amidst the howling wind and rain, which made the roar of the engine barely audible. Quietly, without haste, Ajani cocked both the Cetme automatic and the Kalashnikov assault rifle. He checked his dungaree knapsack and ensured that his spare magazines, grenades and RPGs were in order. He wrapped himself into the green foliage, which immediately camouflaged and enveloped the deadly hunter.

The Land Rover slid to a halt before the pool of water and pot holes, which blocked the road. The driver slowed down and changed into first gear. Gradually, he released the clutch and slid forward. As he did this Ajani watched from his camouflaged position by the side of the road. He strained his neck and looked into the Army Land Rover. The soldiers were all wearing the tell-tale insignia of the Army Pay and Records. And there were the usual money cartons, with their usual identification marks and sealed at the top in regulation manner. And from experience, the pseudo – intellectual comportment of the soldiers in the Land Rover was enough to convince Ajani that these were "Pay and Roll" boys. He had seen enough. With one quick move, he aimed and shot the driver. The bullet went through the ear and came out as a ghastly mass of flesh, blood and bones in the right ear. He died instantly.

The Land Rover rolled forward, shuddered and came to a halt. Second Lieutenant Haruna made a dash for his service pistol in the glove compartment of the Land Rover and drew his sub machine gun at the same time. The two corporals and their body guards at the rear of the vehicle drew their AK47 assault rifles and manoeuvred to take aim and shoot. But the room was too tight and they were too late. The AK47 held steadily by the concealed figure coughed again and again. The shots shattered the side window glasses and carried half the skull of the corporals and the body guards away with them. The Staccato burst also caught Haruna on the forehead as he looked into the bush to take aim. Another shot ran through his neck and reduced it to a mass of tangled wreck. Haruna slumped and rolled into a heap on the floor of the Land Rover. The shocked escorts stopped, dazed as they too fell into the hale of bullets from Ajani.

Ajani waited. Five minutes later, he emerged from the bush, gun held at the ready. He checked and made sure all the occupants of the Land

Rover were dead. Next, he tore open the money cartons. It was all there – brand new notes – all in one-pound denomination. One after the other he removed the bodies and the motorcycles into the jungle and dumped them into a ready grave he had prepared for the purpose. He filled the graves with sand and camouflaged it effectively. Next, he carefully cleaned the vehicle of bloodstains and wound the broken side window down. He checked the dashboard and saw the movement order. It read Abikpo-Emeni. Skilfully, Ajani changed Emeni to Emenike. He went into the bush and dressed properly in ironed army uniforms. He checked himself as he came out and got into the driver's seat. Ajani put the vehicle into gear and drove off. Five miles further, he forked into a side road, which wound through Itu, Abara unto the trunk B road which lead to Emenike. He drove throughout the night and by morning, he had the loot well hidden, the movement order destroyed and the vehicle burnt.

Ajani mingled with the motley crowd as he thrust his way through the web of human traffic. He surveyed the busy Ojuelegba Road around him. Hmm, Lagos! He thought. What a myriad of heads! And a pack of beautiful women!

Presently, two well-dressed gentlemen emerged from a nearby hotel and joined the stream of human traffic. A mouth- watering aroma filtered through the doors of the hotel into the street. Ajani swallowed spittle! He took a second look at the neon lights of the hotel and went in.

There was a little bell by one spring over the door and this had rung as he entered. He heaved a sigh of relief as he was gently carressed by the conducive vapour of the air-conditioned atmosphere.

The wall was covered by some pleated materials. There were rows and rows of alcohol of all brands on the shelf. There were rows of canned beers. Then, there were glass show cases where "Barbecue chicks", "Smoked Monkeys", "Congo meat", "Amukoko Crabs", shrimps and delicious Shagamu "suya" were displayed in rhythm to tempt the appetite and make the mouth salivate. Rows of cooked, peppered and tomatoed stockfish, beef and juicy chicken smiled invitingly at the appetite.

Ajani sat down. For the third time that day, a cold shiver suddenly ran through him as his thoughts raced to the report he had heard the previous night to the effect that the SIB – the Special Investigation Branch – were fast on his trail. He feigned relaxation as he felt the cold re-assuring bulge of the Luger automatic by his side. He curled up his shoulders and called out in an assumed slangish tone.

"Hello princess... gimme two beers for a start."

He heaved another sigh.

This was the life, he thought. The orange neon lightings, the knee-deep ruggings, the burst of quadraphonic jazz music and the aroma of curried stew and peppered chicken were all alien to the trenches and fighting men at the war fronts.

Yet, here was this paradise on earth, in Lagos. Well, he thought, only foolish men suffered and died for the unity of the fatherland. Unity! How many of those boys who died out there everyday even knew the meaning of that abstract concept. Well, he thought again, only very stupid men miss their opportunities. More stupid ones don't even realise when enough is enough. And Ajani was not foolish. Neither was he stupid,he thought.

Ajani looked up to the counter and saw a trendy girl trying to protect her spotless white panties from his gaze. "Jesus", he cursed. He swallowed spittle as his masculine extension between his thighs flexed up muscles for a possible show down. The girl got up. Ajani followed her with his tearing gaze, guided by the fragrance of sweet smelling perfume, which followed in her wake.

The devil! With a series of undulating hip movements and rhythmic bust gyration, the small of her back, gave a rhythmic drumbeat, which put Ajani off his feet and set him in the mood. Yes, this was the life, he thought. He swallowed spittle hard again! If this girl should ever mortal be, he cursed, then "today must be today" for both of them!!

They were both strangers to each other, but the moment Ajani saw that little pretty face, his thoughts were: here was a woman to be loved, this was the kind of perfect feminine beauty he had longed for all his life.

Ajani was suddenly shaken from his thoughts by an apparently distant feminine voice. It was the girl. "Good evening lonely, can I join you on your table"? He looked up and was greeted by an enchanting smile. The girl bowed and the neon lights caught the shadowy curves of her bust. She gleaned and sparkled. Without knowing it, Ajani got up docilely. His breathing was held by a strong aroma of expensive perfume. The girl took the cue. She pulled him close as they hit the dance floor to the pulsating sound of music from the jukebox. She fondled and gyrated to put Ajani in the mood. It did not take long … Ajani gave a convulsive sensuous fit and heaved a sigh of joy as he held to her lovingly. His masculine extension between his thighs rebelled and nodded violently – Ajani was in a sensuous paradise and wished for no other heaven.

Three weeks into the relationship, Ajani woke up one morning in surprise. Under the tipsy state of the previous night, he didn't quite realise how he got to the girls' house. He looked round the house – executive beds and bed spreads, super colour television, super water colour paintings in the bed room, ankle-deep rugging, bucket sofas, and a cosy dreamland stereo – phonic music, whose source Ajani could not trace. The girl, Tonia was her name was awake.

"Won't you go to work this morning?", Ajani asked.

"No. You know, I'm self employed"

"Self employed? How? You mean you are a prostitute"?

"Some call us that".

"But what would a beautiful girl like you be doing in that kind of dirty business"?

"I don't know if I am all that beautiful like you say and … well, you have to be beautiful to succeed in my kind of work. I am self-employed, with an exciting work schedule which I thoroughly enjoy…and the pay is quite good. And I can tell you one thing – it is not a dirty business".

"You haven't answered my question".

"Huh! … You see, only very obstinate children discredit the taste of their mother's soup. I have seen dirtier trades in this town than I have chosen for myself. Do you ever see the moon at noon-?"

"What do you mean" Ajani asked.

"What ever makes you believe that the sun you see at mid-day is not the moon you see at night? Do both of them not provide light? People could call them different names. Afterall, it is the nature of this wicked world, to call black white and white black when it suits their purpose".

"Tonia, you talk in parables I still don't understand what you mean"

"Okay, you say I am doing a 'dirty' trade. But let me tell you ... many a 'clean' man with political power, many a 'clean' man with the whitest garment at church time, symbols of decency and morality have sneaked under shadows of darkness, with faces writing in lust to this very bed to steal a moment of affection and wanton sex from me, their dear Tonia. But to the public, they are clean and I am dirty. Well, I am not bothered ... Not even when I house fugitives like you and..."

"Tonia ... enough ...!!!"

"Don't you play the good man with me!!. I have seen the shady sides of pastors, civil servants, ministers and social crusaders. So I have learned to live with shady people because most of our top bureaucrats and business executives all have shady backgrounds so you are not a peculiar case!!"

Ajani looked up in utter disbelief and shock. After all he had done to cover his tracks, so this innocent looking girl knows something about his past?.

"I don't know what they say you did ... but they say the SIB are looking for you".

There was a knock on the front door and before Ajani could say anything, Tonia went to answer the call. She came back with a tall black man in a black tweed suit. The man had a strong muscular face with jovial, smiling eyes.

"Mr Ajani"? He asked.

A cold shiver ran through Ajani and he took a step back in surprise.

"Yes. That's my name. But I don't think I know you sir".

"Ha! David ... Dave – Dave. You don't know me? I am Adams ...You were my pupil in Ajegunle ... How you have grown!! ... You were quite bright in those days...and suddenly, you disappeared ... Boy, how you have grown into a man!"

"Thank you sir", said Ajani smiling.

"You have had your breakfast? C'mmon, Tonia, get us something to eat".

Over food, they talked about life in the city – the hustle and bustle which Mr Adams referred to as "One mad mass with a common mad purpose". There was a peculiar glitter in his eyes, which encouraged Ajani.

"You are in trouble" he said suddenly.

Ajani shivered and nodded docilely.

"Don't worry. We'll fix it up somehow".

"How"?

"When you are in trouble, like this, you don't gain anything by being alone and sticking to your independence. You have to let people help you. David, you are in big trouble ... you can't fight it alone. You need the support of dedicated friends and sympathisers ... people who share a common bond ... who live and die for each other ...who believe they are one, because they are from one mother. Now if you had the protection of a group of people like that, how would you like it?

"What is the price"?

"No price. There are little mutual contributions you make now and then. But what is important is your loyalty to the general cause for the general good. That you stand for the interest of all members ... that you are prepared to stake your fortunes in the promotion and protection of the interest of all ... That your bond to other members transcends and overrides your bond to your nuclear family and blood relations. And that you'll keep the secrets and tenets of the Union. If you're interested, I'll pick you up here on saturday.

It was a big black house. The house was surrounded by a brick wall towering over twelve feet high. Mounted on top of the wall were spikes and barbed wires to check infiltrators. It was a large house with double steel gates.

Earlier that evening, Mr Adams had come to pick Ajani up in his car. Ajani noticed that Adams, unusually drove himself that evening. He half melted into a corner in the front seat as Adams eased out of the kerb into the road that ran into Ojuelegba. The car forked into Herbert Street and entered the busy Ikorodu road after five minutes. It was a saturday and the traffic was comparatively light. The car drove for twenty-five minutes and slowed down at the Maryland junction. Ajani's heart missed several beats. His whole body was experiencing violent spasms as the heart thumped frantically. The car drove for another thirty minutes. And mid-way into Ketu, it slowed down and meandered into a side road. Finally, it slowed down after a twenty minute drive and entered an untarred sandy road. As they drove along, Ajani managed glimpses of both side of the road. There were no houses. There were giant forests on both sides. Just as he began to wonder where they were going, he sighted the big black house.

The car slid into a massive car park. The park was filled with cars of all makes. Adams parked properly. He drew his briefcase from the back seat and took out a black object. He held the object firmly with both hands and recited some weird incantations. Next, he ran the object round his head and spat away. He sighed deeply. From the other cars, people were emerging, dressed in a mock traditional style. Adams brought out his own outfit from the brief case. It included a calico, a fur-covered wrapper and a white traditional shirt and black baggy shorts.

Adams dressed quietly. When he was ready, he beckoned to Ajani who came over to him. He held Ajani's wrist with his left hand and quietly recited

"… The left hand is the mother's hand … as the mother's breast milk is sweetest … so shall the mother's hand be strongest".

They walked towards the black house through the double steel gates and unto an ante-room, where everybody dropped their footwear and recited certain lines. Adams opened another door and entered a bigger hall. As Ajani made to follow him, he was stopped and led into another room. The door was slammed behind him and he was carefully blind folded. The room was dark and windowless.

After some time, he heard the door open and a voice say quietly, "Let him stand up". Ajani was then tapped slightly on the shoulder to stand up. As he got up, something cold was sprinkled on his head. From the character of the voice, Ajani guessed that the man who ordered him to stand up must be an old man of over sixty-five. Ajani guessed the man was sitting on a high chair directly opposite him.

"My future brother", the man drawled, "they tell me you are fascinated by our work in the Union and you have decided to identify with us... and that you are prepared to give a lot and sacrifice much ... and receive much and give none depending on your fortunes and the dictates of our Mother in the Union ... are you following me"?

"Yes brother"

"No" he snapped "You'll not answer me that way. You'll bow down and bend your knees. And you'll call me Chief... Because you are not yet my Brother'".

"Yes Chief", Ajani corrected himself.

"That's better".

The interrogation continued throughout that night.

At about four, the next morning he was given some literature on the do's and don'ts of the Union to read. He was also given some weird phrases to memorise and recite always.

The drill continued for two months during which Ajani learnt the ranks in the Union – from errands men through executioners to chief executives of the different Compounds. He also learnt their titles, usual mode of dressing at specified ceremonies, the different branches of the Union, the yearly programmes and calendar of the Union, studies and uses of full dress, gala dress and procession dresses and various charms, amulets, incantations for various occasions. On the third Saturday of the third month, Ajani was led into a different room. Here, there were exaggerated paintings of the female bust highlighting a luscious,firmly erect breast. Just before the old man came in, he was again blind folded.

That night,the old man entered the room humming a weird tone.

"Have you heard of the 'Mama Nughe' song before"?

"No Chief".

"You can't have. It is the Full Ritual processional song". The chief hummed a few stanzas of the song and explained some of the lines.

"Mama is off to the market ...

This way ... and that ... way

The roads to the market are many

This way and that way

The market is filled from all the ways,

To the left and to the right

All ways lead to the market

From the left and from the right

The market is filled from all sides"

"Well that is it" the Chief said "You move into the hall with this song and fall into queue in the bigger ante room. From there, you switch to the second stanza of the song:

"Fathers are many and varied,

And only your mother you know.

But here we are

Fatherless we all are

But sons and daughters of one Mother

Listen Mother

Hear us Mother

Protect us Mother

Cuddle us Mother

We have come to your single breast for our milk of life"

The rhythm and melody of this song threw Ajani into nostalgic desires to feel and touch again the mother he lost at age six.

"Ajani, under no circumstance must you sing that song in public unless for identification purposes. Another version of the song, which we have titled "Meek Mother", will soon go out commercially from a popular musician. Any time you hear that number on the National Radio network in the very early hours of the morning, then there is an emergency. This is very important. You must remember it at all times. I'll have to teach you all the basic songs – and all of them you must memorise and sing well before your initiation. Others you will learn gradually at your pace."

The last Saturday before the initiation was a gruelling one for Ajani. "The Chief" entered cursing:

"Have you come again ...
What have you come for?
You can't take my son
No. I say you can't.
Now will I cuddle my son.
And whatever harm that comes to him, must come to me first ...."

"The Chief" turned violently on Ajani. "Now who was that"

"That?" Ajani asked "That was our Mother"

"Whose mother"?

"You and I, all of us"

"Now" said the Chief "What are the marks on our fur-clothes and other ceremonial garments"?

"Seven identical stripes" Ajani answered.

"No. You failed that one Ajani. It is a hidden eye. The hidden eye which only true sons and daughters of our Mother see. The seven rough stripes are only seen on our traditional tools. Remember? The rough stripes are found on our third hands, our chains, our bracelets, our amulets, our rings and our traditional fans. The stripes also form usual secret form of identification in our communications, understood"?

"Yes Chief"

"Okay. Repeat what I have just said" And Ajani repeated everything sheepishly.

"Recite to me the oath you'll take at your initiation"

Ajani repeated perfectly.

"Who is your Mother"?

"I know her. Her name is Mother but we fondly call her 'Mama' she is our Mother"

"Who is my mother?"

"Our mother"

"Who is your father"?

"I have no blood father. I am from and for my Mother. Whoever I call father is any of my Mother's sons or any Brother in the Union who may have done me a special good turn".

"How many breasts has our Mother"?

"One"

"Why"?

"Because she sacrificed the other one to protect and further the wishes of her children".

"Why do we suck her breast"?

"Because Mother's breast milk is sweetest. It is our source of life. It is nectar, which we suck to seek Mother's protection, progress and procreation."

"What is the significance of this"?

"It means that I am prepared to sacrifice anything in the interest of my brothers in the Union who suck from the same breast and all their anointed dependants."

"What if what you want to sacrifice is very close to you"?

"It does not matter. It can't be closer to me than my Mother. And the interest of my Mother is paramount and final".

"Thank you my Brother". And 'The Chief' removed the black hood which had all the time covered Ajani's eye. Ajani blinked as his eyes adapted and took in the scene in the room. He looked at the Chief and at once a glimpse of recognition flooded him. He looked at the face again to make sure – yes it was the Commissioner of Police himself – Ralph Bolade!!.

Ralph Bolade led Ajani into the inner chamber. It was a big round hall, with graduated rows of seats. There were also other initiates and their masters in front and behind Ajani. As they entered, the hall burst into the "Mama-Nughe" song. The initiation ceremony was climaxed by the oath taking. And one by one, the initiates knelt before the statue of

"Mama" and sucked strength, protection and progress from her breast for the first time.

Chapter 3

∽

BOB INENE

"GARRI," A STAPLE food in most parts of West Africa is produced from cassava, ground and fried into starchy small grains. For flavour, colouration and vitaminization, some producers of this grainy carbohydrate add palm oil. But mostly it comes white.

The fifty-ton lorry trudged through the narrow streets of Warri into Effurun. At the outskirts of Effurun, it forked right and headed for Eku. It arrived Eku after one hour's journey, re-fuelled at the Sapele-Asaba intersection and headed for Abraka. At Abraka, it veered into a lonely laterite road that led into the small but socially active town of Abbi.

Abbi is a small town. But it is the headquarters of a chain of Union Farms which dot Abbi, through Amai, Utagba-Uno to Obiaruku and Ogwashi-Uku.

The time was drawing near seven O'clock in the evening. The driver meandered into a side street and pulled up before a big walled compound.

Ostensibly, the lorry had come to load garri for Lagos. But the large store in the compound was only a front. As the evening grew darker, the driver would be joined by a guide and the lorry would move off.

The lorry veered into a sand-diggers road normally used by tipper-lorries. Just before the sharp sand sites it meandered sharply into a bush path. It followed this path for about five miles and forked into a cleared area and parked. About ten minutes later, the lorry was joined by three other lorries and the loading commenced.

It is not known who introduced indian hemp into the country. But the modern era for the weed started with a man, now about sixty-five, called Bob Inene, alias "Old Timer". Inene was a veteran of the Indo-China campaigns in the Second World War. He saw action in Burma and the trenches of Sumatra.

After his discharge from the Army, he tried his hands on many trades, without success. He then moved into Ojota, a suburb of Lagos and opened a small palm wine bar. At the inner room of this bar, he sold indian hemp, the mystery "energy-giving vitaminizer", which he brought back from the Great War.

Just when fortune was beginning to smile on him, he ran into hitches with the law and to avoid frequent harassment from the police, he became an initiated member of the Union.

He set up farms for the weed around Ojota, Bariga and Ajegunle and the swamps of Badiya. But he later found out that the most fertile area for the rapid growth of the weed was around his hometown – the Abbi-Kwale-Ashaka area. Two years later, he introduced the use of high yield fertiliser. Now the weed was in high demand and had earned popular aliases – "stone", "gay", "wee-wee", "gem", "monkey" "stuff", "ganja", "kaya", "flower", "rose", etc.

The four lorries were carefully stacked with sacks of the weed. The sacks were of double cover and the weeds had earlier been dried, perfumed and packed in sealed polythene bags. The lorries were loaded in such a way that sides were left empty. Later when they drove into Abbi, the sides were loaded with sacks of garri – all to mislead any inquisitive eye.

One lorry took a side road from Abbi that led to Utagba-Uno, unto Ubiaruku. From there, it headed through Agbor and Asaba to Onitsha. Another one left through Abraka to Benin. From Benin, it went through Ekpoma, Auchi unto Ilorin. The third one went up North while the last one left through Benin to Lagos.

The paths of these lorries had been smoothened earlier by an internal police signal to all field units resulting from a directive from Police Headquarters:

"Recent developments have necessitated this signal. There have been reports of undue harassment of agricultural workers and vehicles carrying staples and other food items.

This is contrary to the spirit of Operation Feed the Nation and a great disservice to the nation.

All personnel are therefore warned that on no account must vehicles carrying foodstuff be subjected to undue delays at check points…"

The signal was signed by the A.I.G(Operations) at Police Headquarters. Copies were sent to service chiefs and all Police, Military and customs operational units.

Abbi is not the only operational base for the national distribution of the weed. In Akure, a modest farm produces just enough to fed Ondo, Oyo and some Northern States. Vehicles from this base are loaded in Union standard pattern. But unlike truck loads from Abbi, the sides and rear of the trucks are loaded with cocoa beans. These narcotic laden trucks normally move in a convoy through Oshogbo into Ogbomosho. Here they will join the south-north traffic through Kontagora up to Yelwa.

Yelwa is an old fishing town on the Niger. The twin cities of Yawri and Bin-Yawri are surrounded by smaller villages like Hgwara, Mogo, Rofia and Bakin Turu. Together, these towns form the distribution nucleus for the mystery weed. The new town of Yelwa sprang up after the damming of the River Niger at Kainji. The increased height and level of the water displaced and engulfed the old town of Yelwa. The new town, also situated along the Niger is by no means less dynamic and productive in the fishing industry.

The smell of roasting fish is a twenty-four hour phenomenon in

Yelwa. Raw fish from the Niger is first disembowelled. Then they are descaled, salted and put over fires to gently roast and dry.

Yelwa is therefore a base for fish distribution with a network which is almost country-wide. It has an added advantage because of the presence of the Niger, whose many tributaries open into the Nigerian hinterland. And so every day, as vehicles and boats load dried fish destined for all corners of Nigeria, sacks of the weed are mixed and loaded along – for all corners of the country.

Housed in the Soho area of London, "The Tudor" is one of the oldest hotels in Central London. The five-storey building portrayed some of the most historical architectural traditions of ancient London.

The Tudor was originally situated on Knightsbridge before it moved to its present site in 1805. It is a very popular hotel for most Africans;as most of them who studied in London and who were to later spearhead Nationalist struggles; and who would become political leaders back in Africa worked in various menial capacities at The Tudor at one time or the other.

The main gate of The Tudor opened into a parking lot divided into compartments. The parking lot ran round the entire perimeter of the building. Consequently, four strategic doors lead into The Tudor from the lot.

Walking straight into the hotel through the central door, which over-looked the major Soho traffic, a visitor is first confronted by a small but comfortable cloak room, with racks for hats, umbrellas and winter coats. Passing further along through a second door, one came into the main Reception Hall. Here, guests and visitors sat in groups reading papers, watching television and discussing animatedly. It is a wide hall with long tables, running through it.

Further along the corridor, a door opened into a quiet and reserved lawn. There are whistling pines planted in beautiful lines and circles on the lawn. And on most days of the week, guests could be seen seated on easy chairs in heart to heart discussions. Along side the chairs are sweet- scenting flowers and flowerbeds. This particular friday evening, there were two men discussing something very personal in low tones.

The previous year, Bob Inene and his wife had made an extensive tour: Three weeks in London and Liverpool, two weeks each in Hamburg, Berlin and Dusseldorf and an extensive business coverage of the United States. All the national newspapers made headlines out of the business holidays. There was also a network telecast of major points in the tour in a TV magazine programme, Commercial Spotlight.

This year, ageing Bob Inene mapped out a similar itinerary.

He was led to the airport in a long convoy of vehicles. All Union top notchers were present at the airport as Bob Inene boarded a BOAC flight with stop-overs in Kano and Accra, for London. Any close observer that evening would have noticed that Bob Inene did not go through customs and passport control. He would have noticed too that Bob Inene did not use the common transit lounge. Instead, he was ushered into the executive transit lounge reserved for top government officials, National Award recipients and diplomats.

In London, he was received by enthusiastic brothers. His luggage was cleared by UNIFREIGHT – a Union owned clearing and forwarding firm based in London. Unifreight served as an effective link between the Union and the wide European market. It undertook bulk purchases for the Union and settled all its accounts. It also issued quarterly reports on the market situation in Europe and where best to invest union funds at any particular time. Further, it was charged with the packaging, forwarding and shipment of all Union cargo and the general welfare of all members in Europe. Bob Inene was promptly checked into The Tudor.

He was into the second week of his visit to London and was relaxing on bed with a proud sample of the Soho feminine community when the telephone rang. After an understandable delay disentangling himself from the voluptuous female artiste, Bob Inene picked up the phone and drawled ... "Yes. Inene here".

"This is Khan – Patrick Khan some good friends of mine told me you were in town. Are you alone"?

"No. Why? and who are these good friends of yours"?

"They say I should tell you, they are your brothers".

"And what's this all about"?

"I'm sorry to bother you ... but it's business and very confidential. Can we meet on the lawn down stairs"?

"Ok, let me see ... Okay, give me thirty minutes and I'll be right down".

"That's alright ... Thank you".

Bob Inene descended the staircase, his huge hulk supported by a walking stick. He moved into the bar and ordered drinks. . Then he strolled out unto the lawn.

As he walked unto the shade of the whistling pines, an Indian in a well cut carnaby suit went to him and made to shake hands.

"Mr Inene? I'm Mr Patrick Khan".

"It's a pleasure meeting you ... I thought you were English ... from your accent on the phone. So you are Indian – eh"?

"That's right. I was born in Bombay but I have been around London since I was three. So you can see why I have an English accent".

Mr Khan gestured to his table at the edge of the lawn and they moved over to it and sat down.

"Huuh!", Inene moaned as he sat down "quite a comfortable place ... I've enjoyed every minute of my stay here so far".

"Well, The Tudor is fair ... but it's not comparable to the Astoria. It's not even as extravagant as the Hilton Hotel in Nairobi, the Presidential in Kampala or The Federal Palace in Lagos".

"So you know the Federal Palace? Then you must have been to Nigeria"?

"Yes ... O, yes. My intimacy with Africa started about ten years ago. I toured Africa for business opportunities. But unfortunately, there were no useful contacts for me in Nigeria then. So all my investments are in or were in Uganda".

"Why the change in tense"?

"O-ho. It's unfortunate really but you undoubtedly must have heard about the purge of British Asians from Uganda. I lost all my investments in Uganda through that".

"-O-ho!"

Patrick Khan was a slender, tall man with a brown stout moustache. He wore beautifully tailored suits and had the general comportment of a successful advertising executive. He had attended the highbrow Trafford nursery school in North West London as a child. Later he entered a day school to read for his Ordinary Levels and for his Advance Levels. It was while preparing for the Advanced Level examinations that his mother fell ill and later died at the Saint Michael's hospital in North London.

Old Mr Khan, a transport clerk with the London Metropolitan Transport Board harnessed all the family resources to give his wife a descent burial. Since he could not afford to fly the body home, the traditional burial rites were performed by sympathetic members of the Indian community in London.

Patrick Khan wrote the Advanced Level exams and failed. He tried the exam a second time without success. His father encouraged him to do some professional courses, so he enrolled with the Pitman technical-commercial institute to read Accountancy. He received his National Diploma and joined a London firm of pharmaceutical manufacturers while preparing for his professional accounting certificate. It was whilst at the pharmaceutical plant that he learnt one or two things about drug making - both legal and illegal. From the laboratories he saw how chemists manufactured capsules and tablets of all kinds of drugs, including barbiturates, seconels, membutals and morphines,sedatives, analgesics and hormone tablets.

He also came to know Doctor Fabar, who resigned his post as a Consultant Pharmacist at Hammersmith Teaching Hospital to join Braal Pharm as a chemist. With closer scrutiny, he saw how Doctor Fabar occasionally clandestinely prepared morphines and little doses of concentrated heroine. Two years later, he teamed up with Doctor Faber and started financing more of this clandestine drug productions.

But so many unbalanced records were discovered during the annual auditing of raw narcotic stocks and the Braalpharm entrance control accounts. Subsequent investigations disclosed that Patrick Khan had been filching company funds and diverting raw stocks – an amount which ran into a third of a million pounds. The Management met and Khan was subsequently sacked. There were no court proceedings to avoid damage to the good name of the firm and to save the firm the rigours of a long and expensive prosecution.

Mr Khan came home from work after his termination a defeated man with a heavy heart. All attempts to find new jobs failed. The tightly woven employment market in London, having heard about the fraud in Braalpharm gave Khan no chance to practice his trade. He became a very violent and frustrated man. His dismissal without trial, though saving him the ordeal of court trial, had alienated him and destabilised his psychological responses and his pride as an accountant.

Khan combed the whole of London for a new job, with hatred in his heart and anger on his face. He came home dejected. There he found a note in his father's bold hand writing. The note was brief –

"Patti,

Your mother must be crying in her grave by now. You have disgraced the family. You have made me a laughing stock in the midst of the Indian community by your senseless fraud. For the past few years, I have observed you and doubted if you were my meek and gentle patty of yesterday.

Now, I know you are not. Why have you done this to me?

As you read this, I am in the hospital. If ever I die now (which I pray for) I want you to know that you killed me. Patti, you killed me and now I wish to join your mother ..."

The letter was not even signed.

Khan was sober and thoughtful throughout the night. The next morning, he visited his father at the hospital. Nurses told him that the old man had been in a deep coma since he was admitted. Khan went into the office of the Principal Medical Officer(PMO) and held a heart to heart talk with him.

"Actually", the PMO said "the chances are not too bad... I'll say fifty-fifty. This kind of situation is caused by a traumatic occurrence, a stream of fright or spasm of shock ... But generally traumatic enough to destabilise the precarious balance of the mind ... Do you know of any thing that could have caused such a traumatic shock to your father"?

"Doctor" Khan replied calmly, "You know I wouldn't know. A man's mind is not open for scrutiny ... and he didn't talk to me about any problems ... At any cost, I want you to take good care of my father".

Khan rummaged his pocket and stretched out a fat envelope – "Here ... this is five thousand pounds. Do everything possible for the old man, take money for your bills ... and ... thank you in advance..."

Patrick Khan went home and smoked throughout the night. The

next morning, he packed his few things and joined the crowd of British Asians emigrating to Uganda in Africa.

As the plane circled the airport for the final run, Khan looked through the window and the silvery green foliage below. His heart heaved a quiet thump of satisfaction at the beauty of lake Victoria and the surrounding vegetation. It was a British Caledonian flight, from London through Nairobi to Entebbe and it touched the tarmac gently without any hitch.

Several government officials were at the airport to receive the expatriates. Slick chauffeur driven cars were provided to take them down to Kampala. Mr Khan was driven in to the exclusive area of Kampala and checked into the luxurious Victoria Hotel. Perhaps because of his new frame of mind, Mr Khan might not have been as good as an accountant as he had been before. At any rate, he was interviewed for and was employed as a production pharmacist, having quoted and explained his job with Braalpharm in London. Unknown to his interviewers, Khan had never been a pharmacist at Braalpharm, but the little he saw in the laboratory during illicit deals with Doctor Faber, gave him enough to talk about his job at Braalpharm – enough to convince the Panel that he was suitable for the job.

It did not take Khan long to discover that the fertile soil of Uganda favoured the growth of indian hemp. In down town Kampala where the natives lived, Indian hemp which they popularly called "Shanba" was taken in a mixture of coffee in very many spots, as a beverage.

In the ghettos of Ikolo and the back streets of Jinja, the weed was used extensively by excited crowds of teenagers, youths and adults. There was no limit to the stories people told in these spots about the 'good' weed.

Once in Jinja, an old infantry corporal sat in a dim corner of a shack. With a regular slur, he told other users of how the weed served as a source of ideas and courage in battle. He said it was a form of energizer "when I take dis shamba ... Aba! I come see clearly ... I get pictures in my head ... I think fast ... you know like a computer. And dat time, if you give me gun and bullet ... the enemy is finished"!

Another middle aged man from a coffee factory supported the old corporal. He talked about how he could go on for days without food after taking "shamba". He swore violently that after taking the weed, he could perform sexual orgies tirelessly. And that when his wife became too weak on bed, he initiated her into "shamba" and they have lived a happier sexual life ever after.

There were many varieties of the weed in Uganda. Although the Entebbe variety was admired for its beautiful serrated leaf features, the Jinja "Shamba" was still the most famous and far more potent .

Patrick Khan started a big farm in the Jinja region ostensibly to boost raw material production in the area. But in secluded areas of the farm, he experimented with the Jinja variety of "shamba" and came out with astonishing results. He discovered that a mixture of certain types of fertilisers produced astonishing results when applied on the weed. The mixture produced greener, bigger and more potent "shamba". Generally, the mixture increased production and yield four-folds.

Two years later, he resigned from the services of the Uganda government and opened a drug-store and a medical consultancy service in Kampala. Here he continued with illicit conversion of "shamba" into more potent drugs and varieties.

But his criminally-bent mind did not keep check on the political climate of Uganda. And so when like a whirlwind, Field-Marshall Idi Amin put his military stamp on the affairs of Uganda, it took Khan by surprise. It is not immediately clear what motivated Idi-Amin into the subsequent purge. It was true the economy of Uganda from production, through distribution to retail was in the hands of British citizens of Asian origin. Their British nationality gave them free room to manoeuvre and defeat the timid Ugandan Bureaucracy at foreign exchange control and indigenisation.

But the British Asians even did more criminal and sinister things. Although the real cause of their purge is still shrouded in mystery, it is on record that Idi Amin acted with an understanding of the criminal mind. With swift military briskness, he purged Uganda of British Asians,without giving them room to out-manoeuvre the government again.

And Mr Khan found himself on a British Airways flight back to

London.

"It's unfortunate ... really unfortunate ... Did you manage to sell your things before the deadline"? The question shook Mr Khan back to the discussion.

"O-ho that? No way. There was no time for that. They have since all been confiscated by the government".

"I see. So what's your line of business generally now"?

"Same as yours".

"I don't understand".

"Mr Inene ... I am a man of the world. I come with good recommendation from your brothers ... So to be frank with you, I deal in one or two illicit items and I think we can pool our resources and technology together".

"What specifically can you offer in the partnership"?

"I have a wide European network and a growing American market. Moreover, I have developed a successful way of increasing quality and quantity of yields and sophisticated international distribution channels".

"Mr Khan ... it's a pleasure meeting you ... I hope it will even be more pleasurable doing business with you. You'll hear from me at the earliest feasible time – through my brothers,of course".

Mr Khan got up thanked Inene and shook hands, inwardly pleased about the signs of another business success. This time he prayed to the gods of Africa to steer him through this second chance with leniency.

Three months later, Mr Khan flew into Lagos on a regular Nigeria Airways flight from London through Kano. He was met at the airport by the personal assistant to Bob Inene and later checked into the luxurious Federal Palace Hotel in Victoria Island.

The black Mercedes drove into the Ogunlana area of Surulere. It forked into Alhaji Masha, climbed a fly-over, joined a stream of traffic and veered unto Western Avenue, near the National Stadium. As they pulled past, Bob Inene tapped Mr Khan and pointed out the stadium and the surrounding landmarks.

As they drove on the Eko Bridge, Mr Khan stole glances and sank back into his seat in fascination, as he took in the bustle of Lagos. The car forked right and descended gradually unto Malu Road. "This is Ajegunle" said Inene as they drove on "We have many ghettos like this around Lagos ... Here life is miserable. Life is poor and cheap. They call where we are now "The Boundary". Quite ironical, because it happens to be the boundary between life and death. No one dares wonder around here after mid-night. Even a false robbery alarm could do you in but it is worse if you have money on you ... a quick lunge from the crowd, a stab and you are dead without your money and briefcase. Strangers don't come in here unescorted".

A cold shiver ran through the spine of Mr Khan. The chauffeur piloted the car through the wobbly, pot-holed narrow and crooked lanes and side streets, where ominous darkness hid the houses and their occupants. Here and there were wooden and aluminium shacks. Others were constructed of mud and dry raffia palms. Dark shapes of men could be seen defecating publicly by the wayside near muddy, slimy and infested open gutters. These were connected to dingy stagnant pools of messy and sloppy ponds on the centre of the lanes. "There is a police station nearby ... but they know how to turn their face at the wrong direction ... The Police do not come this way of course, except in squads.

Any solitary Patrol is vulnerable. The uniform and his gun are valuable to armed robbers."

"I see. It's like old Brixton or Harlem or the dark alleys of Beirut" said Khan.

"Yes. You got it right. But here in this urban ghetto, I have my largest market".

"How do you do it? They are rather rough as you said".

"No problems. I am one of them. I grew up with them and now I serve them – with some profits. Here I have my biggest network of warehouses".

The driver burst unto an intersection and turned left. Bob Inene stretched forward and spoke to him in a strange language. The driver nodded. He made his way up unto a fly-over and curved unto a bridge. Now, the driver swung the car in a complete U-turn and made for an exit from the bridge. The Mercedes sped on through an open country and climbed unto another bridge. As they levelled up, they entered the heart of town. The Mercedes drove along an enormous ten-lane highway, lit brightly by tall fluorescent mercury street lamps. To the right and left were modern office buildings with intermittently flashing attractive neon lightings. Within a few minutes, they climbed unto a higher bridge. This led them straight unto the Marina and a kaleidoscope of lights. There were tall magnificent buildings with bright, multi-coloured neon lightings to the left and then Apapa harbour with well-lit ships to the right.

The car sped on and slid down from the bridge. It flashed past the Federal Palace Hotel, through the Bar Beach and the Mercedes slowed as it forked into the bumpy and narrow side road to Maroko. Twisting and panting, the Mercedes slowed to negotiate its way through tight bends and curves. They burst into the town and finally the driver pulled into a walled compound.

The driver flashed his head lights thrice and an inner steel gate was pulled up. The Mercedes slid into a large warehouse.

Bob Inene got out, followed by Mr Khan into the echoing blackness of the warehouse. The driver walked round and switched on a bulb. It was a long, windowless garage cum warehouse. Before them, were stacks of sacks.

The Driver rummaged through the stack and brought a small pack. Bob Inene held it and sniffed.

"This is for you Khan" he said. "It is a symbol of my trust and to aid you in your experiment on the suitability of our variety for drug making. I am expecting a comprehensive report on this and our other discussions".

The two men re-entered the car. The driver reversed and turned on the way back. Khan sat back and felt elated. The uncertain part of the deal was over. Tomorrow he would write his report and soon business would be on again.

For the whole of the next week, Mr khan busied himself preparing a report for Bob Inene and unknown to him a sub committee of the Union.

"From all indications" the report began "Our deal is the most lucrative single drug enterprise in Africa today. And from all indication today, climate, topography, soil and environmental conditions and political climate, Nigeria favours the growth of high quality cannabis".

The report continued and ran into pages. It talked about individual efforts at improving the quality and quantity of the weed. Mr Khan talked about his experiment with the Jinja variety in Uganda and how subsequent experiments in Nigeria have proven very fruitful and reinforcing.

"My discussion on and the desirability of my overseas contact for supplies is crucial. With the application of fertilisers, growth and productivity of our item is definitely going to experience a boom. This we can transform into widening our domestic and international market. Re-our discussion, the problem of beating international borders is actually no problem at all. Leave that to me.

On my little research. It has been shown that current international trend indicates that people are fast taking to more potent forms of the original weed. With a few investment in a laboratory – with very cheap items like large ceramic tanks, sinks, burners, multiple heating plates, suction pumps, balloon glass and serpentine tubing, dryers and acids, we could produce a more potent drug – easier to carry, portable, convenient and readily acceptable because of its many functions in the international market".

Khan briefly traced the procedure for the production. How the original hemp leaves should be reduced to base and how in a surgically clean environment the base is filled with acetone. "The mixture should be left to settle and separated from all the other alkaloids. The base acetone batch is then subjected to pressure and filtered through suction pumps. The outcome is then electrically dried to remove impurities. This will produce a different form of pure morphine and no longer a base. From this, other more potent derivatives could be produced".

Every aspect of the report was analysed by the Union sub-committee. Finally it was accepted.

Three months later, the Union acquired land in centrally placed Ilorin. The first set of fertilised weeds were soon planted. It was a bounty harvest. With this new flourish, the domestic distribution network was over-hauled. A new warehouse was built in Kano to redistribute the weed in the area. Mr Khan was sent to Europe and America to confer and confirm with Bob Inene's new customers.

A pharmaceutical firm known as U-Pharm was established in Ibadan, with nation-wide distribution network. Mr Khan was appointed its first General Manager. On the surface, U-PHARM produced legitimate drugs. But now and then the General Manager, with trusted members of his staff – all of them Union members – produced what the firm was primarily established for-the conversion of base cannabis to morphines and other derivatives.

With roaring diesel engines on full blast the two trailers trudged along the countryside. As they sped along, the wind swept the hillside and the bushy rain forest vegetation. The two trailers were of the same make and bore similar marks – UNIFREIGHT.

Uni-freight, a well known registered clearing and forwarding firm with international business links,which apart from its Nigerian operations, had offices in major European and American capitals. The company's logo – a three-legged Monkey enjoyed the good will of the public because of its efficiency.

On the dash boards of the two trailers, there were duplicate copies of way bills, duly signed and stamped at the Tin Can Island Port complex and which indicated that the two vehicles were carrying shoe soles for the Societe Nationale in Niamey, Niger Republic.

Just before Ilorin, the vehicles veered into a dusty wayside road. These all-steel trailers, sealed all round with a barred large doors pulled into the Ilorin farm at midnight. The doors were thrown open and quietly the trailers were loaded with sacks of the weed. When they were almost filled, two rows of shoe soles in cartons were planted at the rear to give effective cover.

The republic of Niger on the fringe of the Sahara desert in West Africa was a land-locked country. The country, plagued with political instability and a weak economy had found it very difficult to be particularly vocal on the international scene to be of any political significance. The devastating drought which swept the region in the seventies further aggravated this bleak state of affairs.

Generous Euro-American donors to the republic following the drought found it difficult to reach it because of its land-locked nature. There were only two flights a week into Niamey, the capital of the country. And it was not even economical to fly the needs of the country, since the drought created a demand for food and other aids far beyond the level generous donors could accommodate.

A cheaper alternative was the land routes. The routes to the Republic of Benin ran from Niamey through Pirin-Ngaure and the junction town of Dosso. It then veered down through Gaya, the three country border town of Malanville, unto Kandi Parakou to Cotonou.

The Nigerian route was more extensive. Ships carrying goods for the Republic of Niger were usually given berthing priority in Lagos ports. But because of the inadequacy of shore handling facilities and the congestion in Lagos, some ships were usually diverted to more distant ports like Warri, Koko, and Calabar which were less busy.

Very early the next morning, the two Uni-freight trailers left Ilorin and entered the major north-south highway. They drove on through Mokwa and Jebba unto Kontagora. Kontagora is an important junction. Here the road forked into two major highways. The first through Tegina unto Sahon Birnan Gwari and Kaduna. And the other through Yelwa, Jega, Sokoto, Illela and Niger republic.

The two vehicles parked in Kontagora where the drivers – both Union members – took their lunch. They resumed the journey immediately after along the Yelwa road, parked full with the new variety of strong vibrant and potent weed which the people of this area call "Ishaka". This is a luxurious variety of heady strength, full grown with fertilisers.

The sudden upsurge in the production of this new variety had generated the need for new and bigger markets. Some of it was consumed in the domestic market and used in U-pharm as base stock for other more potent preparations. But more of the "Ishaka" variety was sent into the international market. Most of it was destined for Europe and America, where people pay through their noses to sniff or inhale what they call "the weed of life".

Two days later, the two trailers pulled up at the Illela border. The trucks were immediately passed on. They moved on to Birinin Kani which is the Niger side of the border. The authorities here looked at the waybills, rubber stamped them and passed on the vehicles.

The vehicles fork left unto the road that lead to Dogon-Duchi unto Niamey. In Niamey, the sacks were delivered to the Union agents, who henceforth would be responsible for the onward transmission of the cargo.

The "Ishaka" variety was the most popular of the Nigerian weeds. When newly planted with fertilisers, it shot out in a pale yellow form. Significantly, it had been found to grow well in almost any terrain. The offensive tropical heat and sunshine gave the plant a very conducive environment for growth. Within four months, the plant shot into branches, foliages and more green serrated, with a strong powerful,aroma. Depending on the terrain, the mature "Ishaka" was either dark and greenish or pale yellow.

All these varieties were freely circulated in most towns by small time links men in the Union like Mallam Wakili .

It was a bright thursday morning and a pedestrian traffic jam stretched from the Yaba bus terminus, through the Tejuoso market unto the Ojuelegba round about. The tumultuous noise of this pedestrian mass movement tucked the individual into oblivion and disregard.

In the midst of this bedlam, a tall slim-built and well dressed man meandered his way through the human web. The man was Malam Wakili, the shifty one. He walked briskly, occasionally keeping a check on his wristwatch for the time. In quick athletic steps, he crossed the busy Ojuelegba road at an intersection and walked past a filling station. He randomly looked through articles on display on the kerb, moved ahead and nodded at a stoutly built man at the barber's shop.

They exchanged greetings and moved on along the kerb. After a few yards, they went into a bookstore on the left. This is a busy bookshop with numerous window displays. It was a normal rule with this bookshop that you must not carry any bag into it. A spot is provided by the door where personal baggages are heaped before moving into the store. The tall stoutly built man dropped the suitcase he was carrying and they both went into the bookshop. They moved round the store and at a secluded spot they talk in low tones shake hands and made to go. When they got to the door, Wakili carried the suitcase. They moved out and immediately went their separate ways. Wakili moved towards the Yaba railway level crossing while his stout colleague went the opposite way.

The Yaba bus terminus was particularly busy that morning. Young office girls who could not stand the hustling crowd stood conspicuously on the kerb, with tantalising smiles waiting for lifts.

The crowd was growing larger every other minute. Suddenly, a bus veered into the terminus and the whole crowd burst into a spontaneous struggle. Pockets were picked. Bags were snatched. And many shoes and elbow stabs were recorded. Wakili pushed into the crowd energetically creating room for himself with a violent head butt and elbow shoves. He made a break-through and took four quick paces to the front door of the bus. He dropped the suitcase between the front door and the driver's cabin and immediately ran back to join the riotous crowd, sending two women and a third man reeling on the ground. In no time, he found his way unto the bus and sat comfortably not too far from the suitcase up-front. He didn't feel elated or particularly smart with the way he had handled the whole operation. It had become a daily routine. He examined himself, gave himself a dishevelled look to fit into the next act.

With a violent engagement of gears and quick clutch release, the bus sprang up and moved into the busy Clifford Street. Wakili got up and moved up front nearer the suitcase. He cleared his throat and announced himself.

"Ladies and gentlemen, you are welcome aboard" he said. "You are the select few that managed to squeeze through the storm and the toil and through hustle and sprained limbs unto this bus. I congratulate you".

An ominous hush fell on the bus. Wakili stretched and inched up to have a clearer view of the whole bus. With red-blood-shot eyes, he surveyed the bus and its occupants. His dishevelled look, his scattered beards, his extra large trousers and his general composure created a mock stir all over the bus.

"You'll find it written" he continued. "The messiah does not lie ... for his word is truth and his person is holiness. Do you now dare to doubt the messiah ...? Yes. I am the messiah. I come when least you expect me to wash away your iniquities ... to make you pure and whole, to make you physically and spiritually clean, to cleanse you of the putrid stench into which you have sunk yourself. I am the messiah. I have come to give you another chance ... to make you survive the wrath of the Lord. To make you acceptable unto the Lord. You will not miss this chance. You must purify yourself now. You must accept the Lord through his chosen messiah. Who will not"?

It was a harsh question. And it was barked with blood-shot ferocity. The whole bus remained silent. Two young men wearing sunshades dared, and looked up. The blood-shot eyes of the "Messiah" caught and forced them to look down. The one nearer the messiah fidgeted and picked up a novel to read to maintain his balance. The "Messiah" brought out a dirty handkerchief and cleared his sweaty face.

"And let it be known" he resumed "That there is no accident in creation. There is no accident in birth and death. Your entrance and exit from this world is programmed by my father from above. And let it be known too that your entry into this bus is part of the large programme made by my father".

There was an agitated movement as murmuring came in from the rear of the bus.

"Quiet! You'll keep quiet! I say in the name of my Lord, you'll keep your mouths shut. Yes. You'll do as I say. You will find it written that anywhere two persons are gathered, there you must find my father. Yes. My father is here. And anywhere we are gathered in his name, shall be for that period his house. Yes. This bus, with its load of hypocrites, sycophants, sinners, winers and diners with the devil, infidels, morally bankrupt and spiritually impotent passengers is the house of my lord ... Yes. This very moment we are in communion to resuscitate you, to revamp and give you a new lease of life ... to fulfil the desires of my lord".

Is it an accident therefore, that out of the multitude, out of the exodus, out of the mob, out of the frustrated throb and agitated mass at the bus terminus, you were singled out for the honour of entering this bus"?

Just then, the vehicle swerved and the two doors of the bus were drawn shut noisily. The passengers were taken aback. Some cowered into their seats, while others nestled their buttocks for support. A churlish and weird sense of fear ran through the bus.

"Now you are afraid. Because the Lord has manifested his presence? Of the motley crowd and agitated deluge that rushed into this bus ... who here can stand before me and say 'I was stronger ... I was healthier ... I was more experienced and I fought more gallantly, hence I entered this bus – who"?

There was no answer. The crowd maintained its silence.

"The Lord has come in human form today, in the person of his son the messiah. And behold you delinquents and sinners, you morally bankrupt striplings, you stone hearted messengers of the devil, you satans, you dogs, you pawns, you are finished. Because after today, the Lord will hold you accountable for your sins. I am just the messenger, I am just the son, I am here in body and spirit representing the will of the lord. You'll not disobey that will because this is your last chance. You'll keep quiet when I tell you to keep quiet because I am the chosen vessel of the Lord. You'll not disobey me because you dare not disobey me. You'll do as I say and when I say it because my will is the righteous will. Yes. It is the popular will, the so sought after will, the will of the Lord, which even now is manifesting his presence by your calm approval of my mission".

The bus moved on. It went past the Alogomeji and Adekunle bus stops. Just before the Loco bus stop, the messiah cautiously eyed the battered suitcase where he had placed it. It was there.

Suddenly, the bus forked into the Oyingbo bus stop, throwing everybody off position. The driver steadied the bus and brought it to a halt sharply. There was a sudden surge as people rushed into the bus. The conductor repeatedly barked a "move forward" order as the surge threw the bus into a violent cauldron. Some of the crowd in a bid to beat others into the bus rushed in through the front door, stampeding everything in their way, including the messiah's suitcase. The messiah seeing his suitcase threatened, rushed forward violently shouting "Infidels, rascals, devils and children of the devil .. how dare you!".

He held the front door and shut it on the face of the on-rushing crowd. He barked at them. "In the name of the Lord, I say scatter ... I say scatter in the name of the Lord".

The crowd looked back in bewilderment. Some of them summoned courage and pointed threatening fingers at the messiah. Others shouted him down in anger. The messiah remained unruffled. "You bloated rascals, you puffy cheeky sinners. Your vain and arrogant anger touches me not. Yes because I wear the armour of the Lord, to protect me against haughty delinquents like you. And my Lord is a merciful Lord, or ...if I were to visit the anger of the Lord upon this stubborn and iniquitous act which you have just perpetrated before his chosen vessel ... ! May the Lord have mercy on your souls".

The driver engaged gear and began to move again. The messiah turned to those inside the bus. "It is written in the book of life ... Two friends shall be in a liquor house and one shall be chosen. From a large family of seven only one may be chosen. From a multitude in a bus stop, only few may be picked and in a riotous assembly, not one may even be called. Yes. So it is written. And only those chosen shall taste of the bounties of my father's house. The rest, will like those we left at the bus stop writhe and wallow in perpetual pain, subjugation, penury and anarchy. For they have been condemned by their own sins while the righteous man will be lent wings by his good deeds, to fly unto the everlasting joy and bounties of my father's house".

The messiah cautiously looked round over his suitcase again. It was safe. By now, he had established his person so firmly on the passengers that no one dared talk to avoid the wrath of the messiah.

Upfront, the conductor clanked coins to commence his collection of fares. In no time, he got to the "messiah." He clanked noisily and asked for the correct fare. The messiah remained adamant. The conductor clanked louder and asked for the fare.

"Yes you shall find it written. Silver and gold have I none. But what I have I give freely. Conductor, in the name of my father, the Lord", the messiah said, raising his hand "I give you bounties of blessings ... I give you peace ... I give you love – all of these you cannot buy with silver and gold. Conductor, go thy way in peace with my blessings".

The conductor clanked noisily steadfastly demanding his fare. "Impudence! Have I not said it before? That where two are gathered in my father's name, there shall be peace, because it is my father's house? And are we not gathered here in the name of my father? Is it not true then that this bus for the moment is my father's house? Young man ... I warn you ... young man, you'll not incense he wrath of the Lord and bring destruction upon this congregation. I warn you again, you will not pique and vex the Lord for his love and anger are everlasting".

The messiah suddenly turned to the conductor with red blood-shot eyes. He extracted a crude crucifix from his pocket and held it firmly to the fore-head of the conductor.

"You will not lurk and prowl around my father's house. You will not snoop into his congregation to meddle in iniquitous acts. And you will not convert my father's house and congregation into a market place, because my father's house is a holy house, a peaceful house and you will keep it holy always. You must not shake the frail and delicate balance of my congregation by battering their conscience for money. Young man, you are warned again. You must not turn this bus into a place for the exchange of money. There must be no activity of any kind that should bring the name of my father into ridicule. There must be no market in my father's house ... And that is to say there should be no collection of fares on this bus!!"

The conductor looked round the bus for support. There was none forth coming. Tactfully and quietly too he moved past the "messiah". In scarcely audible tone, and without the usual clanking he asked others for their fares.

The bus moved on – through the Iddo bus stop unto the Carter bridge. There was a sudden halt as the bus was caught in a massive traffic hold up that stretched further all the way to the Marina. Below the carter bridge, the muddy waters of the lagoon stretched in rapid currents to the left and right. There were little canoes, with half naked muscular men throwing nets.

Presently, one of the boats veered nearer the position of the bus on the carter bridge. A black muscular man, naked but for a loin-cloth strapping down his private parts, stretched fully and threw out his fishing net. He let the net dip, held back by sinkers for a few moments. Gradually, he drew it back unto the boat. It was a big catch and the whole bus burst into congratulatory sighs and applause.

The messiah waved towards the lagoon and warned. "A few minutes ago, the catch of the fisherman was safe in the depth of the lagoon. Until now some have lived like you here. Others hushed and dubious. But the miracle of the lord, manifested in the puzzle of death and creation has flushed them out today into the net of life. It is true you ignorant lot will think they were trapped in the net of death. No. You are wrong. It is the beginning of another journey more lively than the life they were used to. Is it not written in the book of life? How the Lord made people fishers of men? I am here in your midst today to realise that promise. I am here armed with the net of the Lord to catch men for salvation and the kingdom of my father. How many of you here will like to share of the joy and everlasting life in my father's kingdom"?

"The messiah" looked round. There were affirmative nods from nearly all. "The messiah" gazed at a young man in sun shades and pointed. "You? ... You rascal – Have you not defied the word of life for ephemeral things ...? Have you not cheated and polluted your young blood in pursuit of dubious gains? young man ... I see a bell chiming, I see heads ... a sea of heads ... But your head is biggest ... I can see a guillotine dangling over your head ...Young man ... pray for forgiveness ... pray seriously I see trying times for you ... you have soiled your hands with blood and rebellious spirits. You have polluted yourself and your innocent blood now crying up to my father for justice. Young man ... will you confess your sins?

The bespectacled young man looked round from one face to the other. He looked up at the hard glare of the messiah. He could not stand it. He cupped his face in his hands and burst into tears.

"The Messiah" turned abruptly, panting and pointing angrily at a corner of the bus.

"Yes. Here they are reeking of iniquity. Yes. Here they are enemies of progress, masters of pillage and thievery. The elephants and midgets of iniquity. How dare you mingle and blend into my congregation? I know you. I know you all. Bringers of darkness. Bringers of disasters and calamities. Messengers of Satan and his creed. How many innocent men have you led astray? How many have you erased permanently from the face of the earth. I see them in their innocence waiting for you at the alter in my father's house. You can't avoid them. Like a meteor, you have struck at random at the followers of my father. You have put families to shame and sorrow. You have broken the bonds of couples. You disciples of Satan, what do you do with all that blood? What do you do with all those limbs? What do you do with all those neckless heads, which even now are reeking in putrid decay in your dubious concoctions ... Yes. I see you all. The merchant man in your midst rich in his blood- stained hands, armed with illicit concoctions of money making. Now he is hoodwinked and he sees the world through your devilish eyes. And who is that government worker with you? The one in a white shirt and a tie. Now I see you clearly. You believe not in merit. You lack mettle and you have been absorbed into the whims of this cruel people. Have you not long battered your conscience? What about those ten percents which gradually rose to twenty percent? Has your cruel dispensation not starved millions of my father's children? ... so the new regime has caught you in a mesh and you have paid money and mortgaged your conscience to this murderous brutes, to salvage you from your present mess? Today you shall not succeed. I warn you. You have come into my father's house in search of merchandise for your ritual concoctions. You have come in search of a human lamb, to be led dumb to a slaughter in appeasement of your devilish wooden gods? And all this, just to cover your dirty tracks and maintain your office? Officer, I warn you. This time tomorrow, you would have been a victim of your own god".

The messiah paced down the bus. He whistled a religious tone aloud and the atmosphere in the bus livened up. "They are all here – mischief makers, mugs, murderous maniacs and malcontents. They are here mixing with the gentle and chosen ones of my father. They have made my father's house a haven and a sanctuary for enemies of the book of life.

"They have conspired and woven a snaring web over the humane and gentle flock of my father ..."

The bus engines suddenly sprang into life. The driver gently eased the clutch and the vehicle slid down gradually unto Idumota. "The Messiah" paced up the bus and stared harshly at the passengers. He brought out a small bundle of religious tract and started to distribute them.

"This is the word of the Lord ... It is the word of life" he said "but I know the vampires in your midst ... satanic errand boys and all their running dogs will not bother about the word of life ... Yes. They all believe they have seen life already. But in the name of the Lord, I warn you to desist from your satanic paths now. Come to the Lord through the book and the word of life and you shall be saved. You think you are living now ... but it is not until you come into the glamour and splendour of my father's house up yonder that you will begin to realise how lost you were. Pray ... I say pray today for eternal joy in the splendour of my father's house ... In the beauty and elegance of the everlasting home of my father ..."

The messiah paced down and suddenly wheeled round. He stared fixedly at a young woman at the edge of the bus –

"You ... Yes. Have you not disobeyed the laws of my father? Swear by the book of life ... Take this oath by the word of my father ... Have you not wantonly displayed yourself for material benefits. Have you not assembled with vile and cruel hearted devils and embroiled yourself in opiatic mixtures? Have you not given them courage in their dark deeds? Have you not poured forth promises of love and satiation in woeful ecstasy even after their commission of deadly acts? You feigning, devilish mercenary of the flesh. You worm-like mercenary of the night... Have you not climbed unto copulation in the dark of nights with devilish strangers ... Tell me did the Lord join you in holy wedlock with anybody? With what authority do you then entwine and fornicate in an alliance not purified and blessed by the Lord ... Young woman ... Repent now ..."

Just then, the bus pulled up at the Leventis bus stop on the Marina. The Messiah looked round warily. Stealthily, he picked up the battered suitcase – which all this time had been dropped carelessly in an obscure spot at the front of the bus. He waved to the passengers –

"A word is enough for the wise ... Those who have ears ... let them hear". He paced down the Marina into a car park. There his contact was waiting. He handed over the suitcase packed with wraps of hemp over and quietly; they both went their different ways. It was mission accomplished for Akin Adeola alias "Pastor Wakili", alias "Jagu".

Most of the weed got to Lagos from far away farms through the Bob Inene network. Once it got to Lagos, the distribution "leg men" took over. They spread the weed to bars, restaurants and nite clubs. They push up to hotel foyers, barber shops and cinemas.

∽

The Nigerian Christian Union Church was situated near a noisy market that served the people of Agege. A parish of the Lagos Diocese and one of the many branches of a chain of Union churches founded by Pastor Patrick, the general environment of this densely populated area was that of disarray and general poverty. But inside, the church emitted a luxurious and enchanting aura. The wear and tear and the unpleasant stink of the environment outside contrasted sharply with the serenity and fragrance of the church. In the cosy atmosphere of this church, Reverend Benson Ajanaku reigned supreme. Here his regal person served as an intermediary and a bringer of light and hope in the quest for the Lord and salvation. Here the advise of the reverend was held sacred.

There were two kinds of worshippers at the Nigerian Christian Union Church. There is the one, whose ultimate desire is a union with the Lord and an everlasting abode in the house of the Lord. This same one was driven by inner faith and spiritual unity with the purity that is the Lord and the simplicity of the Lord's ways as in the Book of Life. He believed that the communion with fellow christians and the purity of the relationship with the chosen one of the Lord were basic for the cementation of Christian brotherhood and a prelude to life everlasting.

The second took the church as a purely business venture. He had hazy ideas about God, faith and all that a true church stood for. His foggy ideas were further blurred by his belief that the church was an extension of the Union – built to serve certain purposes. His church attendance was a hollow guise to appear holy and peaceful and to pass on essential information through the presiding priest.

This day, the reverend personage of Benson Ajanaku ascended the pulpit in all purity and spiritual ebullience, flanked by church wardens. He opened the church service calmly and proceeded to talk about honour. Honour he said did not spring from being great, or being popular or being wealthy. He said honour sprang from the esteem and deference showered on an individual not only by his kind but by all.

He said true honour sprang from being recognised for selfless devotion to your community and being showered with blessings and purity from the Lord for honesty and integrity. True honour, he said, was therefore not the sole making of an individual but a property held and monopolised by the Lord, to be shared to his deserving children and anointed ones.

Reverend Ajanaku warned his congregation about the danger of the times – "These are troubled times" he said "I can see evil moving like a rat in the dark in the minds of many ... I can see people snooping into the dark to meddle in iniquitous acts ... Many have defied the Lord and have allied with bringers of darkness, destruction and calamities ... But I am up to the task and whosoever comes to the house of the Lord shall be saved. Nobody can incense and incite mutiny in the house of the Lord ... May, the Lord's name be praised". And the whole congregation shouted "Amen" in unison. The church choir immediately burst into a melodious hymn.

Just before closing time, Reverend Ajanaku cleared his throat for the special announcements. For the initiated, this was a crucial aspect of the service. He announced two forthcoming marriages. These were followed by an announcement that the family of Mr and Mrs Inene had requested for special prayers to guide the country in the prevalent shaky political situation. Special prayers were also to be said for the speedy recovery of the father of one Ajani and for the house of Bala.

For the initiated, these special announcements of prayers meant more than prayers. They were coded messages of "house meetings" in the Union.

The choir burst into a closing hymn and gradually the congregation began to disperse. But some in the congregation went up to the reverend to receive "spiritual blessings" and send important messages through the reverend, to be received throughout the Union network. During the special "Spiritual Blessings" too, those who stayed behind were told the specific dates of the "House Meetings" in the union, announced earlier in the church service. This Sunday, the Reverend also informed the select group that stayed behind for blessings of the arrival of the MV Damba-Damba in Nigerian waters. Later still, the members of the church "laity" – all senior members of the Union – stayed back to hold secret weekly "milk and honey" rituals at the sacristy.

∽

The MV "Damba-Damba" held a steady course as it made its last approach into Nigerian territorial waters. One nautical mile later, it dropped anchor a short distance from Ogogoro village, a shorter distance still from Komos Island.

Not many people know of the existence of Komos Island. But many had at least heard of Ogogoro village. It is about two hours journey by engine boat from Komos Island to Ogogoro village. And this small island represented an important Union gateway.

The skipper of the "Damba-Damba" peered through his binoculars at the fading horizon of Komos Island. He managed to pick out a small weather-beaten jetty and about three men standing at the pier head. The details were not clearly visible but another sweep with the binoculars revealed giant mangrove aerial tap-roots and swamps, a dozen suspended huts and dark green tarpaulin tents.

The three men standing on the pier head each had a high-powered binoculars. In the early burst of dawn, they picked out the complete profile of the ship. They studied the ship intently. There was no one on deck, but the "Damba-Damba" showed signs of activity as it bounced in rhythm with the waves. They panned the binoculars left and right until they picked out the name of the ship on its bow.

"Good", the leader of the small group said. "Fredo, … Sho-boy it's our boat. According to the boss, it is supposed to leave and to call at the Tin Can Island tomorrow evening. The boat is on its way back to America. It brought a consignment of drilling equipment. They say it has been off-loading drilling bits, pipes, chemicals and oil well cement for the last one week in Warri. The captain has decided to pick on a few sacks of Cocoa and crepe rubber at the Tin Can Island in addition to the palm oil it took on at the Burutu port".

"So when are we loading" Fredo asked.

"Possibly the day after tomorrow. The boss promised to call us on the radio. The whole deal has been worked out by Mr Khan any way. So when we hear from the boss, we load. No problems at all". They strolled unto the damp earth and moved behind the huts. Hidden under the thick mangrove tree lines were two strong boats. The three men got into one of the boats. It was an executive sporting boat. The "Mama 1" and "Mama 2" looked graceful and beautiful against the shiny dark waters. These two boats were bought and registered by a Mr Benson – of the Marina Boat Club – for sport fishing and pleasure cruising.

The "Mama 1" and "Mama 2" rode gently, secured aft and fore to giant mangrove trees. A dark winding tributary ran through the thick swamp forest and overgrowths into the interior.

About 2 am the next morning, the long awaited call from Mr Khan came through. It was a simple coded message (Mummy is waiting …) The high powered radio receiver in "Mama 1" picked it up, loud and clear. Later, a visual survey confirmed the deal – the three quick light flashes from the bow of the "Damba-Damba".

"Sho-boy" got into "Mama 2" and ran an experienced eye over it. He looked at the double Yamaha engines and kicked them into life. Next, he checked the optimum revs of the engines and the cooling system. Satisfied, he went into an adjoining cabin and looked round. He stepped out gingerly and signalled Fredo to take over. "Sho-boy" went into "Mama 1" and repeated the routine.

It was not by accident that "Sho-boy" moved round a boat with such ease and familiarity. Shomuyiwa, alias "Sho-boy" started life as a dock-worker. Three years later he was promoted gang head over a casual labour force at the old Customs Quay on the Marina. But Shomuyiwa was an ambitious young man. He lobbied all the appropriate departments for a professional sea-man's passport, to no avail.

In frustration, he stowed away on the Norwegian liner – Hibiscus Oslo – in a bid to get away from all the frustration and make it outside Nigeria. Fortunately for Shomuyiwa, the "Hibiscus-Oslo" made a repair stop over in Las Palmas. There "Sho" saw the bustling melting pot of Las Palmas for the first time. There were all manner of shipping in Las Palmas. From rusty-creaky ancient merchant men to slick oil tankers. There too, "Sho" saw the intricate smuggling – which spread into wide networks all over the world. And this was a period when there was a dearth in deck-hands. "Sho" was quickly taken on by the "Uruogo Maru" – a Japanese freighter with world-wide routes. For over four years, "Sho" traversed the world visiting every major capital and port – on the "Uruogo Maru". Until, they brought a consignment of Japanese general cargo to Lagos. "Sho" arranged and sold most of the goods on the high seas to smugglers based in Ogogoro village. He disappeared into the night thereafter, with a fat purse pinched from the captain's cabin, the first and second officers and the boatswain.

"Sho-boy" untied the mooring ropes and the "Mama 1" slid out gently. He made a full turn with Yamaha engines barely coughing. "Mama 2" followed a respectable distance behind. "Sho-boy" held course for about five minutes and gently manoeuvred the boat to the port side. Gradually he slid into place side by side with the "Damba-Damba".

A shadow appeared, ran a torch light over the two boats and went back. Three minutes later, after a coded identification, the loading process started. as they loaded, the cargo was transferred into less conspicuous spots – into personal cabins, below decks, oil rooms, into storage rooms and into the electrical maze. By five-thirty that morning, the two boats bounced off, lighter, their erstwhile narcotic cargo now safely stowed unto the "MV Damba-Damba".

By the turn of the year, the Annual Conclave in a major policy decision instructed that all Union exports had to be centralised under Alhaji Bako's "front office" – Omega Associates. To facilitate all operations, the "front office" acquired Cocoa processing plants in Ondo and Crepe rubber factories in Bendel. Thus, side by side with genuine exports of rubber and cocoa, all Union narcotic exports were neatly packaged in crepe rubber bundles and cocoa cakes and freighted through regular shipments to affiliated companies in Europe and USA.

There was an old saying credited to the legendary Mother of the Union:That a man must do three things in life – plant seeds of his kind, make silver and gold to his fullest and live long enough to enjoy his spoils. And these were the cardinal promises of the Union.

Nobody has factual details on how membership of the Union guaranteed fertility, wealth and longevity. But it was true that most Union members were rich men, with enough to eat and spare. But the details of how they actually made their wealth were hidden in the tight- knit social fabric, secrecy, conspiracy and extreme weird rituals of the Union.

In the absence of official Union versions, so many stories had been put forward by the inquisitive public to explain the unknown. Stories of vast nation-wide conspiracy in robberies, corruption and smuggling. Stories of month-end sharing of money realised therefrom. And stories of vast metaphysical powers … of how human life was central to the claimed wealth of Union members; how so many innocent citizens announced missing were actually murdered and their spirits made to bear money by some weird and highly occultic rituals.

Although not all members of the honoured Union portrayed visible signs of enjoying the material benefits which membership of the Union conferred, most of the stories about wealth associated with membership of the Union were fuelled by the stupendous wealth of known members and their secretive lifestyles.

Whilst the rumours persisted, an internal restructuring of the organisation to present a much more acceptable public face was unfolded by the Union.In the new structure,the organisation was divided into four autonomous departments. Each department was named a "compound" and all the supporting services from the research agency, protocol, communication and bureaucracy were brought under a fifth Department, a purely service department with unrestricted powers of supervision, co-ordination and elimination.

At the All-House Convention of the Union held thereafter, David Ajani was returned unopposed as the head of Department One – Ajani Compound. Bob Inene was also elected the head of Department Two – Inene compound. Chief Olatunde Ashakoleh and Inua Bako were elected heads of Department Three and Four respectively.

In keeping with the hierarchical pattern and line of control in the Union, the Compounds were further broken into Houses and the "houses" into "Blocks" and "Gates" for effective control. Still along this line, it was not unusual to see newly created "houses", "blocks" and "gates" openly seeking government approval through national dailies:

"This is to notify the general public that "The Crew" – a socio-cultural association situated at No 7 Ajakameme street, Ikeja, Lagos has applied for registration under the Land Perpetual Succession Act Cap 98 of the Laws of the Federation of Nigeria...

Anyone wishing to object to this name should send its objections to the Permanent Secretary, Ministry of Internal Affairs, Ikoyi Lagos, within twenty-one days of this publication..."

Through this method,a semblance of legality and openness was foisted on an otherwise very secretive cult. Of course,it would be a useless and most futile exercise for any member of the public to attempt to object to the registration of "The Crew" or any other union- affiliated club for that matter. Apart from the grave danger involved, there were members of the Union planted all along the official bureaucracy to make sure that no such objections ever got to the desk of the Permanent Secretary.That was how all the component units of the Union were given legally recognised and accepted personalities in a very structured manner over a period of one year.

Mr Khan had a very busy day putting things in order in the vast secret underground laboratory of Unipharm that night. At about five O'clock he walked into his office to clean up. As he went in, he beckoned to his personal assistant, Dick Opoleh.

"How did it go"?

"Fine. They've changed everything".

"So how did they do it"?

"Well … Nothing you can't achieve with money … I greased all their palms – from clerk.. upwards.

"So now it's all in order"? Mr Khan asked, betraying his anxiety.

"Yes. The register now shows two of us as the sole owners of the firm … and the bank too – it's all settled … any cheque signed jointly by us is valid … "

"Opoleh! That's a brilliant one. Now we'll move when we are ready. The last heavy consignments we sent abroad have been delivered in Italy. Quite easy … you know with the new government, security has not been very tight …"

"That reminds me … they say the new military ruler in Uganda has called on all expelled British Asians to come back and rebuild the economy." "That's wonderful…everything is falling in place nicely as you rightly forecast".

"Yes. Infact I have sent somebody down now to prepare the grounds for us".

"Don't worry about the details of your Uganda move …Me? I am headed for London to continue my studies and live a quiet life..As we agreed, all the proceeds from the shipments we have made this month have been lodged in our secret bank account"

" Tomorrow we'll begin actual preparations. We will start making transfers of funds from our local operations into the account in London…I tell you,we will never be poor again in our lives…good..see you tomorrow".

"Alright. So tomorrow then".

"Yes. Tomorrow".

Opoleh walked back to his office gingerly, bubbling with excitement.

He sat down, made two phone calls and stretched his legs full-length on the table. He heaved a deep sigh. So at last, here was an opportunity for escape after so many months of planning.

Nine months earlier, Dick Opoleh was a trusted Union worker. Within the Union membership they called him "The Shadow" because of his effective but unobtrusive surveillance over Mr Khan. A graduate of History and Politics from the University of Ibadan, Opoleh was recalled from Post Graduate work on African Cultures and Political Systems to assume duties in U-pharm as a Personal Assistant to Mr Khan. It was hoped within the decision making level of the Union, that Opoleh would understudy and eventually take over from Mr Khan when the time came.

Chief Ola-Bembe Opoleh, the ageing father of Dick Opoleh was a high- ranking title member of the honourable Union. And under normal Union family tradition, Dick being the eldest living son of Chief Opoleh was initiated into the Union immediately after his graduation from University as an associate member;with his full membership deferred until he was of age and ready to "suck Mother's breast". The associate membership initiation was a source of joy to Dick then. As a prominent member of the Afro-League at the University, he had imbibed bold pan-Africanist cultural ideals. He therefore looked at his initiation then from a purely socio-cultural perspective. To him then, it was a re-birth of sorts and a re-identification with his African roots. The extremely weird traditional rituals which preceded the initiation gave him feelings of oneness with his African ancestry.

But as he began to operate within the Union in his daily dealings, he gradually began to realise that there was a lot of evil lurking within the membership of the organisation. He started to have doubts about the integrity of the source of his father's wealth.

In June of that year, he met Jumoke,a born-again Christian, a charming girl who was to further change his perspective and drive a wedge between him and his father.

Just after six months of courtship, Dick became genuinely interested in Jumoke and The Word. He became "Born Again" and studied the bible with an unrivalled fervour.

He began to see his father in his dreams, consorting with evil men. Guided by the Holy Spirit, he began to condemn the Union openly in the house before his father. His father in turn threatened him with eviction from his house if he persisted in his rebellion.

When Chief Opoleh returned to meet Dick and his fiancé in deep praise worship and cleansing prayers in his sitting room upon his return from a midnight Union Conclave ritual, that was the limit. That night, he banned Jumoke from the house and nullified all previous arrangements for their wedding. That night in deep prayers, Dick asked for the Lord's guidance and protection. Emboldened by the Holy Spirit, he went into his father's bedroom early that morning to confront and challenge his unchristian ways.

The father was nowhere in the bedroom. Dick called repeatedly and thought he heard deep breathing in the direction of the giant wardrobe in the bedroom, his father was nowhere in sight. He approached the direction of the deep breathing and flung the wardrobe door open. There, to his surprise, his father was stark naked in deep ritual incantations ... down on his knees in supplication, cuddling and sucking the breast of a dark,one-breasted female wooden sculpture!

"Father! What are you doing"?

Silence.

His father continued with his sucking, interspaced with incantations, totally ignoring Dick's presence. In a fit of anger, Dick struck his father's exposed head with his Holy Bible. The Bible was one of those strong hard cover type. When he struck the old man he merely wanted to shove him aside. But the force of the blow threw the old man off-balance, railed his head against the concrete wall and he passed out.

In one swift movement, Dick took hold of the lifeless wooden sculpture of the one-breasted naked woman, smashed it on the ground. He rushed with the broken parts of the wood into the kitchen and set them ablaze. He supervised the burning, pouring fuel repeatedly into the bonfire to ensure complete destruction. When he returned to the bedroom, his father had come to, but still dazed. Dick took a long, hard stare at him in disgust and cursed:

"You are a disgrace ... how dare you worship this ugly ritual idol in this house of God ... father ... you will burn in hell ... just like your effigy in the kitchen ..."

"Oh ... Dick ... you burnt her? What have you done? I am finished.. eh! you have killed us all ..."!

That was nine months ago.

Back to the office on this quiet night when he had perfected his escape plans with Khan,Dick Opoleh read through a file on foreign pharmaceutical developments for the rest of the evening. He stopped suddenly and pulled out his brief case, checked his passport and that of his fiancé,bundles of foreign currencies and nodded in satisfaction. He cross-checked one or two items contained in the file with a recent magazine and pulled up to go. He came out, locked the door and walked down the long alley, acknowledging the greetings of the roving night guards. He went down the stairs, peeped into the laboratory and walked to the car park.

From the shaded light from the laboratory he saw the shadow of two men, walking towards him. As they came nearer, he saw they were well dressed and looked gentlemanly. The shorter of the pair moved forward with a gesture to shake hands.

"Good evening, Mr Opoleh ..."

"Hello ... I don't think I know you too well ... but you seem to know me".

"Ah-ah – Mr Opoleh ... How can you say a thing like that? In any case, I am Mr ..."

And with that he took the hands of Opoleh, in a vice-grip of a handshake.

A mild shiver immediately ran down the spine of Opoleh. He felt groggy and dizzy. There was a funny peaceful feeling in his mind – even as his heart raced, frantically at all time peak. With one final struggle, he tried to hold himself straight as he began to slump groggily to the effect s of the chlorofoam applied in a wet towel by the other gentleman from behind. He struggled frantically to talk but nothing came out. The lips hardly moved. Gradually, he blacked out and faded into oblivion; as the second man squeezed more of the chlorofoam vapour into his nostrils.

A car roared somewhere farther up the park and pulled up. It was a white Mercedes saloon – shinning white and ironically in sharp contrast to its dark devilish and dubious occupants. The two men led the unconscious Opoleh into the car and drove off.

The car burst unto and joined the busy traffic heading towards the Gate area of Ibadan. The occupants of the white Mercedes rattled merrily as they crawled along with the traffic. About thirty minutes later, they were out of town and speeding along the Ibadan-Ife road. Midway, they forked right into a small dusty road. The car held course for some time and turned into a smaller road. About eleven O'clock that night, they entered a small sleeping village. The car slowed down considerably. It meandered into a side street in the village. It eased into a small park by a walled-off house and parked. The driver opened the back door and the two men held Dick Opoleh, and led him into the dark confines of the house.

Chapter 4

ESHEGUME "ESAU" AGABA –
THE FINAL WORD

WHEN DICK CAME to, he found himself in a dark circular room. A charcoal fire farther down the room provided an ominous glow in the otherwise dark room. He was seated on a native bench and made to face the direction of the glow. Strangely enough, Dick had got back some of his courage and balance. The room had a traditional pleasant smell. There was an acrid smell of local herbal insecticide.

Dick looked round. But for the native bench, there was no other form of furniture in the room. There was a mat – carefully rolled up and tucked away in a conspicuous corner of the room. Just then, there was a flurry of movement to the right of Dick and an old man, with a walking stick for support walked delicately into the room. He staggered towards the edge of the room and picked up the rolled-up mat. Next, he moved farther behind the fire place, spread the mat and bent to sit down. As he made to sit, the two men who brought Dick rose, muttered the Union greetings and went down on their knees with eyes shut. The old man sat down, picked a glowing twig from the fire, held it before his gaze and shouted – "Igbu ne gbu" three times into the still night. The two men echoed the call in unison, rose up and walked back to the doorway.

Now, Dick felt a little at ease. So it was a Union affair, he thought. The old man threw something into the fire, and a tick black smoke rose up. He held up his hands to the two men and they promptly walked out into the dark night. The old man held his bald head in his palms and started staring intensely at the fire. He held the hard stare for about five minutes and laughed out aloud, his eyes still stonily staring at the fire. As he stared harder the colour of the flame flaring from the fire began to change. First into blue. Then white. And in quick succession, blue, green, yellow. And at last black. The old man laughed out again and looked up. Now the eyes were hard and stony. The eyes were black and dormant. No twinkle. No sparkle. These were dark unseeing eyes, like eyes of a vulture before a desert feast. Then without warning, he began to speak –

"Do you know me"

The voice was from a distant. It revved and whirled round the room. It took an eternity before Dick could mutter a reply.

"No".

"You will not know me … Never! – Ha-ha-ha … you cannot know me … The key to your eyes and memory is blocked in my heart … No you cannot know me – Not your kind".

The old man put his palms over the black fire and yawned and there was an immediate change. Sitting behind the fire was an old cranky woman in a loin cloth. She had deep-sunk sockets which held white bulging eyes. But for one long inscisor on the upper jaw, she was toothless.

For the first time that night, Dick was really afraid. He turned to run out, but he could not even get up. He tried to shout. But the lips were glued. From a distance he heard the old woman speaking in a sexy feminine tone – "Don't you know me"? Dick fainted and blacked out immediately. When he came to, the old man was back in his position. He was speaking again – "You are not even a man and you have chosen a clear path of destruction … Ha-ha-ha….?"

"Nobody ever sees me twice. I am an escort. I can lead you to fortunes and glory. I can also lead you to doom and demise. There is nothing I don't know ... You were well read ... you worked hard for us – until recently. Yes. That was when you decided to ally with a foreigner ... a slippery one ...a traitor and a girl,with a bible in one hand and destruction in the other... ha-ha-ha – when the lion goes berserk and devours its kind – there must be a reason" And he burst into a ritual song. Suddenly, he stopped singing and started reciting some weird ritualistic lines.

"I am 'The Okpohrokpo'. Yes. 'Okpohrokpo'. Huh! The Lion! That's my name. I never strike from the rear and nobody out-runs me. You are in the house of the Lion. You are in a Den. Look at me ... Have you not seen me before"?

Dick looked up. The old man's face had changed dramatically into that of a lion. He bared and snared his fangs. Dick was almost fainting again. The Okpohrokpo changed into his human self again.

"Haven't you seen the lion before"? He asked.

Dick thought ... As for lions he had seen many in zoos ... But The Lion? That was a different story altogether. So it was no fairy tale afterall. The Lion? Faintly, memories of the legendary Okpohrokpo flooded Dick. The Lion. And now the more he thought and reflected on the living legend,the more he was gripped by convulsive shivers down his spine. The Okpohrokpo – the invisible and invincible Spiritual Leader of Department Five.The steward,gardener,cook and spiritual guide to the American founder of the Union. The Final Word. He almost fainted again.

The" Lion" was almost as old as life. He was older than the Union. According to the legend, he was born in the village of Egume, near Ankpa around the Benue tributary and Christened Agaba.

Local gossip had it that Agaba was a victim of the visitation of the animal kingdom on his father. The local gossip had it that on a hunting trip once, his father had scoured the whole length and breath of the forest, with no animal to shoot at. In desperation, he had brought out a calabash and his secret talisman and invoked the spirit of the animal kingdom to send forth animals before the barrel of his gun and charm them into obedience.

The animals came, led in long procession by their queen – the beautifully striped and coloured antelope.

In his haste, the father had forgotten the basic taboos and don'ts of the talisman. He shot the first animal that appeared. It was The Queen! The whole procession burst into a mutinous rage. The father invoked another charm and disappeared from the scene immediately. The animals trampled and scoured the scene. They picked his father's human odour and trailed it to his home. And there without anybody knowing, they cursed the household and cast a spell on the pregnant wife.

And so was Agaba born prematurely six months after. Seven days after his birth he was christened traditionally by the father. And that day was his last on earth. He did not wake from his sleep to see the next dawn.

In desperation and deep mourning, the mother moved whatever was movable from the household and made arrangements to make for her kins in a distant village near Ayangba. She set out for the futile trip the next morning with little Agaba on her back. All through the packing and the trip, the young Agaba cried continually and sorrowfully. The maturity conveyed in the deep-throated cries of sorrow of the young Agaba, so surprised the mother that she hurriedly bundled the young boy on her back and set forth for the long trip immediately.

But she was not to see her kinsmen again. Twenty miles from the village of Ijillo on a lonely bush path, she had her first premonition of danger. First, there was a sudden change in the weather into bright floral sunshine that penetrated the foliage of the thick jungle of the bush path. Then appeared the mysterious owl. The owl according to the mythology of her people was seldom seen during daytime. And when it appeared at all during the day, it came as an escort to the great beyond.

Suddenly, the whole jungle was caught in a loud uproar. So deep-throated was this roar that the whole jungle shook and shivered at its impact. Next, there was a high-pitched weird whistle, climaxed by the roar of a lion nearby. At the sound of the roar, the mother made a quick dash aimlessly along the bush path, losing valuables and loin cloth as she frantically but futilely sought refuge. Before she could realise it, the supporting loin-cloth and calico holding the young Agaba to her back snapped and the baby fell with a dull thud to the hard earth.

She turned back to retrace her steps and pick the fallen baby but suddenly the area was enveloped in a violent gale and wind-storm. The jungle foliage gave a vacuous staccato whine to the pressure from the whirlwind, the vegetation bowed and shuddered as the sheer force of the gale bent and uprooted century-old mahogany and iroko trees, Palm trees were uprooted and tossed aimlessly. Old, solidly-built oil-bean trees were picked up like feathers and made to swing in the air like flying saucers. A nearby tree was lifted and swung violently in the direction of the mother. And all she could utter as she was struck down dead was a hysterical "Ahh..". People later surmised she wanted to scream – "Agaba why are you doing this to me"? But Agaba was no longer there anyway. He had gone with the evil wind for orientation and grooming.

Agaba!! The Lion!!.The one who started out as a steward to the White Master and who initiated him into traditional African rituals and local lore . The one who now sat on the Right Hand of the Holy One – Pastor Patrick! The Spiritual Leader of the Union! The Lion!! It was all over then, Opoleh thought.

The morning light was now breaking in the horizon and a clear-headed sobriety overtook Opoleh. The whole room was now mortuary-quiet. Suddenly, in this oppressive opaque silence, he found internal warmth and solace. An over-powering light feeling over-took him in a trance-like evaporation of the skin from the main body.

In that state he found joy and serenity as he bowed in reverence to The Lion. The tables were now turned. This time, The Lion had changed from his aggressive stance. He was now the high priest petched on his alter and looking down on Opoleh with piety. Opoleh was in turn prostrate in respectful adoration, devotion and communion.

The Lion! Like one who had a supreme duty of worship and benediction to supervise, he glared with inner lustre and serenity. Suddenly, The Lion burst into weird ritualistic chants invoking spiritual guid-

ance for the dead and those about to go death's way. Sprinkling incense
into the fire for libation and ritual sacrifice, The Lion roared. There
was a mysterious echo as his spellbinding chants gripped the room in
choking suffocation. In a gramarye that incorporated magic lore, necro-
mancy invocation and exorcism, the Lion recited chant after chant and
wrapped it all up with a solemn prayer:

"Forgive them Mama those that trespass against you ... forgive them
for their ignorance ... forgive them who conspire with strangers to steal
from you...forgive them who betray you to foreigners...forgive them for
their rebellion!!.

Mama ... for you are too meek, too gentle ... too protective of your children ... for you are so protective of all of us that you vowed that whosoever
shall soil one finger with a threat to contaminate all other fingers shall have
that originally soiled finger excised from his system ... so protective that
you have put us all into a fortress and a stockade to shield us against the
evil omissions and commissions of those who have sinned against you so
that the virus of their shame and betrayal shall be contained without harm
to your beloved children ...

Mama ... for you are so good you sacrificed one of your milky, succulent and juicy breasts to us and for us that we may live and prosper
so that we may walk across all of life's journeys under your shadow and
protection...so that we may live to be grateful for your provision of a
bountiful harvest and forever sing your name in praise. Mama ... That
whosoever disobeys your injunction and brings shame to your children
and brings disorder to your rhythm, that bares and snarls his teeth and
threatens the peaceful sojourn of your flock shall, even he be one of
yours be excised and carted off from your flock like a cheap renegade
and made to pay the price of his folly.

Now sitting upon the mantle of your throne, have you not directed
me to convey your pity to this your straggler.

Now! ... May your children sing forever in your praise ... May your children suck forever juicy milk from your breast of life ... May your bounty
flow forever uninterrupted to your children. May your nectar be the breakfast of your children. And may your children walk all of life's journey under

your shadow, behind the beam of thy light. May all that obey you enjoy your kindly favours......

And above all may all that threaten you never live to tell the story ... your children ... your sons ... your daughters shall and will always remain one with you to cast out all that threaten you, including your own very lost flock.

All these you have already accomplished! And so shall it be!

Then The Lion burst unto a melodic song quite familiar to the "Igbunegbus" – the executioners in the Union.

With that signal, Opoleh was led sheepishly out to the cold misty morning where death was lurking and where he would pay the supreme sacrifice at the toll of dawn.

As for Mr Khan, the newspapers were not very sure of how it happened. But it was reported that his Audi had skidded and veered off the Ibadan Expressway on a notoriously murderous stretch sending the expatriate General Manager of U-pharm to his death in the swamps on that notorious stretch of the expressway; that morning.

Chapter 5

∞

INUA BAKO

"ALHAJI" INUA BAKO was born in Birkin-Kudu, Kano in the early 1900s. The son of Mohammed Bako and Halima Amina.

Inua attended the Tundu Wada primary school in Kano, where because of his scholarship, he was recommended to the Government Craft school Angunwar Rimi for further training. He later became an instructor at the Kano Craft School before proceeding for a one-year Local Government Course at the Kano Institute of Administration, with emphasis on Administrative Law.

He worked briefly with the Kano Local Government Authority before moving to Kaduna as an Administrative Officer in the Northern Nigeria Civil Service . Later, he was posted as Administrative Officer in charge of Jos, Shendam and Keffi.

By 1950, he had worked in virtually every major town in the then Northern Nigeria. In 1951, he was was transferred to Lagos and appointed Secretary of the Joint Task Force charged with procurement of war material for the use of Her Majesty's Government during the resettlement of veterans of the Second World War.

No one was quite sure of when Inua Bako became a member of

the Union. But it was rumoured that while serving in Lagos after the Second World War, he had an effervescent social life, which led him to cross paths with the Union.

In the late fifties at the old Can-Can Crazy Horse Nite Club, Inua Bako met and courted Bunmi Laniyan for the first time. They had a riotous and crisis-ridden affair, which culminated in a fight and later death by concussion and internal bleeding from a blow struck to the head. It was rumoured that some "good friends" cleared the whole mess for Inua Bako – and that was it.

Once initiated,he rose rapidly and became the undisputed "Mr Fix-it" of the Union by employing his numerous administrative skills,legal training and suave public relations personality country-wide. By 1960, he was already the Head of the Union's Department Four – Omega Compound – and quite appropriately Inua Bako floated the limited liability firm of Omega Associates that same year.

Department Four-The Front Office- was somewhat like the Administrative Headquarters of the Union. Some of its weird functions read like fiction. But no institution or person for that matter had successfully challenged its arbitrary power, conquest and breaches of the law.

Omega Associates – the front office of Department Four – paraded extremely well-trained and highly competent professionals in what the company called "Communication Techniques".

These men and women, very suave and glamorous mostly owed their positions to one form of Union connection or the other; without knowing it. The uninitiated amongst them mostly thought they owed their appointments in Omega Associates to some high uncles, personal pull or political clout. But the truth of the matter was that every employee of Omega Associates was related to the Union by blood in one way or the other.

Since the evolution of the Union, frequent tactical changes to put the organisation on proper course had been taken by Department Four. But the aim had always been the same- to run the Union and thereby run the life of the country through this clandestine apparatus.

The Union was a unique phenomenon peculiar to Nigeria. It was very doubtful if it had any true counterpart of parallel strength and enormity anywhere in the world. Perhaps The Mafia! Perhaps the Union Corse!! Or perhaps the Knights Templar!!! Perhaps, but even if they had parallel functions, none of these organisations could equal the Union in the means of regulation of speech, socialisation, rituals and thought control. Definitely none could equal its draconian means of regulation and its selective infiltration into every sphere of Nigerian life. That was why it was often said that where there were ten or more gathered, there may be one Union member,thereby creating fear and suspicion amongst non-members . Without this fear, the Union may have lost most of its capacity to control its own membership and achieve set goals - the acquisition of wealth and power for its members, terrorisation, extortion and subversion of society if need be.

The Nigerian frontier post at Illela, Sokoto State was not a particularly busy one. There was a constant pedestrian international flow across the border post and customs officials who perfunctorily waved everybody on. The peak of this traffic was on fridays when people as far as Dogunduchi in Niger Republic travel to the Sokoto market to buy and sell and to attend Jumat prayers. Private vehicular traffic increased during the week-ends when people on both sides go on social visits.

But occasionally, there was a remarkable commercial traffic in smuggled goods which the new Customs Area Administrator was poised to stop. Having received intelligence reports of an imminent crossing of the Illela Customs post of a large convoy of trailers, he moved from Sokoto to the border post in readiness for the challenge. Several earlier Union moves to get him transferred,compromised or recruited had failed to yield results. Thus on this sunny saturday morning ten 30-tonne weight Fiat trailers,bearing Union goods for delivery in Niger Republic bore down on the border post at full throttle. The new Area Administrator saw them early enough and braced up for the challenge, waving to the first truck to stop. But it didn't. Instead it bore down on the shaky wooden frontier barrier and brushed it aside. Foolishly, the new Area Administrator moved into the approach line of the trailer waving his swagger stick to stamp his authority home. But the only authority around that sunny morning at Illela was the combined roaring horse power and grinding weight of the approaching Fiat trucks. When they finished with the new Area Administrator, there was very little left on the sands to be related to any part of the human anatomy.

In the late sixties, a contract was awarded to the firm of Mother-Earth Dredging to clear the Niger River of its numerous sand-bars to make it navigable all year round. The contract was renewed in the seventies to clear the River up to the new Onitsha River Port. But by the next year when the port was commissioned by the federal government of Nigeria, the sand bars were back again blocking essential traffic of goods to the Onitsha port.

An agreement was reached thereafter for a continuous dredging and maintenance of the river to make for free flow and year-round navigation. The agreement reached with Mother-Earth Dredging for this continuous clearance of the River Niger involved so much money that eye-brows were raised in many circles. Especially when Government wrote into the contract that the firm was to be paid four years in advance for every four-year term.

A proper legal document was then drawn up, authenticated by the Federal Ministry of Works and passed to the principals in the contract – The Federal Ministry of Transport – for the appendage of the signatures of all affected.

But for four months, the file was held up in the office of the Director of Coastal Navigation (DCN). Routine checks by the Union revealed that the Director was "appalled by the colossal sum and terms of the contract" and had refused to be "party to it". Further attempts by the Union to seek the Director's co-operation and change of opinion failed.

Since the Director was not prepared to re-consider his stand on the issue, the Union was left with no other alternative. Two weeks later, he was dismissed from Government service having been found guilty of "divided interest, breach of the code of conduct terms for public officials and nepotism" arising from his "ownership of numerous construction companies with massive Government contracts." The Mother-Earth contract documents were of course promptly signed by his successor.

Men of the "front office" as employees of Omega Associates were fondly referred to by initiated members of the Union actually functioned as Sales Representatives. That was why their education and backgrounds vary widely. Engineering, Pharmacy, Communication Sciences, Humanities, Music, Nuclear Physics, French. Just any course at all. Once employed by Omega Associates, a fresh employee was put through a rigorous training course with the sole purpose of sharpening his communication skills in his area of basic training. For these men represented the interest of Union affiliated companies in such diverse areas as communication, construction, transport, and manufacturing. In addition, they were expected to update regularly their Fact Files on key personnel of their respective areas of interests. Consequently, Omega

Associates possessed information on members of the Intelligence community, The Office of the President, The President's Cabinet, The Military, Nigerian Security Organisation, The Police, Customs, The Manufacturing Association of Nigeria, Banks, key members of all the political parties and associations, journalism,academia, trade unions and student unions.

These Fact Files which were updated regularly were closely studied by "Alhaji" Inua Bako and a select group of initiated Omega executives. From the files a list of potential new intakes into the Union was drawn up. This list was drawn up after a thorough study of the usefulness of the persons involved to the Union. Usually, any recommendation was accompanied by a comprehensive background information gathered after a long period of study.

Employees of government establishments who are in influential positions and can "make things happen" or have access to "when and how things will happen" in government were particularly curried and recommended. Also employees of private companies who can influence award of contracts, distributorship, supplies, etc were also courted. But every new recommendation for contact and possible initiation into the Union was based purely on merit and must correctly specify the basis, motives and categorisation of the person's usefulness to the Union.

Once the list is confirmed, the task of contacting and "convincing" those affected that the Union way was the best way was mapped out by the select committee. Usually, the method of approach could be derived from the psychological and sociological profile of the person as contained in the Fact File.

For instance any evidence of immorality, alcoholism, deviant and pervasive tastes, criminal record, criminal disposition, likes, dislikes, evidence of fraud, evidence of financial difficulties and compromising information that would "convince" the "subject" was explored. And as a last resort – threat to the person's life. This comprehensive study and enticement into the Union was reserved only for those whose position and influence would be beneficial to the Union. All others usually seek out the Union; solicit membership for protection, progress and communion. And many requests were usually turned down.

∞

The Mercedes-Benz Saloon sloped down from the Eko Bridge unto Ijora causeway and veered sharply into the National Theatre Boulevard. At the car park marked "Entrance E" the car slowed down and parked neatly.

A smart personal aide alighted briskly from the Mercedez-Benz and opened the back door. Inua Bako stepped out sprightly.He was a tall handsome man,. still very much erect in his gait with greying hair and firm carriage. Today, he was spotting one of his favourite D L Rue matted velvet suits.

The afternoon was very hot and stinky but he felt cool and calm as he approached the turnstile to Entrance E. As he approached, a hail of recognition went through the small crowd gathered by this special entrance to the main bowl of the National Theatre.

As he moved into the foyer one of the young Omega executives ran over to him.

"This way Sir"

"Is everything alright"?

"Yes sir"

"What about the air-conditioning"?

"That has been fixed Sir".

"Alright. Tell Mr Okwechime that I want a complete media blitz for this one ... But no mention of my name ... In any way. Right"?

"Right sir".

Once inside, the cool air conditioning whipped across his face. He savoured it. The hum of voices in the hall had a deep-throated reverberation about it.

One of the hostesses hired by Omega for this assignment came forward, bent low and handed him a copy of the programme, showing him the way to his seat at the same time. "Welcome Sir" she said.

97

"Is this all you are offering me" he asked genially.

"No sir. There is the show itself and light entertainment thereafter … It's all in the Programme booklet sir".

"Okay. Let me see you after the light entertainment bit. Entrance E. Get in the car and wait for me. Is that alright"?

"Yes Sir". She nodded.

The Special Guests were all seated in the front row. He shook hands perfunctorily with some, hugged some affectionately and waved to others before sitting down.

This was good. This was one aspect of the job that kept him ageless and happy after all the behind the scene intrigues.

There had been so many of these, he had lost count. But this was special. It was challenging. Not the industrial hustling stuff. Not commercial. Not well connected recruitments. Entertainment – and all the glamour and neon lights. This was the life. This was what kept him going.

Just then, the National Anthem started playing and there was a shuffling of feet as everyone stood to attention.

As everyone sat down after the Anthem, he took another look at the hall. They were all there – celebrities in music, literary world, theatre, Top Ten Award winners. Producers and Directors. Rows and rows of dignitaries. And of course there were also rows of standees.

In a way, this was a "Thank-You" show of sorts. From the artistes to the Union and from the Union to the public. All of it put together by Omega Associates.

Just before the opening of the show, the two young men came over. John Imoni. Now, four years after, not very many people could even relate the name to this international celebrity that now bowed before Inua. They now know him as JI – the Hitman.

"Thank you sir, am grateful for everything" said John as he presented an autographed record to the Alhaji.

"You are a good boy. You deserve all of this". He shook hands with him for the first time since he had known the boy.

Next, was the film producer, Tony Dibia. Inua gave him a hug and

a cordial pat on the back. As he sat down, the voice of the Master of
Ceremonies droned on:

"Ladies and gentlemen, you are welcome to Success. On behalf of
Omega Associates, you are welcome to this special appreciation show
appropriately tagged: Lagos Give and Take Jamboree.

The two artistes on parade this afternoon are our own contribution to the International hit market and the World's Who is Who
in Entertainment. Presenting, Ladies and Gentlemen, the Riverside
Mellow hit whose name spells like money!! And his name has brought
money too.....

But that was later..."

At the beginning, it looked dicey to the son of the ex Can Can steward. Armed with a few tricks learnt hanging around pubs with his old
man., he had begged his way into being taught how to play the guitar
very early in his life. And he didn't lose his head. He combined his guitar playing with whatever education the teachers of the Local Authority
Primary School in Badiya, Lagos offered.

Just when he thought the sky would be his limit and was doing well
with his guitar and the Baptist Academy Obanikoro education, misfortune struck. The Can Can was pulled down to give way to new urban
developments – and Pa Georgie was left jobless.

But Pa Georgie had been around nite club gates for too long not
to have seen many of the seamy things that happen at night when
men are drunk. Like the brawls, the hustlers, the killings and the
strangulations!

But he was always a wise man. He kept his mouth shut when the
vivacious girl seen with Inua the previous night disappeared without
trace. And that was why he swore to secrecy after his initiation to the
Union. And he was properly rewarded too.

As the years went by, Pa George and his son had forged a close association to raise money.

Pa Goergie invested his small savings in a neighbourhood bar where
Johnny's guitar drew a lot of clientele. But he had a bigger dream which
he told to the old man who then put everything he had together and

gave Johnny enough money to make a 'demo' tape.

The old man did not know what a "demo" tape was. He didn't care. But he had confidence in his son. For nine months, Johnny took his demo tape round the recording companies – EMI, Decca, Polygram, Rexel, Babel, Grylord. But he had the same evasive comments from all of them: "The voice is too mature for a young man". "The age is difficult to promote", "No previous exposure", "His music has no commercial direction", "The commercial value is not worth the investment".

But the boy was street-wise. He took his demo tape elsewhere. To Inua Bako. For two weeks, he tried, to no avail. But he persisted. Somehow, the boy knew there was some kind of relationship between his old man and Inua.

That friday morning was his lucky day. Inua was on his way to his office when he saw the boy at the lobby.

"So you are in already" he said "Okay come in let's settle your problem". and so was the problem settled – with a phone call to Rexel. An Omega executive in that field was sent over to straighten out the details and "give sound production guidance,with a reasonable contract"

The debut album was a rave. Inua took the challenge by the horn. Rexel did the production and recording. Omega did the promotion.

The three subject press,radio,outdoor and television advertising campaign was launched with:

"I am Money..

Take me"

This was to firmly establish the name I-M-O-N-I

The next subject switched the name around:

"Imoni – Jay

They call me J-I."

And the last was to firmly hit the name home.

"Imoni-Jay (The Hit Machine!)

The money is right on cue!"

Four years and ten international hit albums later, he was worthy of Inua's hand shake.

Tony Dibia read the jaded copy of "The Outlook", for probably the 40th time that morning. He turned the pages of the magazine involuntarily with every article and every photograph in the magazine etched in his sub-conscious.

Presently, on the door opposite the ante-room where he was sitting, marked "Director National Production" two ladies in revealing thigh-length skirts came out of the office and walked out. He yawned and looked imploringly at the secretary seated opposite in that direction. But the secretary was too busy admiring her make-up in a pocket size mirror to notice.

He looked at his watch and confirmed that he had waited for ten hours in his 40th attempt to reach Abdul Azeez, Director National Productions and probably the most powerful man in television in Nigeria.

The secretary made to put her things together, looking at her wrist watch. "Time to go home – you think you will like to leave a note" she said perfunctorily.

"No I will continue to wait"

"But he is gone. He took the back entrance – sorry I thought you knew ... he is gone out with the two girls you saw just now"

"Huhh" it was an involuntary cough of frustration that spoke of all the bottled up anger on Tony's chest as he clutched on his pilot recording and synopsis and made to go out.

But that was five years ago before Omega. Before the death of his father. And the performance of customary burial rites before the father's interment. And as the eldest son of Pa Dibia, he agreed to be initiated into the Union as requested by his father. Once performance of the traditional burial rites of Pa Johnson were over, one thing led to another and Omega Associates took over. Five years later, Tony Dibia was the most popular independent producer in Nigeria. Omega productions had bought the peak viewing hours of fridays through to sunday and put Tony's programmes on the slots exclusively for national viewing; and it became a big scramble for everyone to get home and watch Tony's irresistible offerings on the tube. And now, he was a Holywood celebrity.

Chapter 6

◯◯

ASHAKO

BY THE LAST light on that rainy day in July 1968., Ashakoleh Imienyi alias "Ashako" was ready. He checked the dug-out canoe for the umpteenth time. He had left his Oguta base four hours earlier using bush paths and jungle tracks., the likes of which Biafran and Nigerian troops avoided. He had skirted all military locations and reached his traditional staging post, the River Asse, a tributary of the great Niger, on the outskirts of Ndoni.

'Ashako' moved through the thick of the night, skirting Aboh in the Midwest, berthing in a solitary spot between Ozoro and Ashaka on a tributary of the River Niger. He dragged the dug-out canoe on shore and camouflaged it effectively.

That morning, he was at the Ozoro market on the Nigeria-held Midwest mingling with the crowd. Window-shopping, he haggled perfunctorily before making a detour to the stall of his regular customer-a Union member. They chatted over kolanuts, agreed a sum, he paid and departed. That night, he took delivery of twenty-five bags of cassava brand edible salt and set back for his return journey.

Two days later, he was back in Oguta, the salt securely stashed away. In Biafra, where salt was greater than gold, that made 'Ashako' an instant millionaire in the Biafran pound, that is if he did his business in Biafran pound.

But long ago, a sixth sense warned Ashakoleh not to commit his assets in the Nigerian pound into Biafran currency. The subsequent sheer worthlessness of the Biafran pound convinced him of his foresight. The ensuing thriving black market all through the war ensured that the Nigerian pound continued to be in circulation-even inside Biafra.

Not even Chief Obafemi Awolowo's master-stroke of changing the Nigerian currency could stop Ashakoleh. As soon as the announcement on the impending currency change was heard in Biafra, he had set sail, arriving in Ozoro,on the Nigerian side of the then raging civil war to discuss with clan and family heads of the Union who ensured that the conversion of his assets to the new currency was done smoothly.

Although he had voluntarily enlisted in the Biafran army in 1967 on his return as part of the grand exodus harkening to the clarion call to come home, his early combat experiences at Obollo-Afor convinced him that his survival would depend not on his gallantry but his sixth sense. He subsequently suffered enormous "shell-shock" at the epic battle of Opi junction, became one of the "artillery boys" that were to become very numerous in the course of the war, discharged himself from the army and went back to the safety of his village in the rear to convalesce.

With the fall of Enugu to Nigerian troops and the movement of the Biafran capital to Umuahia, the concentration of military traffic slowed down, "Ashako's" business forays. While he now made fewer trips, the scarcity thus created had naturally pushed prices up astronomically. But then, threats, blackmail and actual search and confiscate trips by soldiers had also increased. To safeguard his wares, he had to relocate to a safe haven in a virgin jungle;where he cut out a massive under-ground storage bunker that he effectively camouflaged with natural foliage.

Just at the beginning of the rainy season in 1969, Umuahia the seat of government fell and all the personnel and authority of the Biafran government had to move again. This time government business was not concentrated in one town but scattered around Owerri, Etiti, Amala and Uli with the naval headquarters remaining in Oguta.

By the time Umuahia was lost, there was virtually no will to fight left anymore in the Biafran populace. The Biafran Army strength had been so depleted by desertion that fresh conscriptions were ordered by army headquarters. The conscription teams combed all nook and crannies, villages and hamlets for able-bodied men to bear arms. Hitherto passed over elderly men and those dropped on grounds of ill-health, including the "artillery boys" were picked up routinely for combat service.

At that stage, Ashako took a decision to leave town permanently and settle in his bush camp by his storage bunker. It was at this camp that he heard the surrender of Biafra that fateful January evening of 1970.

After years of hardship, hunger and deprivation, the end of the war heralded another frustration for Biafrans. The official Biafran currency in circulation was not recognised by Nigeria and was infact illegal. To cushion re-entry into Nigeria, Biafrans were given a few Nigerian pounds per adult in return for all their millions of Biafran pounds. Ashako saw this development and discerned a unique opportunity for a good investment.

All over Biafra were red-eyed hungry ex-soldiers whose only worldly assets were left-over arms and ammunition from the war. And could do anything to have some Nigerian money in their pockets.

Ashako analysed this immense business opportunity and set up shop immediately buying off war surplus, with emphasis on pistols, automatic rifles and light machine-guns; with accompanying compatible ammunition. With a reasonable investment of five shillings per pistol, one pound per automatic rifle and three pounds for light machine guns, he had converted his bush storage bunker into a healthy armoury at the end of one month.

The private armoury was made up largely of .45 Berettas,. 45 Lugers, Smith and Wessons, and 9mm service pistols. For rifles, there was the 9mm FN (Fabriquen Nationale), the 7.62 AK47 (Kalashnikov), 7.62 Madsen, the 9mm Cetme, Uzi, Sten and SMC. There were also MS-1 and MS-2 and more than ten thousand rounds of ammunition.

Although Ashako knew that his private arsenal was a sound investment for the future, he was also aware that post-war Biafra offered very little opportunity. He therefore made up his mind to return to Lagos three months after the war.

Lagos! Nothing had changed that afternoon when he alighted from the lorry at Yaba bus terminus. As he gathered his battered trunks and walked down the ever-busy Ojuelegba road, he wondered what his old abode at Adebiaye Street would present. Number 192 Adebiaye Street looked as derelict as ever. The ageing three-storey building stood towering over the neighbourhood and the adjoining railway line in decay.

The fifth room on the right on the ground floor used to house the Adebolas. He made for the door and knocked. No reply. He knocked again but some children playing football in the central passage told him perfunctorily that there was nobody in the room.

Room Nine, opposite had been his abode for years. He turned and knocked on the door . After three knocks, a female voice answered as the door creaked open noisily. The lady had obviously been asleep. She yawned lazily as she took in the shape of Ashako.

"Yes"? she asked.

"Sorry … Afternoon … Actually I am looking for anybody I might know from way back".

"So? Who might that be"?

"What of the Adebolas in the room opposite". Ashako asked.

"Adebola? Nobody like that living in that room".

"What of Baba Niyi" he persisted.

"For where? This man! … what do you want. You don't know who you are looking for … so better go away..abi,you dey find another thing"She asked in pidgin English

In her outburst, Ashako thought he could faintly discern a slight Igbo accent in her speech. That gave him hope and he decided to explore further.

"Actually … you see I used to live here".

"Where? This compound?".

"Yes. This compound. Infact, this very room" he emphasised.

"Really? So where are you now"?

"Nowhere really. I have just come back ... the war ... you know".

"Chinekeme-o! Nna please come in ... Heh" She exclaimed.

Ashako went in and was offered a seat. Everything had changed. The feminine touch in the room was over-whelming. Everything was crisp, neat.

"So you are Ibo"?

"Yes-o ..."

"Huuh!! Please have something to drink" she offered, opening a small bed-side refrigerator.

He had a drink. She cooked and they ate. And they talked. Her name was Uchennaya Mba. Although she was from Mbaise, she was born in Lagos and stayed in Lagos all through the war; with all the persecution, the registration and temporary incarceration and the loss of esteem.

"So how was the war?" She asked.

"Bad ... very bad. I would rather not talk about it".

"Okay, I understand".

They talked about everything. About Lagos, about accommodation and jobs. At about nine that evening, Ashako had to break the all-important topic.

"Uche ... you are the first person I am meeting in Lagos. Fortunately ... we are one ... I will need shelter for sometime before I can find a place. Please, can you help? ... Please!"

In the excitement, Uche offered her place but Ashako was to understand her trade and routine much later. She worked most nights, sleeping out most nights when business dictated. That marked the beginning of their cohabitation and eventual marriage four years later.

The next day, he visited the Apapa based Peugeot Pick-Up assembly plant where he had worked as a fitter before the war. There, he learnt that the company had shut down its local assembly plant and now imported fully built up pick-ups from France. Baba Sani, his amiable foreman who introduced him to the Union years ago had died the previous year in a motor accident. Discussing his situation further with the Staff

Manager, he was told that the company had no immediate opening for a fitter but that a man with his kind of experience might be needed in the new Volkswagen assembly plant on the way to Badagry.

So to the new assembly plant, he went the next day and luckily, there was an opening for a skilled auto machanic/fitter.

Established in the early seventies Volkswagen of Nigeria Limited was a joint initiative between Volkswagen of Germany, the Federal Republic of Nigeria, The Lagos State Government and a few other investors. At the factory situated on the Babagry Expressway, Ashako was to pick back and refine his long lost skills in a hurriedly organised refresher course. The main body parts for the Volkswagen assembly plant were imported direct from the Volkswagen factory in Wolfsburg, the main factory and administrative centre of the Volkswagenwerk AG. At Wokfsburg, sheet steel was ran direct into pressure and the bare parts for the front sections, rear section and roofs were produced. The presses shape the sheet steel in a precisely controlled working rhythm and parts and moved them into conveyor belts for packing, crating and straight on through quality control to the export jetty for international supplies to Volkswagen worldwide assembly network,including the plant on the Badagry Expressway.

The Lagos factory where Ashako worked therefore essentially welded the various parts together to form cars. The giant robotic welding machines which welded and joined the pressed steel parts together to form the main frame of the vehicles were semi-automated to handle the two hundred or so spot welds that held the vehicle together.

The next stage of the assembly line involved another hundred or so spot welding to connect the front and rear sections with the roof of the vehicle. Overhead conveyor chains brought the front, rear and roof sections together. All the sections were aligned with accuracy and the welding was automated for a few minutes and all the sections were joined in one rigid unit.

Next, the body was moved on a conveyor to where the sealing welds were carried out. Now the bare body was allowed to fall into queue as it moved on to other points where doors, fenders, front and rear hoods were installed.

The hollow car was washed and dried alternately before being immersed in a full tank of primer paint. It wass taken out for a second layer of paint, which gave the paintwork its thickness and durability before the final finishing coat was applied using hand-held spray guns and finally the car was baked dry at high temperature.

The final quality check was on the Roller Test. The vehicle was accelerated through the gears on metal rollers. Highly sensitive measuring instruments kept a constant check on the exhaust emission, brakes, ignition timing, engine dwell angles and idling speed. After a last visual check, the vehicle was ready for the market and left the assembly building for the parking lot.

As an experienced hand from the first Peugeot Assembly plant in Apapa Lagos, Ashako went through the Volkswagen induction with flying colours and only two years after, he was made a Floor Supervisor. The pay was comparatively very good and the welfare perks were enormous. These afforded Ashako the wherewithal to settle down quickly, move into a bigger apartment with his family which by now was growing rapidly – with the birth of two children.But he had even a better source of income- the sale of weapons from his secret armoury with very huge margins to the underworld.

Four years later, he resigned from the Volkswagen Assembly Plant and set up Union Motors an integrated auto sales service workshop on Ikorodu Road, with funds provided by the Union.

"A metallic Silver-grey Peugeot 504 SR salon with registration number LA 9811 BD and chassis number NU06207 parked at 18A Ageni Street Palmgrove, Lagos was stolen in the early hours of 20th November 1984. The car belonged to Mr Tonye Willex of the All-Stars Bank – Anyone who has any useful information about the whereabouts of the car should ..."

The announcements on the radio continued reeling off thefts, armed robberies with violence and two deaths – all involving car thefts in one night alone. To listeners of the radio announcements that morning, the thefts were repetitious and only added to the statistics of car thefts and related deaths in Nigeria, which was growing at an alarming rate.

The importation of luxury cars was restricted by the Nigerian government during the Nigeria/Biafra war to curtail foreign exchange expenditure. The post-war oil boom threw open the floodgate to the importation of all manner of luxurious cars. So too did it account for an alarming increase in the rate of car thefts. By late 70's and early 80's auto thefts had become so numerous and sophisticated that the nation's law enforcement agents looked helpless in the face of their assault. Once considered a business for unserious drop-outs who wanted joy-rides and would sooner or later abandon the car, the new wave was the handiwork of professionals who had developed the business of car theft to a fine art.

By a conservative estimate, Ashako Imienyi had a hand in 80% of the cars that were stolen in Nigeria during the period.

He had an organised syndicate that operated through Union operations in Niger Republic, Republic of Benin, Togo and Cameroun. In Nigeria, key Union officials in the Department of Customs and Excise, The Licensing Authority, Insurance, Police, Ports Authority and the Union of Road Transport workers ensured a hitch-free operation. Above all, he had the arms and ammunition to arm car theft squads round the clock.

Although the Department of Customs set up the notorious "Red Squad" in 1979 to track cars stolen in Nigeria and smuggled to neighbouring countries for sale, the squad's activities were short-lived – at least the Union ensured that.

In the case of the stolen car of Mr Tonye Willex, the lonely broadcast of the particulars of the car over the Radio Nigeria network worried Ashako. The car was originally planned for sale in Cotonou in the republic of Benin and was to have been spirited across the previous night to the new owner who was waiting in Cotonou. But these radio announcements! Something would have to be done to the radio end, he thought.

Convinced that the news of the theft was by now too widespread, Ashako decided to switch to "Plan B". And by the next morning, the car had been issued with a new vehicle number BD 2700WF. A new vehicle Licence valid for the next two years was procured. The purported vehicle licence which was issued in Warri, Bendel State in the sum of forty pounds gave the owner's name and address as Isaac Odetayo of 11 Gbadamosi Avenue, Bariga, Lagos. Also procured were an assortment of other fake documents – an International certificate for Motor vehicle, complete with facsimile official seal markings, a back-dated Insurance certificate and official receipt of sale.

The car was then re-sprayed in maroon, the bumpers changed to American specifications and a sun visor installed. The car was later delivered in Cotonou without any hitch.

For other cars snatched that weekend, their destinations were different. The cars as they were known by their former owners ceased to exist the moment they were driven into any branch of Union Motors. There, complete stripping was done and the results of the cannibalisation would then be crated to Union Motors Spare Parts Departments as stock of spare parts for sale in the open spare parts markets around the country.

By the early eighties, a scared and concerned citizenry had started installing extra security gadgets in cars. Pedal locks, steering locks, fuel cut-outs, computerised immobilisers and alarm systems. But these devices succeeded only in scaring away joy ride car thieves. For the professional Union operatives, the ground rules had changed. Union gangs on the prowl, became more ruthless, business-like and fast. There was more detailed planning, reconnaissance,ruthless use of weapons and deaths. Cars were no longer stolen when parked, but violently snatched with guns blazing.

With this development, Ashako's investment in arms and ammunition at the end of the war began to pay off handsomely.

A Mercedes-Benz 230 saloon car was snatched at gun point on Webb Road, Ikoyi. But carelessly, the car-jackers left behind a bunch of keys. And Mr Tunde Oweyemi, the owner of the car and the Director of Coastal Navigations picked up the bunch the next morning and hoped that Police investigation could start from there.

But he was mistaken. That same morning, while reviewing the operations of the previous night with his team at Union Motors, the issue of the missing bunch of keys came up for discussion.

Presiding over the meeting, Ashako stated his utmost disappointment at the sloppiness of the boys and warned the sector leader that the Union cannot afford more slips. It was thereafter resolved that the sector leader should retrieve the bunch immediately and offer Mr Oweyemi the appropriate inducements.

And so that morning, the Sector Leader dressed in an immaculate flowing "agbada" national dress, well cut-out expensive jewellery and displaying elegant carriage and exuding success drove into Mr Oweyemi's premises in Ikoyi in a white Mercedez saloon ,parked and rang the door bell, waiting expectantly. After a while the madam of the house peered through a maze of metal protectors.

"Yes. Can I help you" .

"Oh-Yes, Madam. I will like to see Mr Owoyemi".

"May I know you? I don't think he is expecting any visitors".

"Just tell him I am from the Police to discuss his car theft".

"Ah Police", Relief flooding into her eyes as she quickly drew the door and protectors open. After a while Mr Oweyemi came down, exchanged pleasantries and invited The Sector Leader to his study.

"Ehe ... I appreciate this timely response. How they beat all the security around Ikoyi and Victoria Island to get away with the car still beats my imagination ... "

The Sector Leader cleared his throat and in a cold,menacing voice said "Mr Oweyemi, I am not from the Police but I have called here to offer you a sound guarantee that you can go about your business in this town unmolested ... that this will be the last time any car belonging to you will ever be snatched ... And to re- assure you ... your Mercedes-Benz snatched by some of my boys early this morning has been returned. Infact, the car is parked outside down your street."

He stopped and looked Mr Oweyemi sternly in the eyes and continued "All I will require from you now is the bunch of keys that my boys unfortunately dropped in their undue haste this morning during the operation and the whole issue should be considered closed. Of course I do not need to remind you of the severe consequences of allowing what has transpired here today to get to anybody ... And I mean anybody, including your wife, Mr Oweyemi."

Mr Oweyemi was shocked with disbelief. This elegant gentleman? He offered a feeble resistance. "But I have already reported the case to the Police and they have the bunch of keys ..."

"Mr Oweyemi" The Sector Leader snapped, "Don't stretch your luck. Yes you have reported the case on the phone and the keys are still with you. You are to make a formal report at the station and hand the keys over. The DPO told me all about it".

At the mention of the details of his telephone discussions with the Police, Mr.Owoyemi knew that he was totally ensnared.At that point, he broke down in fright and handed the keys over to the Sector Leader.

∞

All through the Lagos Give N Take Concert, Obode could not relax. The casually hinted appointment with Inua Bako left her in anticipation and trepidation. And since that chance first contact, Obode could not take her eyes off the strange man in a well cut suit. His speech at the concert was flawless, moving and most romantic.

Obode liked music and entertainment generally. But the hint at the political import and value of the two artistes on parade? No. She didn't see that as she was not very political. She was more concerned about the basics of life – food, shelter, clothes and the good life. But this strange man with effeminate handsomeness … with a bright twinkle in his eyes that could talk music, business, love and romance side-by-side effortlessly in Ibo, Hausa, Yoruba and flawless Queen's English had a charming personality that was most compelling.

The show over, Obode delayed for a deliberate twenty minutes before joining Inua as planned. She approached him, packing her hair backward delicately, rolling her hips and projecting her burst firmly as she did so.

"I am sorry sir, I kept you waiting." as she stretched her hands to Inua for a handshake. " My name is Obode Woemene and I work for …

Then she felt the piercing gaze and the forceful charisma of his stare.

"O.B.", he said caressing her hands warmly. She felt a flush of electric current run through her as a lingering excitement clogged her speech and left a strangulating lump in her throat.

"O.B. That's what your friends call you isn't it?"

"Yes. But how did you know?"

"Never mind" he said as he held her hand and led her to the waiting car. As they walked side by side, he felt a sudden longing for Obode. He looked through her well-proportioned carriage. As he looked, she grew ever prettier. Her skin was ebony with a lush radiance that was most captivating. Her frame was ample and sprightly and the overall beauty was alluring and natural. But then it must be said that Inua's eyes were very experienced in these female matters. And that he found very few women attractive and seductive.

Obode Woemene was not quite surprised at the way events were unfurling. True, she knew she was pretty and many men had confirmed that by their lecherous overtures. But she had always wanted a man who would give her a sense of security – not necessarily marriage – in a big city like Lagos in the absence of parental guidance. After a go at formal education spread between Harbour Road Secondary School in Port Harcourt and Our Lady's Girls High School in Effurun near Warri, she had moved away from her father, an Ijaw from Sagbama in Rivers State and her mother an Urhobo from Kokori in Bendel State to Lagos to seek for greener pastures.

She was newly arrived in Lagos when a frantic message came through from Port-Harcourt announcing her father's death, victim of premature retirement arising from the closre and subsequent rationalisation of jobs in the state –owned Pabod Corporation where he worked. Her middle class family had immediately been thrown into grinding poverty. Obode was then forced into paid employment prematurely. She was barely nineteen when she joined Plus-Point, the advertising agency as a Front Office Executive – a euphemism for Receptionist. While the job offered a salary that was barely enough to sustain her high taste, the occasional perks offered by visiting prosperous clients were regular and handy.

Her main sustenance however came from a chance interest indicated by a client. The agency had been in a model casting session for an advertising campaign for a new body cream. After three failures in as many casting sessions to get the right girl, the client had casually mentioned that the ebony, tall and supple beauty that he had in mind suited somebody like the Plus-Point's receptionist for instance. And that was the cue the Creative Director needed to make Obode up properly for the role. And ever since she had functioned as a successful model, raking in more than twenty times her salary in modelling earnings every year.

That night, in the palatial home Inua called The Temple, they sipped a mixture of cognac, Lemon, lime and ice cream as they kissed and made love alternatively on the rug. With freezing air-conditioning and tucked into the warmth of a comfortable duvet, they made love over and over again until they fell asleep in each other's arms.

The next morning, Obode was up early. She had breakfast prepared and generally tidied up. When she returned to the bedroom, Inua was up. She drew the bedroom drapes and the rising sunlight flooded into the room. Inua stretched on the bed warmed and aroused by the early sunrise. Next Obode entwined and led him to the adjoining bathroom, drew a pale of warm water and proceeded to lather his face and shave an overnight growth of beard and moustache, taking time to pick off strands of grey. A combination of the warm water on his skin and Obode's sensuous fondling of his face and hairs aroused his erotic instinct and before long, they were making love again in the bathroom.

"Oh, my god … " Obode moaned at the end of it "how long is this going to last?",she complained,in obvious anxiety.

"Forever. If you want".

"No, don't kid me, I have heard of your track record with women … and I am honest enough to ask what time I have been allotted …"

"Is that what you wish for yourself?"

"Not wish … but I am being frank."

Roughly and very violently, he pulled her to him and as he entered her forcefully, he muttered again "OB … I promise you … this is forever."

Obode and Inua spent more and more time together. In Lagos social circles, they became inseparable. They spent weekends together at Tarkwa Bay, played polo, visited the Happyland Park and strolled on the white sands of Paradise Beach on quiet nights.

"You amaze me. Six months now and I thought all you wanted was a fling".

"But you know it. That you are different. Special. I will give anything to keep you … except that as you know too well, I am not the marrying type and I don't want my life encumbered by parental worries. So no children."

"But why me Inua, what do you find in me that is not elsewhere and why don't you see other girls anymore"?

"Well … come to think of it, you are so natural … so well brought up.. so surprisingly pragmatic and malleable that no sane man will but care for you and make you his responsibility. And moreover … I love you…I love you Obode" Alhaji said, dragging her to him "but you know I can't marry you because I don't want to hurt you."

"But why?"

"There are aspects of my daily life I am not proud of and can never speak about and I have sworn never to get third parties to suffer unduly because of that."

"Why ... Why.. what is there to rob us of this fine thing we have to-gether?" ...

"Stop it!",Inua barked violently.

He continued, looking agitated and in obvious anger.." You will keep quiet and never probe this issue further. Have I made myself clear?" He bellowed the question with a dark stare and naked crudity that complemented his wild flashing eyes. Presently the dark eyes assumed a distant look as his faint face looked Obode through menacingly. With a swift motion, he pinned Obode to the edge of the sofa, frantically tore off her clothings and penetrated her forcefully. She was dry and not ready for him when he entered. But she endured the pain ... and the humiliation. At the end of it all, Alhaji stood straight, his penis bleeding from the rough contact.

"Obode" he said quietly" I am very sorry ... but we have to understand each other." He stalked out of the sitting room, had a shower and slept off. Now in his sleep, he looked almost like a baby.

When Inua woke up, Obode was beside him on the bed. He turned to her and he could see the moist and hurt in her eyes. "Is there anything wrong?" She thought for a moment. She sighed and held her breath and spoke haltingly "I want you to know that I understand you – totally. I want you to know that I know how well you love your work ... the long hours, the long meetings and your exercise of power." She stopped abruptly.

"You do OB?. Go on...tell me.. you know I like your candour".

"Yes. I will never interfere in anyway with your job, your power brokerage, your meetings or your friends. I only want to be given a fair chance to be allowed my little space to be devoted to you, to make you happy – No. To make us happier."

"Thank you very much." Inua said "we are one with each other already and nothing is going to change that".

That summer, they vacationed together. It was a World Tour starting with a visit to the new apartheid-free South Africa. Then to England and unto the United States and the holiday resorts of Acapulco, in

Mexico. This, once a year vacation became a regular routine for the next six years.

Three weeks after their return from the sixth summer trip, Inua paid a routine visit to Obode's Surulere flat. That night, he drove himself. He had a cognac which he sipped directly from the bottle, all the time savouring the timeless youthful beauty of Obode. When he was through with the drink, he took her hand and they got into the Mercedes convertible together.

"Where are we going tonight?" She asked. He wouldn't tell her but just nodded forward with a wry smile across his lips. They drove through Alhaji Masha Road, unto Western Avenue, straight into the new bridge to Victoria Island. They drove for a while around Victoria Island taking the fresh coolness of the Bar-Beach before ascending another bridge that led to the new Ikoyi Park Lane Development project. Finally, they came to a well-appointed, split-level storey building nestled into a hilly outgrowth and over-looking the lagoon.

"What is this Inua".

"This ... What do you mean this?"

"I mean the house?"

"Oh ... The house? It's been ready for sometime. Just thought I should surprise you with it this night. It is all for you – a token of my love for you, congrats darling."

She jumped from the car and ran through the house. Every single room was furnished tastefully, with the kitchen fully equipped.

Inua opened a drawer in the bedroom and beckoned to her "Here darling are all the papers for the house – everything is in your name. She stared at him unbelievably. "Inua ... I will always be yours ... forever."

Two weeks later, she moved into the house – her house. And three months after, she got pregnant – by choice.

For three months, she managed the pregnancy secretly without arousing Inua's suspicion. By the end of the third month, she resigned from her job as Client Relations Manager with Plus Point Limited ostensibly to do a six- month Fashion Designing Course at HarrowGate Polytechnic, London. Although Inua objected vehemently, she had her way finally, stressing her need for independence and eagerness to do away with paid employment as good reasons.

Once in Britain, she changed addresses twice, relocated to Dublin where she finished a course in Fashion Designing and had her baby – a boy. All the while she made monthly visit to London to post letters to Inua in Nigeria using the London address known to him.

Her eventual return to Nigeria was shrouded in utmost secrecy. She had taken a flight to Port Harcourt and from Port Harcourt; she had journeyed to her mother's hometown in Kokori, Bendel State. There she had told her mother the complete story – how the child was a token of her love for Inua. How despite the fact that he didn't want children and marriage, it would have been a share waste not to have a token of their love and romance as a living memento.

And so it was that the boy – already three –months old with the ravishing beauty of his mother and the stillness and strength of his father was quickly adopted and raised by his grand mother. Although there was no mistaking the source of the deadly twinkle in his eyes, the boy was named Onini – The Leader and Ogaga – Strength, after his maternal grand father. Onini never lacked for anything. With a steady supply of funds from Obode in Lagos, his grand mother ensured that he got the best. He also grew up to be street wise in the traditional lore of his grand mother's people.

Soon after, his grand mother moved back to Port-Harcourt to as she put it "get close to her late husband's people and give Onini quality education in Port-Harcourt" as she approached old age. Another reason she didn't voice out was that she wanted little Onini to have a taste of a good urban life and grow up more cosmopolitan.

Onini grew up strong and street wise in Port Harcourt. He had just finished Secondary School when the Nigerian Civil War broke out. Adventurous, he joined the Biafrian Army. Fought gallantly with the Commandos during the war, and proceeded to the University of Lagos for university studies immediately after the war.

Following repeated playing of the popular Reggae tune "Meek Mother" on the Network Service of Radio Nigeria, it was obvious to all initiated members of the Union that a matter of very serious concern was brewing. That saturday evening, The National Conclave of the Union was holding an emergency meeting in the new wing of the Federal Palace Hotel. The venue of the meeting – the Four Presidential Suites on the last floor – had been booked two weeks earlier and were occupied since the previous night by the visiting Managing Director of Unifreight Overseas, London. The Presidential suites were screened and re-screened for hidden bugs and when they were declared sterile, four portable transistor radios were switched on at different frequencies as scramblers to neutralise all bugging devices, if any in the rooms.

At four that evening, the only door leading to the Presidential Suites wing of the hotel was locked by two Union field operatives who then took over security duties on the floor, although dressed in hotel uniforms. By seven that evening everyone was seated. At a nod from David Ajani, Professor Dapo Shobowale, the only non - head of Department allowed into the Conclave rose to present his report. It was a long report painstakingly put together after the Union's National Commission had initiated the exercise some three months earlier. The day's session essentially therefore was to approve the Shobowale Plan.

Professor Shobowale discussed the report all over. The origins of Nigeria and its colonial history. Nationalism and the emergence of Political Parties. Independence struggles and Independence. He then meticulously traced the history of the First Republic and its failure in 1966, the Second Republic and its failure in 1983 and the Fourth , Fifth and Sixth Republics and why they also failed.

He then traced the economy of Nigeria from agriculture through oil and gas to steel. His conclusion was that given the men and material resources available to Nigeria, there was no reason why the country could not challenge the best nations on earth in terms of standard of living, infrastructure,science and technology and a life more abundant for the common man;given the right leadership. The Paper therefore posited that a systematic acquisition of political leadership in the country was crucial to the attainment of the Shobowale Plan by the Union.

The Professor rose meekly from the corner chair where he was and flipped on a laptop computer at the head of the room. He succinctly traced the problems of ethnicity, self-interest of elites across the geo-political zones of Nigeria and youth restiveness against the backdrop of failed leadership. With examples from other countries where the military had held sway, he concluded that development may continue to elude Nigeria as long as the military remained in control.

The solution he posited was to have an organised, co-ordinated and dedicated brotherhood to run the nation and move it ahead. "And what other such organisation exists today better than the Union?" he asked rhetorically. He then traced what was to become the famous DDT formula – Disinformation, Destabilisation and Takeover – stages and concluded with a time frame for achieving complete takeover.

"Thank you Prof. for a well researched and most enlightening report. I take it that we are all guided by patriotic thoughts for this country. That apart from the main thrust of the Shobowale Plan; that there are also Union interests to be protected. We will be in charge of everything. Gentlemen from Police through the Army to the sale of oil and gas and award of contracts ... Once again, thank you very much Prof." Alhaji Innua Bako said amiably.

Professor Shobowale sat down and the floor was taken over by Bob Inene. As the oldest and most respected brother, the comments and views of the head of Inene Compound carried much weight.

"Brothers", he said, clearing his throat to underline his deep guttural voice. "These ideas are not entirely new ... Infact, they have been under consideration for some time ... but the reason we have not progressed them has not been for lack of courage. I think we feared that we might pollute the Union with negative political values – greed, competition, indiscipline, tribalism, nepotism, you name it!" He stopped abruptly ... cleared his throat again, looked around and continued. "But if we rightly think now that this time around, we can control these things ... by all means let us go ahead."

Ashako Imenyi then took the floor.

"Although the Great and Invincible one is not here, as should be expected, proxy of the Holy One mysteriously got to me this morning so I have the authority to vote on his behalf" He stopped and flipped through the voluminous report again. "Brothers, are we not contemplating the declaration of war on the Federal Republic of Nigeria? And if so, have we got the means and the finance .. Please pardon my ignorance but I have been through this report twice, the implementation of what we now call the Shobowale Plan and the financing of same is taken for granted … so,where will the money come from?"

Professor Shobowale quickly took the floor, bowed to the Heads of Compounds and proceeded. "Sirs", he said, "The omission of source of funding and operational details was deliberate. I did not want to appear presumptuous by usurping the authority of the Conclave to make such decisions." There was a perceptible nod of agreement all round the table which re-assured Professor Shobowale to add "On the issue of war declaration, you will find that on appendix four, that after the initial destabilisation, all that will be required is the elimination of just one man and the resultant systemic state of flux will ensure that our brothers will take over. Thereafter, the eventual hand over to the Union will be under the authority and supervision of the Federal Military Government of Nigeria".

"Thank you Professor … Good. Very good. I think you can now excuse us … so that we can look at your proposals in greater detail … Once again, thank you". David Ajani said conclusively.

After a further six-hour debate, the Conclave adopted the Shobowale Plan and moved that Ajani Compound should handle the destabilisation and elimination of key personnel while Bako's Compound would handle all finances.

∞

The crowd on Broad Street was now uncontrollable. Swelled by a throng of office workers and traders, there was now a complete standstill of all traffic – vehicular and pedestrian.

It was over 10 pm and even civil servants who closed since 3.30 pm were still trapped in Lagos Island and environs.

In far-away Ikorodu Road, Festac/Mile 2 junction and down-town Ketu,Agege and Isheri the traffic bottle-neck was unprecedented.

And in the absence of official explanations for the traffic gridlock, the rumour mill was agog with stories of an attempted coup and how fighting was still going on to wrest control of Dodan Barracks from the coup plotters!!.

For forty-eight hours, life in Lagos virtually ground to a halt as those trapped on the Island spent sleepless nights in their cars and the mainland was in complete disarray. Government's attempt to give an official reason to the cause of the bottle-neck and nip the coup plot story in the bud only succeeded in fuelling the rumour further.

In attempting to piece the origin of the problem together later, The Guardian newspaper had reported that coincidental multiple crashes on Eko, Carter and Third Mainland bridges started the traffic obstruction from about mid-day.

And towards dusk, other crashes and vehicular break-down and obstructions on the Western Avenue flyover, the Yaba flyover and the Orile-Iganmu interchange further exacerbated the situation.

By 7 pm that evening, two men on a motorcycle had under cover of darkness thrown a timed explosive device into the hose compartment of a fuel tanker caught in the gridlock on Eko bridge. Similar explosives were also installed on tankers and a luxury bus on the third mainland bridge, Iddo, Ikorodu Road by Fadeyi and the flyover in front of the National Stadium.

By 8 pm that evening the explosives were detonated. The ensuing massive explosions and fires gave birth to the rumour of the coup attempt. And the rumour in turn led to panic which created more accidents and bottlenecks, hysteria and resultant gridlock.

Twelve hours later, scores of fire fighters, police and military helicopters were still fighting hard to put the blaze under control. With every detachment of Army and Mobile Police headed towards any of the emergencies, the more credibility the rumour of a coup attempt assumed. Such was the fear that gripped the populace that forty-eight hours after, the entire city was still in shock and nobody could venture out. It took a personal announcement by the Head of State and Commander in Chief to re-assure frayed nerves. And gradually Lagosians started trickling back to work until life returned to normal again. The entire operation had cost the Union only a few manhours and explosives.

One month later, a mysterious fire and an explosion in the National Grid Control Centre of the National Electric Power Authority (NEPA) threw a third of Nigeria into darkness for over two weeks. Just about when a bye-pass was being installed, another severe explosion destroyed six central control transformers resulting in a a further one week black-out; nationwide.

As the Union destabilisation acts shifted into high gear, the Conclave had to meet again to give a go-ahead. Without realising it, events that had been set in motion had attained a momentum of their own. Of the two next targets picked, only a timely Conclave intervention saved these monumental institutions.

A decision to have local refining capacity of petroleum products was taken in the late fifties. By 1960 a company known as BP-Shell Petroleum Refining Company of Nigeria was established with a decision to have a refinery at Elese-Eleme, near Port-Harcourt. The Federal Government of Nigeria later signed a tripartite agreement with the two international oil companies and acquired 50 per cent shareholding in the resultant Joint Venture. To reflect this development, the Company's name was changed to Nigeria Refining Company Limited, and by 1965, the refinery was fully operational. Production in the refinery started with an initial 35,000 barrels per day in November 1965. With the substantial damage suffered by the refinery during the civil war, the Federal Government had to spend an additional seven million pounds to bring it on stream again after the civil war. By 1972, the Government acquired a further 10% shareholding in the company bringing its equity participation in the refinery to 60% . The company experienced tremendous growth and by 1991 a Petrochemical Plant to use materials from it as base stock was formally launched by the visiting Zimbabwean President, Robert Mugabe.

However, following the phenomenal industrial growth and upsurge in demand for petroleum products in the early seventies, the need to build another refinery was discussed and agreed. In 1971, the foreign consultant appointed to determine the best location for the second refinery, BECIP chose Warri,in the heart of the Niger-Delta.

By 1974 when actual work commenced, the capacity of the refinery had been increased to 120,000 BPSD and the need to link it with existing pipe network gathering systems of the oil companies had been taken into consideration.

The Italian firm of Snamprogetti, member of the ENI Group of Italy undertook construction of the refinery specially designed to handle Shell's Ughelli Quality Control blend and Chevron's Escravos blend. Like the Port Harcourt refinery, the Warri refinery also had additional Petrochemical facilities installed near it in 1990.

By the 1990s, refinery capacity in Nigeria had been increased following the opening of the Kaduna refinery earlier and the commencing of the Japanese built second refinery in Port-Harcourt.

Petroleum too had assumed a most significant role as the engine room of Nigeria's growth, responsible for over 95% of foreign exchange earnings. To earn this amount, the country depended on export of crude oil through two petroleum export ports located at Forcados and Okrika.

Following the operational implementation of the Shobowale Plans, the entire refining and petrochemical capacities in Port-Harcourt and Warri;and the export outlets at Forcados and Okrika were put in line for destruction.But a quick Union Conclave decision saved the situation at the nick of time.The decision was conveyed to the assault team that since the Union was not interested in inheriting a scorched earth, a frontal assault on the refineries was not in anybody's interest and must be halted immediately. Thus a decision was reached that striking at the Nigeria's jugular by a systematic destruction and destabilisation of all the petroleum export terminals was a preferred option.

To avoid the numerous sand-bars of the Niger-Delta and to accommodate the high dead-weight of super-tankers, the Escravos/Forcados tanker loading platform is located far away at sea, about 14 nautical miles away from the control centre and Tank farms on the islands. A long pipeline runs from the islands to the tankers loading at sea. While fears had always been raised about the possibility of diverting oil over this long stretch of under-water pipeline that was hardly patrolled,the target of the Union attack was the Beachhead and Loading Jetty itself. It was the loading Bay that was pulverised and sunk on a rainy friday night.

That same night, the Okrika jetty, situated on the Bonny River, some 49 kilometres from the sea was also blown up. The Okrika jetty had always been accident-prone. The jetty delivered products to tankers of about 25,000 tons at the outer berth while lighter coastal vessels of about 1,500 tons capacity and barges were loaded at the inner berth. The jetty had suffered repeated tanker collision with the result that even before the Union attack,its landing head was split and separated from the main body. That jetty was dealt a further severe blow in the dawn friday attack.

For three months after these attacks, no export of crude oil could be made. Emergency repair contracts were awarded to Julius Berger and Westminster Dredging to resuscitate the jetties. In the mounting insecurity following the attacks, the Nigerian Navy troop carrier and coastal landing craft NNS Ambe and the frigate NNS Agbakara were deployed to the two jetties on constant patrol and to give sea cover to a company of soldiers dropped on the two locations from the Amphibious Battalion in Effurun, near Warri.

The Union's war of attrition was beginning to have a telling blow on the government. Whereas session after session of the Security Council could not identify the source of the constant sabotage, a Security Report read at the last session of the National Security Briefing indicated a strong popular support for the sabotage efforts as possible attempts to discredit the military administration and stampede them out of office.

While repair work was in progress on the Okrika jetty, a Shell-NNPC drilling team was busy on the offshore drilling rig SEDNETH-5 in the Ikang/Aram oil field. Built in 1981, SEDNETH-5 was a new generation drilling rig with a capacity of drilling wells as deep as 10,000 metres. The rig was anchored on a 50,000 pound weight with a 4,000 feet, four inches wire leash attached. The rig, submerged up to 400 feet had a stand-by helicopter and a spare helipad. Apart from the operational area, it had a residential area consisting of accommodation for three tool pushers, two geologists, two engineers, two drillers, fifty general duty technicians,mechanics, floor/derrick and catering staff. The rig also had provisions for cinema/video hall, games room, cafeteria and library.

Faced with a wide expanse of an unending sea, rig life was extremely boring; and because it was also extremely hazardous, beer, spirits and hard drugs were officially banned. So were other substances that could lead to mental distortions and wrong judgement. And usually a duty tour of seven days maximum was operated. Seven days in which socialisation was restricted to work colleagues on board and movement restricted to the work routine on SEDNETH-5.

On this monday morning, the duty shift on the SEDNETH-5 was rounding off, with barely four hours to the end of their duty tour. Very soon, the relief team,on operational rotation was expected from Warri to take over the running of the rig for another seven days.

The Tool Pusher checked his watch as he made a few entries in the drilling log book. Thereafter, he continued his Handing Over Notes to the Tool-Pusher of the arriving shift who would be on board for the next one week. Suddenly, he heard an explosion and saw smoke billowing up from the direction of the port window. He got up and walked over to the Master Control Room.

John Ebiyemi, age 44, a native of Mosogar near Sapele was on board as Tool-Pusher. As Tool-Pusher, he controlled the entire rig, with drillers,geologists and petroleum engineers reporting to him, all working hard to make a hole. In a way he was like a battalion commander, with all the authority to take decisions on the spot as they drilled into the depth of the sea to find the black gold.

"Where was that explosion from?" he asked.

"Looks like the engine room" somebody answered.

By now, more smoke was billowing. He raised the engine room on the intercom and confirmed that there had been a small explosion, but it was under control.

"What caused the explosion?" be bellowed.

"Still can't explain it. There had been an on-going are welding by the landing platform and there had been a light spark...whether that could have triggered an explosion down below ... Honestly, I still don't know..."

"My God! What do you mean you don't know!! ... And what have you done? No direct alarm to me and you sit on your ass there ... you want to get us killed? Don't you understand procedures anymore?"

He turned to the radio operator and shouted; "Get Safety Department in Port-Harcourt and Warri on the radio immediately. Tell them we have an emergency here. Explosion and fire. Can't trace the source. And put out an area-wide distress call ... No! Give me the radio."

He then proceeded to call Port-Harcourt and Warri giving them details of the incident. Next, he broadcast a MayDay distress alert stating the position of SEDNETH-5. Three ships answered immediately. One of them was NNS Agbakara.

Mr Ebiyemi then sounded the ship's alarm. At the sound, the drilling operations were shut off and everybody aboard as in earlier safety drills was expected to assemble at designated muster positions.

Suddenly, the Tool Pusher felt the platform sink below him and in seconds, he was drawn down, down and down. The platform was a huge structure, with a height of about 250 feet from the bottom pontoons to the top of the drilling tower. He realised then that the rig was sinking. He heard a bang. And another bang. Initially, he thought it was the boat buffeting against a large wave. Then, another sudden bang and the entire platform tripped over. Another explosion ruptured two of the main support struts for the platform and flung the derrick away.

There was now a general panic. People were running and screaming desperately in total confusion. Some had fallen and had been trampled upon. Others panicked and jumped into the deep ice-cold sea. A life-boat was quickly lowered and about a dozen men quickly scampered on board, but a strong wave picked it up almost immediately and smashed it against the anchor wires, tipping the men into sea.

Several others dashed for safety vests and put them on. Just, then, the boat tilted even further, spilling some of the men into the sea. Everything was happening quickly now. Another explosion engulfed the whole engine room in darkness as it billowed large suffocating smoke. The platform tilted more and more. A few of the men managed to get three boats working.

Just then the NNS Ambe arrived on the scene and sent out five rescue boats immediately, while calling for reinforcement.

There was a final explosion as the boat finally submerged. Everywhere, men were clinging to boats and rubber rafts. Ratings on the Ambe threw more and more rafts into the sea. As the men clung on to the rubber rafts, it was biting cold and some were vomiting uncontrollably.

First there was a sound of a helicopter, then two helicopters and soon the whole sky was full of choppers in a massive rescue effort. The helicopters from the Nigerian Airforce Force Helicopter Squadron in Port Harcourt made swoop after swoop, scooping up survivors and taking them to the nearby NNS Ambe. In four hours, the rescue operation was over and out of eighty-six men,including some of the early arrivals on the new shift,catering and security staff on aboard the SEDNETH-5 when it sank, only thirty-six survived the accident.

The incident sent a sense of outrage across the oil industry. Relating the incident to other sabotage acts on the oil industry, the National Union of Oil and Gas Workers reasoned that in view of the insecurity in the industry, it was unsafe to continue work until the Federal Military Government could guarantee the security of oil workers.The Union therefore declared an indefinite strike and work stoppage until the government could guarantee security.

The Federal Government subsequently set up a judicial commission of enquiry, where the survivors of the accident were made to re-live the trauma of the sad experience. The Panel spoke to the tool-pusher, Mr Ebiyemi twice, went through 200 memoranda, analysed drilling instructions/procedures, maps and technical reports.

At the end, sabotage was ruled out of the incident. It was confirmed that a wrong data which erroneously gave the drilling depth as an oil zone had misled the tool-pusher into using a low mixture of brine for the over-pressure. Unfortunately, the drilled depth was actually a gas zone as later geological data were to reveal. The resultant inadequate suppressing brine pressure led to a gas leakage and a blow-out; which in turn was ignited by an on-going arc welding; and then finally a collapse of the main drilling platform,derrick and living quarters.

The Report however, noted that occurring so close to some earlier acts of sabotage in Okrika,Escravos and Forcados, all in the oil industry, the accident created a fore-boding which did not augur well for the industry.

Chapter 7

THE ADEKUNLE OJO Memorial March was the most controversial
and volatile event on the social calendar of the University of Lagos.
Students wanted it and looked forward to it. The Government and the
University authorities dreaded and wanted to avoid it. Since 1978, when
a peaceful protest by students of the University over escalating cost of
living was met with Police firepower that left Adekunle dead, nothing
had been the same again on the anniversary of that march.

The date had become a rallying point for student activists .In discussing the impending rally at the Park Lane home of his "Aunty Obode"
with Inua Bako, Inua had reiterated the imperative for; and why an
active and vocal students agitation was crucial to rallying public consciousness on the need to effect a change in the national life and the de-
plorable standard of living of the masses.Onini therefore went back to
school with renewed vigour and conviction as preparations commenced
for the annual march.

That year, the massive deterioration in the standard of living since the
removal of all forms of government subsidies was sufficient to galvanise
the student body. From Jaja Hall, through Moremi Hall, to the notorious "Mosquito Republic" annexe of El-Kaneni Hall, Students were bristling with preparation. The crowd at Mosquito Republic was joined by
the even more notorious off-campus residential extension at Bamgbopa/
Abule-Oja;which was in turn swelled by street urchins,vagrants and the

unemployed as they sang in unison towards the University of Lagos Main Campus.

Presently, three-bus loads arrived the main gate of the university from the Medical School at Idi Araba. Behind them were another five bus loads in the yellow "molue" colours of the Lagos public municipal transport. Inside were three hundred members of the National Union of Road Transport Union who had come to march in sympathy and solidarity with the students.

An unusual stillness began to descend on the main boulevard of the campus as the hands of the clock drew nearer the hour of ten in the morning – the appointed time for the rally and march. And as if on a cue, everybody started moving towards the forecourt of the Haile Selasie auditorium. And never had so many people assembled for an Ojo Memorial rally. All along the streets, from the Iwaya Entrance to the Lagoon Front, people were moving in one general direction. Some with torn dresses as if on Rag-Day parades and all with placards criticising the government's policies. A group of students with bullhorns emerged drunkenly singing the popular Unilag chorus: "All we are saying …Giver us our Rights …"

Not to be outdone, another group arrived with a more powerful bullhorn drowning the now chaotic atmosphere with a more militant chant in pidgin English: "we no go pay … we no go pay! High, high school, fees, we no go pay!"

The crowd hailed their emphatic chant in unison.

Suddenly, the bullhorn erupted and switched to the attention-grabbing Unilag call sign: "Shegbue!"

And the crowd responded in unison.

"Hey"

"Shegbue"

"Hey",

"Shegbue"

"-Hey",

"Shegbue"

"-Hey".

"Great...Akokites"

"Hey"

"Grreeaatt Akokites"

"Hey"

"Ggrrrrreeeeeeaaaaaaatttt Akokitesɪɪɪ"

"Heeeeeyyyy!!!"

"Are we Fools?"The man with the bullhorn asked a rhetorical question

And the crowd yelled "No!"

"Are We Slaves?"

"No!"

"Are We Nigerians?"

And the crowd yelled a long

"Yeee ...ss!"

With that the bullhorn changed the chant to:

"We no go gree – o, We no go gree"

Government Power ... we no go gree!"

It was difficult for any student of the University of Lagos not to respond to that chant. The whole crowd broke into a spontaneous roar of emotional approval as one and all thought of all the abuse and misuse of "Government Power" on their persons.

Even as they sang, the crowd swelled. The Old Timers – elderly students usually to be found in the Faculty of Education- having a go at acquiring a university degree in old age marched on – clad in motley suits and jackets. Behind them was the most dreaded group on the campus – the Pyrates Confraternity with their typically morbid full dress red regalia, complete with skulls and crossbones.

So much crowd and the atmosphere was getting electric. People were everywhere as far as the eye could see. People were petched on all balconies of the old and new Senate buildings. An intensive electricity passed around the stands as everybody caught the tempo of the assembly. The Palm Wine Drinkers Club in their traditional white cotton jumpers and robes came in next, each clutching and drinking from a gourd. As they joined the crowd, they looked weary and spent. But that did not stop them from contributing a few "Comrado" chants to the gathering.

Presently, the whole crowd burst into a frenzy as the Students Union bus emerged from behind the Senate Building. A roar of applause and recognition shook the gathering as three men disembarked from the bus. Events were moving very fast now. As the three Students Union representatives climbed up to the auditorium verandah, the crowd was gripped in frenzy and ecstasy:

" Presido ... Presido ... Presido..." a chant of recognition ran through the crowd.

The tallest and most eloquent of the three men raised a clenched fist and the gathering kept still in obedience.

"Greeeeeee...eeaaaaaattttttt Akokites"

"Greeeeeeee...eeaaaaaaaaat Akokites"

"I say Greeeeeeee ... eeeeeeeee ... aaaaaaaaatt Akokites"

The crowd burst into a frenetic yell and they responded to the call sign from the Public Relations Officer of the Students Union,Onini Ogaga.

Tall, svelte and smooth Onini Ogaga was a thespian with oratorial talents of immense proportions. Reading the crowd, he knew at once that the way to reach them was to speak the mob language. The usually suave and fluent English language speaker burst into a mixture of pidgin; patois, and Rastafarian chant:

"First of all let us give massive respect to our forefathers ... for their blood watered the land...their tree planting efforts and their decayed bones gave us the oil boom that our oppressors are feasting on today!! ..." This was followed with a big roar from the crowd.

With his voice undulating, he continued ...

"My Fellow Students....let's offer thanks and praises to Almighty Jah for the air we breath and for making it possible for us to be here today ... yeah! For The Lord created us in his likeness – that is why we have intelligence ... and can discern right from wrong."

A big roar and animated dancing followed.

"Let us give maximum respect to all our parents for sending us to school and for all the suffering and sacrifices they make for us ..."

Another big roar.

"Great Akokites…Are we Fools?"

" No-ooo!"

"Are we slaves?"

" No-ooo!"

"My brothers and sisters, let's go out there and tell our brothers and sisters on the streets and our oppressors in Dodan Barracks that we cannot all go to their Defence Academy University … and what is good for their Defence Academy is also good for the University of Lagos.…"

"Good Food"

"Yes…o!"

"Free education"

"Yes…o"

"Water,light,accommodation,books,transportation,pocket money,well-paid lecturers,air-conditioned lecture halls.…."

"Shegbue! Shegbue!!" The crowd burst out in excitement.

"Today, even as we mark the death of our fallen comrade, we shall march on the streets, down the riverside … shout our complaints on rooftops and pull open their deaf ears in their barricaded barracks …"

More applause

"… And I dare them to stop us …We are ready for them this time… We will not be intimidated by anybody.. and let me warn them.…that nobody has a monopoly of violence !!!"

With one final exhortation, Onini Ogaga dismounted and moved up to the front of the crowd. As he did so, chants of excitement and fraternity moved him to wave to all. Then down on both sides of the boulevard, the crowd moved towards the gate chanting a traditional war song.

But even as they marched towards the gate, an under-cover State Security Service agent had radioed their intentions to his Awolowo Road Headquarters and in thirty minutes a squadron from the notorious Mopol 717 was speeding towards the University for an interception.

Mopol 717, led by the Deputy Superintendent of Police, Justine

Auleh met the chanting students, just outside the University gate by Bookshop bus stop. Armed with a megaphone, Mr Auleh told the students they had no permit for the March, that it was illegal and that they must return and restrict their March to the University premises.

But the students were unyielding and Mr Auleh ordered his men into anti-riot positions and to hoist protective baskets and gas masks. Everything was happening fast now. Behind one of the parked anti-riot police lorries, three tear-gas cannisters were fired. The noise of the shot sent a wave of panic across the crowd. And gradually, the students were pushed back to the university gate.

Once at the University gate, the students refused any further orders to retreat and a ding-dong battle ensued with the Police falling back on more tear gas cannisters. Soon, the students discovered an anti-dote to the effects of the tear-gas:kerosine. All manner of fabrics soaked in kerosene were passed round and spread across nostrils to absorb the effect of the tear-gas. And with this discovery, the students were emboldened and surged forward to continue their march.

At the sight of the now surging students, Justine Auleh ordered his rifle section to move forward and aim to incapacitate. As they stepped out in regulation manner and took aim, Mustapha Alli also steeled himself for the next move........

Mustapha Alli was a man of very little education. But in his chosen field, there were very few people like him. A professional to the core, he was happiest when peering through the crosshairs of a telescopic rifle. The only non-Union insider in a massive intricate sabotage operation, he was on a permanent contract with the Union as a hitman.

Mustapha hardly spoke, on account of a stammer and a speech disability since infancy. He was a Recce squad sniper during the civil war and found no useful employment after the war without his guns that he had become emotionally and almost organically attached . At the 'Depot' in Zaria where he was moulded, he was trained to shoot straight and shoot to kill. He had done exactly that ever since and very well too. He had killed without scruples, without emotion and refused to be drawn into political discussions and the rationale for his actions. Once a target had been identified and the money was good, he did his best to fulfil his contract.

On this particular day, he had been briefed and well paid and intended to kill and execute his contract to the letter. Every live shot from the police should be replied mortally to a maximum of ten Policemen hit ... after that he was to disappear from the scene.

The bit about disappearing from the scene was unnecessary. As a professional, he had recconoitered the whole neighbourhood and organised his field of fire and route of retreat. That was when he selected his jump-off position – a crypt on the roof of the College of Education auditorium. From there he had a clear view of the university main gate and as far afield as the St Finbarrs Road; and the University Road as far as the Bookshop bus stop.

Nature compensated Mustapha's speech defect with good eyesight and muscle reflex harmony. His small squint eyes were like the telescopic lens of a camera. He could bring objects into ECU- Extreme Close-Up- situations as necessary when the occasion warranted. While others required a high flow of drug-aided adrenaline to handle high risk jobs, he was naturally motivated, almost mechanical and precise in his efficiency. His muscle tone and reflex had a perfect harmony with his eyesight. He could therefore fire with precision without being conscious of his actions.

And so it happened that with the first sound of fire from the Police, Mustapha had picked two policemen through his silenced, telescopic rifle. He fired...and two policemen lay dead, even as the students were wailing and dragging away their wounded. With another volley from the police, three more of their men lay dead. It was only then as the last one fell down in a grotesque scream that DSP Justine Auleh realise that things were moving in an unnatural pattern.

He checked his men and ordered a rear squad to advance while he radioed for reinforcement and medical evacuation. Next, he checked through the field through his binoculars but could not identify any outwardly belligerent or armed student. But just to reassure himself, he picked on a raggedly looking student, armed with a club. But even as he fired, Mustapha's bullet whipped his head out of shape and he slumped to the ground.

There was total confusion now. Students were running frantically as the reality of the killings dawned on them. In the midst of the confusion, the Police reacted in even more panic by firing random volleys into the retreating students. Mustapha responded with more deadly precision, squeezing police lives away as they showed in his crosshairs. Before the turn of the minute, twelve policemen were down, dead on the hot University road tarmac. The Police broke ranks and retreated in panic and Mustapha packed his tools and left the vicinity. At the temporary cessation of hostilities, the death toll was; four students dead, three injured and twelve police dead, no injuries.

The injured students were rushed immediately to the Medical Centre. There, after initial administration of torniques to stop the bleeding and quick shots of morphine, they were put aboard ambulances and rushed to the Lagos University Teaching Hospital, Idi-Araba.

But the situation at the Idi-Araba gate of the hospital was even more chaotic. Two companies of soldiers had taken over the whole hospital and were virtually ripping it apart. The whole hospital was cordoned off. No one was going out and no one was coming in. Strict orders they said.

The situation was developing into an ugly spectacle. Scores of casualties from road accidents rushed to the hospital were stopped at the gate. A CNN television crew covering the crisis was curtly turned back at the gate. But that did not stop them from recording the anguish of the wounded and dying.

Later that evening, all the events were to be pieced together in a CNN Special Report. The report said Lagos, Nigeria was boiling and that students in retaliation for the detention of the President of their Union had apparently kidnapped an army general and a member of the ruling Supreme Military Council!

The Special Report gave the first hint of the advanced deterioration of the government versus students imbroglio.The Special Report pieced the events together thus: Earlier in the week, acting on a security alert, two truck-loads of anti-riot policemen had stormed a book launching ceremony at the Institute of International Affairs, Lagos. The over forty policemen who poured out of the trucks, armed to the teeth then proceeded to take strategic positions. They pushed open the main doors to the launch venue and in the midst of bewildered guests, marched out briskly to block all exit points.

Next, the commander of the squad, a stout, stubby man with tribal marks walked in menacingly, looked through the rows of invitees and stopped before Kunle Okilo, Secretary-General of the National Association of Nigerian Students(NANS) and said brusquely; "Follow me please, you are under arrest"

"Under arrest? For what?"

The exchange brought the proceedings in the hall to a halt. The dumbfounded assembly watched as Kunle protested vehemently. But to the consternation of all, the policemen all cocked their rifles at a command from their leader. The leader himself drew a service pistol.

"Don't waste my time ... and don't cause unnecessary bloodshed, ... " he said. At the mention of bloodshed, Kunle lost his composure. From behind, two policemen seized him and put a handcuff on him. Another slapped him across the face and shoved him forward. And that was how he was kicked and forced into a waiting car and driven away.

One week after, no official statement had been made about his arrest until the Annual March.

The distance between Idi-Araba and Akoka is made even longer because of the unnerving, winding chronically chaotic traffic between the two suburbs in Lagos. Because they were so far apart and so different in functions, very few people made quick mental connections between the two campuses of the of the University of Lagos located in the two different suburbs.

Whilst the Lagos University Teaching Hospital (LUTH) is a hospital, open to the public for 24 hours and generally accessible because of its location in the centre of the city, the University of Lagos on the other hand with its imposing, almost royal and elitist arched main gate was perceived to be very private and shared a distinct neighbourhood with the Lagos Lagoon. It was not a place you went through to a further point. It was not a thoroughfare to any other point. So you had to have a business there to visit it.

But unknown to many, the Lagos University Teaching Hospital and the University of Lagos, were two sides of the same coin. Most students of the hospital's Medical School spent at least one year at the Akoka Main Campus of the University of Lagos for their Pre-Medical Sciences before moving into mainstream medical studies at the Idi-Araba campus. The two institutions have the same Students Union body and the Medical School traditionally supplied the Vice-President of the Union every year.

So, when Brigadier Ishola Omojokun, the Director of the Army Resettlement School Oshodi, and a member of the ruling Supreme Military Council was to present Easter gifts to a group of disabled soldiers at the hospital's Physiotherapy Ward, he did not think too much of it before accepting the invitation. True, the disabled soldiers were from his unit and he had been instrumental to getting the hospital authorities to create a special ward for them. It was a weekend and he had opted to visit in mufti without his security detail, but with his batman and aide-de-camp. After going round the ward and having made wrapped gift presentations to the disabled soldiers, he was taken to the adjoining ultra-modern, fully computerised Diagnostic and Fertility ward extension of the Maryam Babangida Maternity of the teaching hospital.

Forty years earlier when during the General Ibrahim Babaginda military administration the maternity was commissioned, it was the biggest and most modern of its kind in Africa. The new extension to the maternity- the Diagnostic and Fertility wards were World-acclaimed and were being prepared for commissioning by the Chairman of the Supreme Military Council when Brigadier Omojokun visited the hospital.He built an informal pre-commissioning tour of the facility into his visit to the hospital-and that was where it all started to go wrong.

As they showed Brigadier Omojokun round the ward, there were more than fifty medical students ostensibly on clinical duty,complete with medical coats and stethoscopes around the ward. Presently, the Brigadier's party approached a lobby and the Director of the hospital pushed a button to call for a lift

As the door of the lift opened, the Brigadier, his orderly and ADC moved in to secure it. Next, the Medical Director stepped in, followed by the brigadier's ADC and batman. Just then another lift pulled up. As the doors drew open, the Brigadier was gently shoved and tugged to go into it by a group of white-coated "doctors". Immediately, the lift screeched off to the bewilderment of the Brigadier's orderly and ADC. And that was the last time anyone saw the Brigadier. So it was in response to the ADC's distress call that the soldiers were called in to cordon off the whole hospital and embark on a room-to-room search for the missing Brigadier. And it was the CNN report that gave the public the first hint of the disaster.

The CNN Special Report was also watched by a hurriedly assembled Security Council in the depth of the Emergency Operations Room in Dodan Barracks. A large black table ran the length of the Operations Room. At the head of the table was General Donald Atiku, Chairman of the Supreme Military Council, Commander-in-Chief of the armed forces and President of the Federal Republic of Nigeria. As he reclined his chair and turned his gaze from the television built into a panel on the wall, a hush fell on the room. With a wave of the hand, the Director of Military Intelligence used a remote button to put off the television and a curtain automatically rolled across the face of the concealed television panel.

General Atiku cleared his throat and in a very steady tone opened the meeting.

"Gentlemen ... when we met yesterday at our routine weekly Security Update, little did we know that we shall be here again at very short notice ... I thank you for responding so quickly. Today, we have an emergency of a very different kind ... Yakubu. Please fill everyone in on the details of the events earlier today.

Brigadier Yakubu Wanche was the Director of Military Intelligence. Besides him and the President, there were six other men in the room. These were the inner political and military caucus of the Federal Military Government. The real government behind the government:. The Provost Marshal of the Army. The Chief of Air Staff. The Chief of Naval Staff. The Director General of the State Security Services. The Chief of Army Staff. The Chief of Naval Staff. The Director of Operations and Logistics, Supreme Headquarters,Director of Strategies and Plans,Army Headquarters.

Brigadier Yakubu Wanche commenced his briefing. With a brusque military moustache, his briefing was brisk and precise. In summary he reported, "the abductor or abductors of Brigadier Omojokun are still not known. But the familiarity with which they operated around the Lagos University Teaching Hospital gives us a strong lead and all our cells in that neighbourhood have now been activated."

The apparently standard furnishing of the Emergency Operations

Room was deceptive. Located one hundred and fifty metres below the surface, a maze of lifts and stairways led to this massive underground labyrinth. On the underground Operations Floor, there were living quarters for the 500-man "Lightning Squad" of the Presidential Guard,with sufficient firepower to hold down an enemy brigade strength for at least one month.

Most central to the operation of the floor was the Command Communications Room. This top security room housed all the computers and sterile communication links with all the intelligence organs of government. The room also had access to the computers of Interpol and at least two other friendly foreign intelligence agencies.

The Chairman of the Supreme Military Council cleared his throat and glanced at the occupants of the room. In his usual affable manner, he swung his high-necked executive chair and faced the Director-General of the State Security Service.

"Wole ... so what have we got here? An abduction? Assassination ... What is the objective and who is behind it?"

General Wole Abioye, the self-effacing boss of the State Security Service (SSS), the ubiquitous octopus that was so feared smiled knowingly. Of all the national security agencies, the State Security Service (SSS), had the widest and most powerful reach. From its headquarters on Awolowo Road, Ikoyi Lagos it had a network of agents, reporting Case Officers in all the state Capitals and all major towns. There were also Field Officers in every Local Government headquarters and field agents everywhere: hotel workers, taxi drivers, tailors, journalists, students, mechanics, and prostitutes.

Previously discredited because of its draconian methods and harsh interrogation techniques, it had become the mainstay of most governments since it played a crucial role in saving General Ibrahim Babangida from sure death in the hands of putschists in the famous "Orkar Coup".

Glowing in its new acceptance, a happy General Babangida had changed the name from the National Security Organisation (NSO) to its current name, State Security Service (SSS), and pampered it with extra budgetary funds for state of the art communication and intelligence gathering facilities.

It was infact the SSS's foresight that led to the construction of the massive underground Emergency Operations Room. With lessons learnt from the April 22, 1990 abortive coup of late major Gideon Orkar, when Dodan Barracks, including the then Security Room was pulverised, the new structure was designed and executed by Nigerian architects under the supervision of the SSS.

"Excuse me sir" Wole cut in "I had it in my Special Report circulated to everyone... wherein I advised clearance from the SSS before any public appearance. Brigadier Omojokun received the communication and I am therefore surprised at his carelessness ... ".

"Enough Wole!" The President snapped. "I am equally guilty. Let me confess that I too, am yet to read your report, despite proddings from my ADC. And I personally authorised Omojokun's visit to the hospital, without realising the security implications of course... So tell us – what manner of threat are we faced with?"

Looking exonerated and very much important now, Wole cleared his throat again and continued:

"Two months ago, we started picking up reports of emergent ties and cooperation between elements of the Students Union at the University of Lagos and a violent ultra-secret society. Based on this information, we activated our Search Teams in the two sectors and pulsed all our cells within the university. We also arrested the President of the Students Union as you will recall and put him through dry and wet interrogations but we couldn't establish a link.

Then just five days ago, one of our Deep Cover agents in one of the Pyrates Confraternity decks-the Cassandra Deck- reported a positive link. We followed this lead and could only establish that a kidnapping of a government official was planned. A joint sally of both Cassandra and Panama Decks was planned for last Saturday and the agent was supposed to ferret more information for us." Retired General Wole Abioye paused for effect; providing an opportunity for General Atiku to cut in.

"Wole, you almost lost me there. This deck, sally,cassandra,panama.. you want to explain?"

"Sorry Sir...just fancy organisational descriptors for secret student organisations.A Deck is a school unit or sub-group and a sally is their description of their secret meetings.When they announce their meetings,they talk about sailing and they have secret sign languages for announcing time and venue of their sallies.. sorry, I mean meetings.."

"And these are supposed to be students? Alright.. so what happened to your agent?"

"As I was saying sir...he was to be at this sally last saturday...but by sunday morning, he was dead. Drowned apparently in the lagoon by the university water front...body was found floating...no trace of physical harm. At that point, we thought whatever snippet we received from him was important enough to have cost him his life. Hence my Special Report."

"Who was his controller? And who was your agent's source and contact?" queried the Chairman impatiently, not being a stranger to intelligence himself.

"His controller initially thought it was a questionable intelligence. The agent was in Deep Cover,had been for over three years... and nobody wanted to blow his cover prematurely".

The SSS Director-General's explanation struck a feeling of worry across the table.

"Do we have anybody within the leadership of the Students Union?" This was from the chief of Army Staff, Major-General Amadu Attah.

"Unfortunately no. But even the leadership appears to be in the dark. We have used all techniques on the arrested President and we are convinced he knows nothing"

Just then, an urgent flash appeared on the screen by the door for the attention of the DG, SSS. The DG excused himself and went out, returning with a manilla file.

"Gentlemen" Wole said, looking very worried. "It's the University of Lagos."

"Yes. What about it." Everybody burst out at once.

"You know today is April 18th. It's their usual date for a memorial March for one of their dead colleagues – Akintude Ojo. Because of the earlier reports of a planned kidnap of a senior government figure, we had been deployed in depth for over a week. .....

This morning the March proceeded normally until they got to the gate and were halted by a Police detachment. There was some firing and twelve policemen have been killed."

"What do you mean killed...lynched by a mob or stampeding students or what?? ..." General Atiku cut in, angrilly.

"No Sir. They were shot. Very professionally done according to the report."

"Shot? By Students?"

"That's doubtful. The agent's report herewith says the students were not involved in the shooting. That the source of firing can still not be established – even by those who were under fire."

"My God! What do we have here. Another inconclusive report?" General Amadu Attah who had never hidden his disdain for the SSS cut in bitterly.

"How many under cover agents have you deployed in the university? Twenty... Twenty-five? Twenty-five professionals in the midst of unorganised students and we can't even tell the source of a gun shot?"

"Well, at least it tells us that whoever the students are in league with this time is very formidable and professional too." Wole continued.

But Amadu was not through. "I'll tell you again as I have always done that you go about with all these fancy gadgets of yours to snoop intelligence and I say there is nothing like human intelligence. Can your bloody computers read a man's body language?"

It was a replay of earlier altercations between the two bosses over budgets. The Chief of Staff's dream of a Rapid Response Force(RRF) complete with dedicated and integral air and sea transport arm, interdiction and ground attack Apache gun ships and fast attack gun boats had been killed just three months earlier by Wole's convincing arguments. Amadu was even more bitter when he heard of the subsequent extra-budgetary allocations to the SSS to invest in satellite snooping equipment.

The Chairman, sensing the under-current to the feud moved to de-fuse the tension.

"What else have we got on the University?" His nod hinted the question was general but was more addressed to Yakubu Wanche.

"Yes Sir. We suspect that the real stormy petrel to watch is the Public Relations Officer of the Union.His oratorial skills are extra-ordinary and can convince the students to do anything...and I mean anything"

"What do you mean 'we suspect'?" Amadu snapped. "Suspicion is questionable intelligence. If you don't have hard facts then say so!" he hissed.

"Well, our judgment is based on a psy-profile analysis of the individual. He led the March in the absence of the President and he has been spokesman ever since."

Yakubu Wanche who had an ear-phone plugged on, pointed to the ear-phone.

"I am patched to our main communication line to the scene. He will speak to CNN on the hour, they said. I have called for his file." Even as he spoke, the file he called for rolled out in bits on his laptop. He scrolled down and punched a button, and the oak partition covering the television, electronic map board and other intelligence gadgets slid open.

As Ogaga Onini was caught in the heat of the CNN klieg lights, he smiled to himself.

His secondary school mates back in Port Harcourt would be shocked, he thought. And his former principal! The quiet,self-effacing boy and son of a nobody was going to appear on world-wide television! And speak for Nigerian youths!!

Onini Ogaga was going to get justice for Nigerian Students,he thought proudly. The "timid", self-effacing village boy that was too unkempt to share dormitory apartment with the sons of the rich! Idealistic Onini who all his life had fought to correct the contemptuous appraisal of his person. To be a strong virile man, capable of talking and being listened to. To become a leader. That had been Onini's life-long ambition.

Yakubu Wanche's file on Onini Ogaga said that much. The notations on the file with him indicated a politically ambitious young man, whose tall physical build and quiet, handsome, sneaky nature had constantly masked his big political dreams.

His school records showed a zealot who occupied his spare time by reading the histories of revolutionaries. By sixth form, the report said, he had memorised dates of birth, training, political orientation, course and effect of their revolutions and dates of death of major revolutionaries across the globe. For no other reason other than to complement his understanding of revolutions and the terrorist methods that go with them,he read military science with a voracious appetite. The Chinese, Wu Chei fascinated him. So was the Prussian military strategist, Clausewitz . And the latter day petal theory of Nguyen Van Thieu of Vietnam.

Instead of a football loving, football playing; romantic, sexually promiscuous, alcohol and drugs loving youth – values that dominated his generation – Onini had other goals.

He barely touched alcohol. Drugs were taboo. But he discussed David Sterling and his SAS with nostalgia as if he shared their desert campaigns. His heroes had no ideological or geographical limitations: General Zukov and his heroic defence of the River Don in Russia. The German, Rommel and the exploits of the Africa Korps in the epic battles of El-Alamein, Tobruk, etc in the Sahara desert. General Nguyen Giap and his Vietnamese cunning. And Adolf Hitler for his military mind, decisiveness and geo-political tactics!

The report on him indicated how his secondary school work had suffered because he read what he thought he needed to know unmindful of the prescribed syllabus.

His bitterness against the system started at Kokori Grammar School. Tall, quiet, he was self assured of what he knew and hated to be ignored or underrated. His village background and his lack of paternal upbringing was a constant source of teasing from his school mates. This constant teasings about the early loss of a father he never knew had

taught him one lesson – to be alone without being lonely. The oppressive cemetery-like quietness of his maternal grand-father's rubber plantation where he spent time with his uncle during his holidays prepared
him for the jungle…where he conquered fear. His conquest of solitude
had produced in him a strong will to operate fearlessly and independently. And he expected his teachers and peers to acknowledge this
inner strength in him.

Instead, he was constantly reminded of his fatherless status at every
opportunity. Those who could not match his intellect soon discovered
this was the surest way to humiliate him at every turn and put him
down. He became more withdrawn and more dangerous.

In the dormitory, he was the object of frequent jokes. How in his
early months in the boarding house, he could never handle his cut-
lery properly and would prefer to eat his native "garri" with his bare
hands. Of course several punishments after, he was forced to learn and
conform.

In the male dormitories at Aggrey College in Port-Harcourt, there
were communal toilet and bath facilities. There were no individual
partitions and therefore no privacy. It was here in the bathrooms that
Onini experienced his most scathing taunts. Gifted with a large physical frame, his penile endowment was again certainly far above the
Aggrey College average. It was with reference to this extra endowment
that he was nicknamed "O.D."-"Over Dimension" in his early years at
Aggrey College.

He was forced to keep to himself, usually taking his bath when all
others had departed. This introversion produced in him a solitude that
was extremely stressful.

Thus humiliated and marginally tolerated, he became extremely fanatical in his study of politics, leadership, war and terrorism. He sought
more and more for an avenue to express the inner strength he knew he
possessed. He sought to dominate and through that avenge the constant jocular butts at his physical distortions.

By his fourth year at Aggrey, he started featuring prominently in in-
ter-collegiate debates and was the undisputed quiz champion in Port-

Harcourt.

Onini read voraciously and became more and more obsessed with revolutionary ideals. The more he read, the greater his zeal to punish his detractors. He was convinced that to change the system and create a society where recognition would be given to the contributions of the down-trodden like his widowed mother, society would have to prepare itself for some amount of discomfort. He saw a need to first of all "unleash the furies of hell on the system to create the paradise of heaven."

Surprisingly, all the Intelligence reports on Onini omitted his outstanding military service in Biafra.

Onini mopped his face. The bright klieg lights created a surreal atmosphere around the hall. The whole atmosphere at the University of Lagos Sports Centre was suffocating. With anti-riot policemen swarming all over, Onini looked unperturbed. He walked up the hallway of the Sports Hall making small talk with the CNN technicians and the security men. He shook hands with the sound recordist, a big framed man who gave his hand a gentle pump and a wink.

The security men looked at him with naked hatred. Onini walked up to them returning their hostile stance with a disarming smile. He walked up to the leader of the squad. He courtsied to the officer as he shook his hand; reading his name tag as he did so. "Akioyanmen..That undoubtedly must be from Edo State. I like your long names. Very rhythmic .Very descriptive. I knew one Akioyanmen once, a classmate. Sunday Akioyanmen. He was Ishan, from Uromi. Very brilliant and serious-minded chap. Do you by any chance know the family?"

A flash of recognition rushed through the officer's eyes as he clumsily acknowledged the relationship.

"Yes. I know him. He is infact my cousin."

"You see what I mean. It's a small world, that's why we should not go on shooting at each other"

Just then the CNN anchorman motioned for Onini to come over and get seated. The Klieg light came on again and a couple of voice tests after, the anchorman yelled, "Stand by everybody. We are on air in two minutes." "Roll Tape" he barked again after two minute….."we are on air" The monitor screen showed footage shot earlier in the day... establishment shots of the University of Lagos, the students March and the gun shots and a straight cut to the anchorman.

"Good afternoon, from Lagos Nigeria, what began this morning as a peaceful demonstration by the students of the University of Lagos has left fifteen dead so far and many more injured. The atmosphere at the University is tense; as it is widely rumoured that the National Guard has been mobilised to storm the institution. I am Martin Stafford, and with me to discuss the unfolding drama is Onini Ogaga, The Public Relations Officer of the University of Lagos Students Union."

The camera panned slowly ending with a close- up on Onini Ogaga. Onini smiled innocently into the camera.

"I say good afternoon to the world and a special good afternoon to fellow Nigerians. Unfortunately, this has been a very sorrowful afternoon for us at the University of Lagos... and our fervent hope and desire is that the situation can be quickly salvaged so that we can be rescued from the jaws of our oppressors".

Onini stopped to check on the effect of his opening speech and at a prodding nod from the anchor man, he continued.

"I speak for and on behalf of Nigerian students, majority of whom are born to very poor parent's. Despite our family's hard work and commitment to national ideals, a cabal of corrupt, incompetent and nepotic military leaders and their civilian lackeys have conspired to sentence them to a lifetime of poverty. But undaunted, our poor parents have denied themselves of the basics of life to give us university education. As I speak to you today, 99.9% of Nigerian students are like me – from poor homes and barely etching an existence to acquire university education" Pause.

"Two months ago, the Nigerian Government introduced a new fee structure in universities;with the effect that total tuition fee payable per student would now be One hundred and twenty thousand Naira per term. This, in a country where the average monthly salary is seven thousand Naira!"

Onini paused again for effect. "They tell us at every turn that we are

the future of Nigeria. But how can Nigeria have a future when its youths
are denied education? We wrote to the university Vice-Chancellors to
review the fees. We wrote through all the respected traditional rulers
of this country. Through all the military governors to the Chairman
of the Supreme Military Council to give a kind ear to our pleas. But
their hearts are hardened like stones. They refused to listen to us. And
we called a meeting here in Lagos. Called the media and told them our
plight. They wrote editorials supporting our pleas. Now, the government, bent on restricting educational opportunities to the rich; and to
compel the public universities to raise fees and bring them to the level
of the private universities they have built for themselves with ill-gotten
monies, responded in their usual draconian manner.The government
struck most dastardly : Our leaders were arrested and brutalised and
security agents were sent to the universities to maintain an oppressive
presence in our midst"

Onini cleared his throat and went on. He wore a pathetic demeanor
to visualise the sufferings of Nigerian students.

"Over-crowded dormitories... Students who slept on corridors, on
bare concrete because they could not afford the rents for accommodation. Hungry students who could not afford one good meal daily.
Students, desperate for knowledge who were turned back from using
the university library because of non-payment of library fees. And students who in a show of comaraderie accommodated "squatters" to sleep
on bare hostel floors with blankets, had their blankets seized by the university authorities and the students suspended from the dormitories."

Now adopting a stentorian tone, he inched up his frame and asked
rhetorically

"So you may ask what have we done to deserve this ill treatment?
Here we are ready to learn and make a contribution to our nation. We
read and hear of youths elsewhere who ignore education and take up
drugs and sodomy. We read and hear of governments elsewhere appealing to their deviant youths with pecks and enticements to bring them
back to the path of sanity and education ... And here we are sane, eager
to lean but distracted and frustrated by an openly biased, illegitimate

government that has no mandate from the people."

"That gentlemen is the core of our problem. It is regrettable to note that we have in Nigeria today, a military junta that openly shows it has no stake in the future of our country. Hence, the deliberate policy of disorientation of the youths of this great nation. And while the youth of this nation burn the midnight oil to make for a better tomorrow; the greed and gluttony of a few military opportunists continues to destroy their patriotic aspirations."

Onini spoke further about the sufferings and deprivation of Nigerian Students while their counterparts in the various Nigerian military academies lived in lush luxuries. He paused to mop his face with an handkerchief. The anchor man, Martin Stafford exploited the opening to take over control of proceedings.

"So what exactly happened this morning that got people killed … "

"You saw it all yourself. .. this morning. How a peaceful procession was confronted with lethal automatic weapons. How innocent Nigerian blood was spilled. What did we do wrong this morning to provoke the kind of response-lethal weapons,armour piercing bullets,smoke bombs and the likes that we got?"

The anchor man quickly cut in again.

"But some Policemen were also killed. How did the students get arms and ammunition for the retaliatory shots at the police?"

Onini Ogaga, speaking to a world-wide audience, reacted in genuine shock. For what seemed like eternity, he froze before the camera in genuine concern.

"Policemen? Killed?" He uttered imperceptibly. "Why should we harm a policeman, knowing that as parents they are equally victims of the policies of this mindless government? No, we couldn't have. We are peaceful students. We don't possess firearms. I mean if you gave me an automatic rifle, I won't even know what to do with it. No, there must be some cover-up going on…definitely!!"

The Policemen all around the room looked glumly at each other. They all seemed petrified at the revelation and showed it. But somehow they believed Onini was saying the truth.

"But Policemen were shot and killed today. So who do you think did the shooting?"

Onini held up his hand imploringly, wiped his face again, evoking the sympathy of millions of viewers.

"We abhor violence of any kind. No. We did not shoot. All we are asking for is a chance for the youths of Nigeria to have access to education. For months we have begged for this chance. And today was a continuation of our begging ..."

"So who shot the policemen?" Martin quipped.

"How would I know? Perhaps they had a mutiny. Don't forget that some of the policemen have dependants and children. That they also pay the exorbitant school fees. Is it then not possible that faced with an order to shoot at defenceless students, they mutinied and shot at themselves?"

There was complete silence in the hall. Everybody in the hall exchanged questioning glances.

"We bear no hands in the misfortune that has befallen the policemen and we sympathise with their families."

Onini braced himself up and looked straight into the camera, "We are today impoverished by a corrupt leadership that has institutionalised graft as a way of life. A leadership that has created a new elite out of military men. While the military has the best of everything, the rest of us are denied basic subsistence. And I can tell you that if there is an emergency tomorrow, we the youths of this country will be conscripted to serve in the military irrespective of our current degradation and deprivation;not their pampered,elitist sons in their military academies."

"I am appealing to well-meaning people the world over to come to our rescue. Even as I speak, a vast array of armament is being marshalled against us. Plans are being finalised to attack us by land, air and sea as if the University of Lagos is now an alien territory, harbouring miscreants, bent on insurrection and at war with Nigeria. But we are not afraid because the truth we speak is eternal and I know there are millions of you out there who are even now saying silent prayers for men of wisdom and vision to take over the reigns of government to rescue the youths of this country. Through our sufferings and our spilled blood, we inflict pain and anguish on the conscience of the world. And surely, men of wisdom shall rise up to defend our cause. Thank you."

That same evening, the Supreme Military Council authorised the use of force to flush out the students from the institution to facilitate meaningful search and rescue efforts for their kidnapped colleague. In the ensuing assault, nine more students were killed. But Onini had gone underground. That same night Uncle Inua gave him a bear hug for his sterling performance. He had prepared a passport and secured visas for him and all other requirements for his studies in London. He was sneaked across the borders into the Republic of Benin the next day;and from there to London following a manhunt for him by the military authorities.

Worldwide condemnation greeted the raid on the institution. Amnesty International called for an independent inquiry. The World Bank said it was suspending on-going aid negotiation until there was an improvement in the human rights record of the government. The Nigeria Labour Congress and the Nigerian Union of Teachers called on the government to resign. The British Foreign Secretary through the country's High Commission in Lagos requested the military government to expedite a transition to civilian multi-party democracy and actually called for an immediate time-table.

On the monday following the attack on the University of Lagos, thousands of public employees resuming for duty at the Federal Secretariat at Ikoyi were shocked at the sight of the sole occupant of a taxi parked by the gate. The decomposing body of Brigadier Ishola Omojokun. The autopsy later revealed that he had been sedated to death.

One week later, the Nigeria Labour Congress called on all its members to down tools in sympathy of the students. In a well publicised press briefing, the President of the Congress, Comrade Femi Ajayi condemned the double standards of the military that would pamper students in Defence-related institutions while denying the vast majority of students in Nigerian universities the barest minimum necessary for survival. The congress said it viewed with serious concern the gradual deterioration in academic standards in the country brought about by what it termed a conscious neglect "of that sector presumably to stifle "non-conformity;"and to encourage a drastic drift to private universities owned by the military elite. It then called on the government to abolish tuition fees at all levels of education with "immediate effect", failing which all Nigerian workers would stay away from work indefinitely.

And that marked the beginning of what was later to be known as the "Forty Dirty Days". Dirty. That was an understatement. All over Nigeria refuse took over all major highways as municipal workers downed tools. All patients in government hospitals were prematurely discharged as doctors and nurses joined the strike. Several lives were lost as accident victims moaned and died at the gates of government hospitals, even as starry-eyed gatemen refused to open the gates to the hospitals.

Ten days into the strike, the Association of Flight Controllers, hitherto on the borderline joined the strike. All in-coming flights were advised to seek alternative landing airports outside Nigeria. Radio transmitters and receivers were shut down. Radar surveillance was deliberately sabotaged and abandoned. Long distance radar and altimeters were switched off. The North-South beacons and radio guidance systems at Bida were switched off.

Overnight, Nigeria was cut off from the outside world by air and the few intra-Nigeria air traffic, mostly military had to rely on visual only approach and take-off.

Military personnel drafted to take over and man facilities at key airports found most of the equipment in unworkable conditions due to sabotage.

Water supply, epileptic and inadequate even at the best of time dried up entirely. It was in the midst of this stench and parched throats that the National Power supply workers threw in their cliff-hanger with a nation-wide black-out to support the strike.

At the centre of all these, the Federal Government after initial prevarication complicated matters further when it announced a partial acceptance of the no-tuition fee call from well-meaning Nigerians. Only federal universities directly controlled by the Federal Government would benefit. Students of State owned universities, secondary and primary schools under the control of local government were advised to negotiate with their States and Local Governments. At the same time, states and local governments were advised to examine their finances and implement the no-fee decision on a strictly discretionary basis.

This decision fuelled the crisis even further. Assured of government's lack of will to fight back and smelling victory, the Nigerian Labour Congress struck back: The Demand was non-negotiable and must be implemented nationally.

The strike action continued unabated with mounting suffering.

When on April 16, the National Security Council met for a marathon fourteen hours, the Head of State was set according to sources to deal decisively with all "trouble makers." The Council rose at dawn on the 17th with clear-cut draconian decisions: An immediate ban on the Nigeria Labour Congress. All workers to resume work in 24 hours or face decisive action. Selective retribution were to be directed at all university lecturers and doctors in government hospitals. They were all to be ejected from their government accommodations with immediate effect. And under a long-forgotten statute brushed up by the Attorney General, all the striking workers in so-called essential services – power supply, water supply, air traffic control, etc, were to be rounded up and tried for economic sabotage and treasonable felony. The Head of State was to announce these decisions the next day on the combined radio and television network service from 1900 hours, Nigerian time. With these decisions taken, the Council rose to brace up for the next line of action.

But even as the Council was sitting, the rank of critics of the government was growing. The column of critics by now had expanded to include ex-presidents, ex-ministers and respected traditional rulers. And from 1400 hours the next day the Radio and Television Workers Union, long restrained from the strike because of their essential services nature joined the strike. That immediately scuttled the planned broadcast by the Head of State.

But even so, the Nigeria Labour Congress was not to be taken by surprise as it had received the exact wording of the decisions taken by the Council two hours after the meeting rose.

The National Secretariat of the Congress summoned a meeting of all its officers two hours later. At the meeting, it unanimously passed a resolution to form the Nigeria Workers Union (NWU) in the event of he NLC being banned.

Predictably, the ban was announced on the Federal Government-owned Daily Times and New Nigerian, the very next day. Soldiers were drafted to the erstwhile headquarters of the NLC at Ojuelagba road in Lagos. That same day, the radical press gave copious reports and interviews to the former officers of the congress. "We shall not be intimidated by Proscriptions" the former Secretary General of the congress was reportedly widely as saying.

A fresh underground headquarters was established at the Dairy Research Institute near Gboko. There, a new NWU executive was elected by voting for the former NLC leadership to continue their term of office in the new union.

Thereafter, the President of the NWU, Comrade Femi Ajayi travelled to far-away Ilorin to make his first public pronouncement as President of the new union. In an interview with a private radio station in Ilorin, he affirmed that "Nigerian Workers are ready to stave off the black-mailing tactics of the Federal Military Government. He urged the government to think about the fortunes of the youths of Nigeria and drop its "barrack regimentation mentality". And that the Government's ineptitude threatens the very future of Nigeria as "an illiterate youth cannot solve the complex problems of a thermo-nuclear age."

Asked about his reaction to the 24-hour ultimatum for workers to go back to work, Comrade Femi Ajayi retorted: "If you decree people to go back to work, then you must have the means to effect it. Tell me, are they going to send armed soldiers to every house to force them to work?" Comrade Femi then painted a pathetic picture of education in the country. Primary School education under the shades of trees, with pupils having to cart their own chairs, desks and writing boards to and from school everyday. Dilapidated Secondary School buildings that continually collapse on students during rains and universities! Cramped accommodation, lack of lecture theatres and laboratory facilities, scarcity of books, research funds and exorbitant tuition fees!

"We will continue to fight until the government places the necessary priority on education," comrade Femi said "Just look around, with all our oil wealth, why should we not guarantee a good future for this country by providing a solid foundation for our children?. Look. All around us, responsible governments are doing exactly that. Ghana spends 24.3 per cent of its public expenditure on education. Togo spends 6.5 per cent. Kenya 6.1 percent. War ravaged Liberia spends 4.9 per cent with all its heavy expenditure on reconstruction and rehabilitation. And the giant of Africa? he asked lamentably... a meagre 1.2 per cent on education and 32 per cent on Defence. This is the mind boggling misplaced priority, that we must all stand up against", he concluded.

Chapter 8

⚭

IT WAS A bright, brisk august morning in Sokoto. As Gregory "Bishop" Ibaba scanned through the previous day's edition of the Guardian, he looked up through the balcony at the open expanse ahead of him. The herd of cattle was gradually making up their numbers on the open expanse of land behind the Sokoto state office of the Islamic Trust.

It was amazing the amount of intelligence animals possessed, he thought. For the one week that he had been a resident of the New Idea hotel's extension at Arguwar-Rogo, he had always been greeted with this scene every morning. Promptly at dawn,. cattles in twos, threes, fours, etc from different owners will cover the distance from their individual homes to the open ground in unison.

Unguided, unled, unaccompanied. The cattle will thread their way through traffic, across roads, through shrubs and streets to finally arrive at their common assembly point.

And promptly at thirty minutes past the hour of eight, at a long command from the herdsman, the cattle will all fall in neatly into a column and head for their grazing fields and watering holes.

On this particular morning, a limping cow from Mallam Sabo's stable had limped its way to the open grounds five minutes late. The shock that greeted its eyes when it realised it had arrived late was all too obvious. It sniffed the ground all over. It ran from one end of the ground to the other sniffing all through and galloped to a nearby shed where the herdsman usually stayed. It looked heavenwards and cried loudly into the air. It was a cry of anguish at being left behind by his herd. It sobbed in anger as it trotted away into the distance, galloping vigorously to catch up with the rest of the herd, way, way ahead in its steady march towards the grazing fields and watering holes.

"The Bishop" took all of these in and marvelled at such display of intellect by such a lowly animal.He was an intellectual of sort. Except that his sharp, mental alertness was selectively deployed for criminal gains. Born in Eku in Ethiope Local Government Area of Delta State, a reserved, self-effacing man who was forced out of secondary school in his early teens by the poverty of his parents. Now in his late thirties, he had learnt all the tricks quickly at the General Motor Park in Sapele and paid his dues afterwards.

It had been a rainy night that september. And the second showing of 'Jantar Mantar' at the Olympia cinema that night drew very little crowd. And it was a cold night. A very cold night. Perhaps that was what caused it. He enjoyed the film thoroughly despite the cold.

"The Bishop" got out with the small crowd and headed for what he considered the main event of the night. He had earlier 'cased' two possible targets around Akintola street. He was traditionally a solo operator. And liked it that way. He had put the two targets under close observation in the last two weeks. And had actually had a final "recce" that evening.

But the cold! For, stepping out of the cinema hall, his cold skin had gently brushed the fair skin of this white lady. And an electric current went through his whole system. And right outside as she slid into the front seat of the car besides her husband, she had raised her legs high. A little too high. And "The Bishop" thought he saw what looked like her spotless white panties!

It must be the cold, he complained. But he had also developed this erection, which refused to subside. So, he followed the direction of his penile erection. The white lady. He knew her. Had always seen her playing tennis at the Sapele Club. He knew the husband was some plant engineer or so at the African Timber and Plywood Company. They lived in one of the staff quarters in a very quiet neighbourhood.

'The Bishop' made for the house that night. Waited till the lights were off and slid in through the car port. He made straight for the sleeping quarters and put on the lights. The couple woke up instantly in puzzle.

"Hello, C'mmon make una wake up", he ordered, pulling out an ugly looking locally fabricated pistol. The couple staggered out of bed in obedience.

"Ok. Money! Yes I say all the money you get! put am here", pulling out a Kingsway Store polythene bag.

"Quick, quick No waste time".

The couple rummaged drawers and safes and dropped their personal purses. "The Bishop" looked through the collection. Not bad, he thought.

"You!" pointing at the man, "come here". The man moved forward groggily and before he knew it, "The Bishop" had hit him hard on the head with the strong metal butt of the pistol. Mr Campbell, for that was the expatriate's name, who had only resumed six months previously as Plant Manager on promotion slumped and passed out. He was before then a fitter at the Apapa branch of Bordpak. From his very first day at the Sapele plant, Mr.Campbell had had a running battle of sorts with his new General Manager who did not just like his face. He put it off initially as petty English versus Irish animosity. But it grew steadily into a lack of respect for his professional competence. He found he had to rely more and more on sedatives to sleep. His blood pressure kept rising. And that knock to his head was the final straw. He slumped down and breathed his last! (The Bishop was to learn that he died from the mild blow only much later).

Next, The Bishop grabbed the white woman savagely. He brought her crashing down on the bed in a tango and squeezed her close to him. Surprisingly, the woman responded without a shout. A combination of Mr Campbell's abnormally high blood pressure and fatigue from long working hours had long occasioned a neglect of his matrimonial duties to his wife. Mrs Campbell therefore gave in initially with hesitation and as she began to enjoy it, with wild enthusiasm.

Thus entwined, they did not initially hear the wild knocking of the Duty Driver and the Assistant Chief Engineer at the door. There had been a major breakdown at the saw-milling conveyor that required the Plant Manager's urgent attention.

With a louder knock, "The Bishop" heard, pulled out quickly dressed up and eased out of the room. This gave the cue and emboldened Mrs Campbell to yell loudly for help. Her yells were amplified by the Duty driver and Assistant Chief Engineer. In minutes, the whole neighbourhood was agog with people, including the resident AT&P Security personnel. It was then that "The Bishop" made a break for it; with four quick shots to scare away everybody. But that was all the gun held. Gradually they closed in on him ...

The trial judge had found 'The Bishop' guilty only of armed robbery as the autopsy report on Mr Campbell had exonerated him of culpability and Mrs Campbell having not raised the issue of indecent assault and rape. The Bishop was therefore sentenced to life imprisonment.

Unfortunately, his Union "gate" had presented his case to their "compound" only after sentence had been passed on the case. It had been a particularly difficult case for the Union. Through its prison channels, The Bishop was constantly re-assured that something would be done. And in prison, the Union ensured he was well taken care of. He was made a warden in the prison's church. There, more out of boredom and frustration, he read the bible from cover to cover and became very versed in the scriptures. In prison, he truly became "The Bishop", his authority on the scriptures being unrivalled and un-questioned in the prison cathedral.

The opportunity to spring him came five years later. As a result of serious over-crowding at the Sapele prison where he was serving his term; and following so many widely reported deaths, a committee to decongest the prison was set up. Fortunately, the Committee was headed by a Union member. Only serving prisoners with light offences were supposed to be paroled or pardoned. But somehow, The Bishop's name got on the list and five years and three days to the day he was sent to prison, he was set free and has served the Union faithfully since then.

By pre-arrangement, four of them met that morning at the Kangiwa
Motor Park. They boarded the Argungu-bound bus separately. It was
the holy month of Ramadan, and the lean looks of most of the passengers conveyed their commitment to abstinence. As Tofi Jibo made to
sit down, he brought out his prayer beads and greeted everybody in the
name of the prophet. 'The Bishop' watched in amusement from the rear
of the bus. He knew his team well. Very well. Tofi Jibo, also known as
"Mugabe" was a smooth operator, a real master of disguise.

On the run since February 1992, he had lived well with his disguises,
changing locations from time to time.

Born of relatively wealthy parents at the village of Nor in Benue
State, he was a tall well-built and extremely handsome man. When
he was only seven, his father resigned his job as a village teacher and
moved to Gboko. With his new job as Purchasing Officer at the Tyre
Department of Denen Tofi Limited, he made good money on the side
and gave young Tofi a good education and good opportunities. Six years
after, the Dunlop people wanted an agent in the area and promptly appointed him.

The handsome Tofi Jibo therefore had all the opportunity to take a
normal education and settle down as a respectable Tiv leader. Instead
in his fourth form at Gboko College, he joined the Army, enlisting as
an "Other Rank" a decision that was a big blow to his father.

His education and intelligence helped. He made steady progress and
had made Sergeant by 1992

In January 1992, Tofi Jibo had completed a gunnery course at Kachia
in flying colours.Back to the Ikeja Cantonment in his first weekend on
return from Kachia, he was at his favourite bar at the Mammy Market
at the Ikeja cantonment when he looked up to see the young kinsman
staring at him intently. Across from him on the table was a young
sub-altern from his state called Mvenga. In the Army, despite the fu-
sion of ethnic groups, ethnic loyalties were still extremely strong and
important.

"So how was your course?" The sub-altern asked him.

"Good. Very good. But I thought some of the guns were a little old-fashioned. I mean with laser and computer guidance systems all over now, I was a little disappointed with the old fashioned sighting methods."

"So did you tell them that at the end of the course?"

"No, how can!"

"You see that is our problem, we allow things to go down the drain before we complain ... Well, well, these people are just not fit to run anything."

Despite the ethnic affinity, "Mugabe" knew the discussion was straying into very dangerous terrains. So he asked Mvenga a direct question.

"Is there anything wrong?"

"No Mugabe. But would you like to make some good money?"

"Depends on who is paying" he answered.

"The source is solid. And there will be other rewards. This is the big one.......

You are good Mugabi and I want you to give me close support in this operation"

A deafening silence closed in on the twosome. Mvenga had said the unutterable.

"Mugabi" broke into their native dialect.

"You may be my superior officer but that's a stupid pass to make. People get shot for less. And I am sorry I can't do it. I have a wife and two children to care for. My father's Dunlop dealership in Gboko has been offered to me ..."

"Shurrup!"

The subaltern held out his hand for the traditional Union handshake. This is our thing. There are lots of benefits for the Union. Money. Promotion. Progress for our people. I trusted you because you are one of us that's why I approached you and you open your mouth to disrespectfully talk about operational security. Will you or will you not?"

He was immediately persuaded. That morning of the putch, he was at the Obalende Road, Ikoyi, where he had led a crack section that created a bottle-neck at the secretariat junction and sped down to to the

Broadcasting House in Ikoyi. But the small tank section deployed at the radio station had been stubborn;and had required a lot of fire-power to suppress,but he eventually achieved his objectives and cleared the way for the senior officers to drive in later to make their recordings....

But back at the cantonment that evening when he knew things had not worked out, he had promptly asked his wife to braid his hair, dressed in his wife's Senegalese boubou and disappeared ...

The bus stopped for a few minutes to pick up more passengers at the By-Pass Round-About, where Adebola Edu also picked up the day's papers. Midway into Bodinga, Adebola Edu disembarked. "Casablanca" as he was more popularly known made for the direction of the numerous tables of onions on sale by the wayside, passed them by and proceeded towards a group of bungalows at the end of the street.

Stealthily, he slipped into a bush path that led to the perimeter fence of the new Sokoto International Airport. He took photographs of the shrubs around the fence, the runway turning point and slid into a small burrow, effectively hidden by the over-hanging vegetation.

Twenty five minutes later, he picked up air-traffic communication on his special frequency modulated handset, tuned to the Sokoto airport frequency.

"Come in Five November Yankee Alpha"

"Five November Yankee Alpha here. Altitude eighteen thousand feet. One Eight thousand Feet. Do you copy?"

"Roger. Five November Alpha. Altitude 1-8 thousand Feet. Whisky Tango Seven Zero Seven.

You are cleared to land on runway Alpha Zero-One. Please proceed Velvet Oscar Alpha. Out"

Ten minutes later, the plane touched down and taxied down the runway in reverse thrust. Just by where Casbablanca lay hidden,the plane slowed down to walking pace and executed a slow turn. Casbablanca sighted it as it made the sluggish turn and snapped. Thereafter, he packed up and left.

"Casbablanca" used to be an able seaman. He was an honest man who worked hard on the Liberian registered "Morning Glory" assiduously and saved up everything he earned. And everything he saved, he passed over to his wife to use on a building project he had embarked upon in his village in Ajah. With the rapid expansion of Victoria Island in Lagos, Ajah in no time became part of the new high-class suburb. And he then considered dropping his sea-faring ways to pick up a shore-based occupation. That was when on his next leave, he realised that the building project had been in his wife's name all along. And that the wife had filed and completed divorce proceedings and was actually now living in "her" house with her new husband.

He lamented his woes to friends. And one discussion led to another until he ended up in the Union. Thereafter revenge was sweet and swift. On his former wife and her new lover.

The wife and her lover disappeared without trace;and he secured a proper transfer of title to regain his property.

Through the support of Union friends, he raised money and bought a dug out boat. The boat was built up and fitted with two Yamaha Almarine engines and with that, he launched himself into business. Plying the tributaries and rivers of the Lagoon and hugging the Atlantic shoreline on smuggling runs between Epe, Badagry, Seme, and Porto-Novo in Benin republic.

His business prospered. With regular smuggling runs which he extended as far as Lome and Tema; he mobilised Union funds and bought a second-hand barge and tug-boat. He continued to render personal service to his customers – mostly Union traders on the West Coast. Despite the blanket cover provided by the Union against police and customs harassment, he used all the experience acquired sailing on bigger ships to fortify his boat against seizure.

Through discussions, he was introduced to a 'brother' with the right technical knowledge. The brother, an engineer with Siemens communication installed a mobile two-way radio communication on the tugboat. The radio had microcomputer characteristics with re-programmable frequencies and "cloning" possibilities. The boat was also installed with a portable hand-held radar , direction finders and sonar detectors. Armed with these gadgets, unexpected in a junk tug-boat and def-

initely too sophisticated for the coastal patrol capabilities of the Police
and customs, "Casbablanca" sailed the coastal waters of West Africa
unchallenged.

For the Sokoto assignment he had chosen the frequency enhanced
Motorola handset HT 750C. The set was small, rugged and battery
operated. Tough enough to withstand all weather conditions while in
use. The set also had frequency memory locks – one of which had been
locked into the Sokoto Airport Traffic Control frequencies.

As Casbablanca packed up and withdrew from the airport perimeter area, another member of the team was crouched in thoughts under
a shrub. He was calculating angles, distances and charge capabilities.
As usual his mind was racing, thinking ahead of the job. He got up
straightened his bones noisily and smiled. This was going to be easy, he
thought. That evening he held final discussions with "The Bishop" on
their requirements. As the Staff Officer to the Bishop on this mission,
it was his duty to plan all the logistics and requisitions. The Bishop
looked through his requisitions and smiled.

"Joe-Joe. Haven't you forgotten something?"

"What may that be?"

"Failure!"

"I never plan to fail."

"All the same, you have to plan for it. What if the pilot alerts the control tower before we are ready? What if there is a military escort for the
plane? And the get-away trucks? what if they arouse suspicion?"

"Well ..."

"No – well Joe. These are just possibilities. But what we have is a
solid plan and your requisitions are in order." They looked at each other
meaningfully. Each with his different thoughts. For Joe Ofili, alias
"Ofege", the gentleman robber; life was a bundle of surprises.

In the last six years, he had operated from Bamenda in neighbouring
Camerouns. From Bameda "Ofege" had pulled armed robberies in the
Makurdi – Enugu – Onitsha axis. He had a neat set-up. In Bamenda,
he ran a flourishing night club and a successful spare parts business. He
therefore had a perfect cover for his frequent trips outside Bamenda to

ostensibly buy spare parts and new records for his discotheque.

Ofege was born in Ubiaruku in what was then the Midwest of fairly well-to-do parents. At least his father provided the only form of resident commercial transportation from Obiaruku to anywhere in those days. The Obiaruku Express fleet was then made up of two Bedford lorries and a Morris Mini-bus. The vehicles made regular trips to Onitsha, Benin, Warri and Oyoko. With proceeds from this thriving transport business, Joe was given a good education. At Saint George's Obinomba, he was so intelligent and so gentle, that the reverend fathers had marked him for distinction in the final School Certificate exams. All seem to be going well. The father had sold one of the aging Bedford lorries and bought a new Mercedes-Benz 911 truck – a rare achievement then. And he had made a total aggregate of sixteen in his mock school certificate exams.

Until that morning, in August of 1967, when the Biafran Army did the unexpected. Over-running a defenceless Midwest in one day. Of course, all the schools were shut and Joe found himself wasting away at home. An ominous silence and a feeling of unease descended on the area. To avoid the boredom of those days, Joe volunteered to ride as apprentice driver on one of his father's lorries – the new Mercedes-Benz 911.

Four months later, with the Midwest once again back in Nigeria and Biafrian forces pushed across the Niger into Biafra, Joe was preparing to go back to school when his whole world fell apart. That morning, Nigerian soldiers had raided the Central Motor Park in Warri. It was rumoured that an attempted landing at Onitsha had ended in fiasco and urgent reinforcements were required to sustain the push. The soldiers who came to the park to commandeer vehicles for this mission saw a good choice in Pa Ofili's lorry and it was promptly commandeered. The lorry's regular driver scared of the likelihood of exposure to combat handed over the keys of the lorry to Joe and disappeared. At gun-point, Joe was ordered to the tactical headquarters of 9 Brigade of the Nigerian Army in Warri. That night, he drove the lorry in a convoy of sixty other lorries to Asaba.

The vehicle and Joe technically became part of 9 Brigade. He made regular supply visits to Warri, ferrying foodstuff to men in the front. At Saint Patrick's College where the Forward Operating Base of 9 Brigade was located, a kind-hearted NCO taught Joe basic gun-handling skills. As the NCO put it, Asaba was a combat zone and it was only proper that all operatives in the area, including conscripted civilian drivers should know basic military craft.

Six weeks into this unstable life, Pa Ofili showed up suddenly one morning at the Saint Patrick's garrison. Fortunately for him, the soldiers were all on morning parade. He traced his lorry to a secluded corner, where he saw his son, dutifully gauging the oil lubricant level, water level and other checks. At the sight of his son, he broke down in tears. It was too much. The loss of a lorry! And the loss of a son!! All to a war that he was ambivalent to. He held to his son in a tight embrace and swore. He confided in his son that the lorry was bought with some down payment and a loan from a thrift society. He lamented that he had continued to service the loan from other sources and that the Army authorities have confirmed that commandeered vehicles were sacrifices individuals had to make for the speedy prosecution of the war. As such he said, no payment was to be expected from the army for his commandeered lorry . That morning, they conspired to "steal" the lorry at the slightest opportunity. That chance came two weeks later. Sent on a replenishment trip to Warri, Joe diverted the lorry through the sleeping town of Umutu to Amai – the hometown of his maternal grandfather. There, the lorry was hidden away and Joe was sent far-away to Sabongida-Ora to continue with his education.

But it was not to be. The emissaries who came to him at school were uncharacteristically undiplomatic. They told him how the Army's Provost Department had traced his father to Obiaruku and how under military escort, he had been tortured and led to Amai to recover the lorry. And was then summarily executed for sabotaging the war effort! And that Joe himself, as an accomplice was also on the Army's wanted list.

Procuring a gun and ammunition in war-ravaged Midwest was relatively easy. Thereafter, Joe went underground. Sniping at solitary army vehicles on the Warri-Asaba road. He picked his spots at random. Waiting patiently. And when he struck, it was decisive.

That evening when he sighted a Staff car, flying the pennant of a battalion commander, he made up his mind to stop the random killings if he succeeded. Joe had picked his spot well. A steep incline with numerous pot-holes. Two Land-Rovers followed, with men and mounted machine guns. But when the vehicles slowed down to walking pace, Joe had ample time to ensure that the first shot mattered. The rear right door glass window exploded into smithereens. And with it, the head of Lt.Col. Kayode Alabi. A second volley silenced the commander's batman and driver. The escort convoy reacted quickly with opening rounds into the thick jungle. But Joe was petched up camouflaged on the trunk of a giant oil bean tree.

As the shooting continued, the commander's car started rolling down the incline. It caught the escort convoy unawares, smashed into the lead Land-Rover, which in turn glazed the second vehicle, over-turning the occupants. In the confusion, Joe melted into the thick undergrowth. He travelled up-north to Katsina-Ala; and eventually settled in Bamenda.

He had remained in deep cover ever since, striking at pre-determined targets. He had carefully chosen his targets all through the years. And was extremely rich and influential in his adopted Bamenda. His Union Compound was in the Ariara area of Aba – a town he frequented for his spare parts business.

With all recce for the Sokoto operations completed, "The Bishop" and "Ofege" travelled to Onitsha to arrange procurement of all the items they required. Deep into the building materials section of the Onitsha main market, they made contact with "Ashako's" front office man.

He was head salesman at a store that dealt exclusively with nails. Presently, "The Bishop" entered the store.

"Good Morning, my brother"

"Morning ... brother, friend ... customer ... what do I call you now?"

"'Brother' will be okay. Please we need nails. Very long nails …"
"How long?" The Salesman asked.
"Very long ones – for unconventional jobs."
"Oh That? You better come inside then"
The Salesman nodded towards the inner sanctuary of the store. Once inside, they shook hands, initially cautiously and on realisation of the special Union sign in the handshake, warmly.

"What kind of job do you have in mind? Small, big? And do you want the nails complete with the wood-work?"

"Yes. All of them" The Bishop replied assured. "Ofege, over to you."

They talked on and on for over two hours. High velocity armour-piercing bullets. K.3 sub-machine guns. Gridiron MK7 rocket launchers. Stanilov Quad 50 multiple band machine guns. Grenade launchers. Plastique, detonators, fuses, primers-silencers. The items were all delivered to and pre-loaded on a Union Inter-City"Luxurious" bus that night.

Chapter 9

The highest Conclave of the Union met that week. And after a review of different phases of "Operation DDT" it gave its approval for the commencement of the last phase-the final push.

The signal was received by all cells that night. On the network of Radio Nigeria "Meek Mother" was played three times in under three hours that night.

Since the early 1800s, Sokoto had occupied a very important place in Nigeria. Located on the north-western extreme of Nigeria, it was the seat of the Seriki Musulumi and the centre of islamic scholarship in Nigeria.

Even before this, the town had always provided an attraction for islamic historians, especially students of the jihads. Here in the bosom of mother earth was buried the great jihadist and founder of the Sokoto Caliphate, Othman Dan Fodio. His royal tomb continued to be of immense historical, cultural and tourist benefits to the town till this day.

With the creation of North-Western State and later Sokoto State in 1975, the need to promote the state's immense cultural heritage meant that the tomb of Othman Dan Fodio had to assume a new significance. The Palace of the Sultan of Sokoto from which all Islamic religious instructions emanate also assumed more significance.

But the most commercialised cultural event in the old North-West state continued to be the Argungu Fishing Festival. Argungu, located about a hundred kilometres, north-west of Sokoto town had grown from a mere village to a bustling tourist haven;complete with a Three-Star hotel – The Argungu Fishing Village.

Since the 1930s the Argungu Fishing Festival has had political significance beyond the town's boundaries. Reportedly, started as a social forum for inducing friendship between the then frequently feuding Fulani and Kabawa tribes, the festival assumed international significance in the 1970s.

Originally, the Emir of Argungu in consultation with his council announced the date of the festival and subsequently organised it. As the custodian of cultural rites in the town, the Emir would summon the town's "Serikin Ruwa" literally the "chief/owner of the river", to perform all relevant cultural ceremonies and the necessary rituals to purify the water and cleanse it for the festival. These rituals would ward off all disasters and invite all the fish from hiding. Significantly, in the history of the Festival, no drowning has been reported despite the large number of participants.

The Festival that year was to be held on Saturday the 31st of November . And apart from the traditional rituals, the Kebbi State Ministry of Culture and Tourism had taken over a large chunk of the organisation of the Festival from the natives. A million dollar extension to the Fishing Village Hotel and general infrastructural upgrades had been completed. The road from Sokoto to Argungu had been reconstructed with gleaming macadam and wide aprons. A saturation level national campaign on national television and international campaigns through tourist agencies, all ensured that the year's festival was going to be one with a difference.

The Festival started with a grand opening by the State's Military Governor, after prayers by his Royal Highness, The Sultan of Sokoto. Agricultural shows then featured with cultural displays and parade of cattle, horses, camel and donkeys.

In the evening of the first day, local wrestling matches were held. Clad in provocative war-like costumes, with charms and amulets tied on their bodies, the wrestlers fought both on the physical and metaphysical levels.

The second day featured various water sports. Sleek, dark flesh com-peted vigorously to out-do each other in the delicate art of bare-hand fishing and wild-duck catching. "Kabenci" displays of canoe racing, un-der water endurance tests were also featured.

The third day. The climax. The fishing competition proper. The fishing competition had held on the same stretch of water for many generations. Towards the Berni Kebbi end of the town, the water ran straight at the northern tip and swept through a series of rice paddies and shrubs, before curving away into the distance.

Hence, all along this straight stretch, men with dark oily skins equipped with hand nets and gourds stood waiting for the all-important signal to dive in. That year, there were over three thousand fishermen poised on the banks ... waiting. For one year, they had been forbid-den from fishing in this river. And now the one who came out with the biggest fish today would get a handsome cash prize of one million Naira! Unprecedented! But that was all part of the hype that had gone along with the promotion of the Festival. Half a mile long, the contes-tants lined the banks of the river. Waiting. The tension and excitement amongst the fishermen had reached fever-pitch.

But just before the signal for the fishermen to splash off, sirens were heard in the distance. No one had been sure. But the Head of State had hinted that he might witness the final events at the Festival. True, advance security men had been combing the whole village inside-out. Secret Service men had been mingling with unsuspecting natives in the town for one whole week. But nobody was sure, except the Union.

The Presidential convoy drove to a smart halt and the Head of State, Commander-In-Chief of the Armed Forces ... President of the Federal Republic of Nigeria stepped down to a rapturous applause. Cameras clicked and flashed. And an expectant hush descended on the scene. From somewhere, a deep voice announced:

"The President of the Federal Republic of Nigeria" The National Anthem followed. Thereafter, all were seated. Waiting for the most exciting climax of the Argungu Fishing Festival. But before the signal for the Fishing to commence, a side attraction had been prepared in readiness to help settle down the President before the main event.

With traditional horns blaring, seven young men were led into the main arena. The men each had an earthen pot. At a command they each filled their pots with water. At another command they sank slowly into the water and rested the pots on their heads. With the pots delicately balanced on their heads, they swam in unison across the fast flowing river. From one bank to the other. Amid cheers from the excited crowd and with melodic traditional music accompaniment, the now frenetic crowd hailed their dexterity. It was a sheer carnival, with myriad of colours.

At last, the signal to commence came and all the fishermen splashed into the water amid music accompaniment. Forty-five minutes to one hour later, it was all over. The fishermen all returned to land with their catch. The weighing was really not necessary. It was only a formality. As Mallam Mohammadu Bah's catch was truly extra-ordinary. Standing twelve feet tall and five feet at its widest point, the catch was truly incredible for a barracuda! And to have caught it with only just a hand-held net!

Amid cheers from the crowd, General Atiku, Chairman of the Supreme Military Council, Head of State and President of Nigeria, stepped forward gingerly to present Mallam Mohammadu Bah the top prize – one million Naira.

The Security people cleared the way as the Military Governor symbolically handed over the prize catch, which was dangling from a suspended hook scale to the President.

The scale swivelled past General Atiku. Just a little too much to the left,and Mohammed Bah moved forward to restrain the swinging scale and the prize catch for a photo opportunity. That swivelling scale saved the General's life. For a second before that moment, General Atiku's head was within Mustapha Alli's rifle cross-hairs. The shot from the silenced AK47 tore into Mallam Bah's catch, veering slightly as it tore into the suspended scale. With a clang, it ricocheted off the main metal support board for the scale and hit a grinning Mallam Bah fully on his chest.

Mallam Bah, hit the ground with a thud. As he fell his blood oozed out of a torn artery, spraying blood aimlessly. In that instant, the sprayed blood left General Atiku's immaculate Number One dress bloodied.

The Security people moved in briskly. They cordoned off the whole area and hurtled the President and Mallam Bah's body away. With sirens blaring, the Presidential motorcade sped off the scene in a controlled frenzy. A mortuary quiet that arose more out of surprise than shock, for not one person in the crowd understood what had really happened, enveloped the entire Fishing Village. Since the sniper's gun was silenced, no one heard any shot and Mallam Bah's slump was initially passed off for exhaustion. But the blood! More surprise!

The security people raced across the River in a boat, combing all the shrubs on the opposite bank. But Mustapha Alli trained to survive in the jungle was gone. His only regret was the miss. A very costly miss. The most important target of his career. And a miss! Next time, he won't be that lucky, he cursed.

Officially, it was flown into Nigeria in the early weeks of April 1984. This was during the early revolutionary days of the Buhari/Idiagbon regime. But the customised Gulfstream was ordered during the Second Republic by the Shehu Shagari administration as the flagship of the Presidential Fleet.

When the Gulfstream, christened "FGN Victor" arrived at the Airlift Command hangers of the Nigeria Air Force at the Murtala Mohammed Airport that morning, it marked the beginning of a media controversy. The media questioned why the Presidential Fleet should possess so many aircrafts when Nigeria Airways, the Federal Government-owned flag carrier was ailing, and getting all the flak because it could not cope with high passenger traffic.

But so many years and five governments after, the Presidential Fleet now bristled with more modern aircrafts. Two customised Super Falcons. One Customised Long-distance Boeing 747, now officially christened "Victor 1" One Tristar and four Super Puma helicopters.

The fleet was run and maintained by the Airlift Command of the Nigerian Airforce. In its over thirty years of existence, the Command has had its headquarters moved first from Kano to Lagos, then moved to the unused airport at Ibadan where it was based for five years until it moved again to Lagos and finally to Abuja; next-door to the Presidential Fleet. The responsibility for day-to-day maintenance, procurement and flight operations of the Fleet was handled by the 501 squadron of the Airlift Command.

Following the crippling nation-wide industrial action embarked upon by the Nigerian Labour Congress, the Presidential Fleet and the routine military air traffic control personnel were deployed to provide priority skeletal air service for essential movements by public officials.

So it was that the Gulfstream now re-christened "Eagle One" was prepared in readiness for a top priority trip. For the purpose of the trip, the entire cabin had been stripped of all its cosy seats to make room for its emergency cargo.

Early that morning, the cargo arrived. Two cash transfer armoured trucks from the Central Bank, under tight security escort, the trucks disgorged crates of new currency notes.

Two hours later, the cargo was fully loaded and secured under the watchful eyes of the aircraft commander, Wing Commander Eke Nwichi. To fly the second seat with him on the No 2 seat as navigator/co-pilot was Squadron Leader Ben Ipaiye.

At precisely 9.30 that morning Nigerian time, Eagle One was ready for take off.

"Start engine One" Nwichi ordered.

"Starting One" Ipaiye responded.

They continued the same ritual for the two main engines and the tail engine and gently nudged the aircraft towards runway Zero One for take-off.

"Open full throttles" Nwichi ordered. The plane roared as the full throttle squeezed compressed fuel through her jet engines. The whole body work shuddered as it was held back despite being egged on by the firing engines. Meantime, Nwichi and Ipaiye scanned through instruments and ahead on the runway intermittently – altimeters, pressure gauges, engine thrust and revolutions, radar. "Injection" ordered Nwichi. At last, the emergency Air Traffic Control cleared "Eagle One" for take-off. With the release of the brakes, Eagle One burst out in relief, achieving a speed of 100 m.p.h. in five seconds. At another command, Ipaiye lifted the control yoke and the Gulfstream responded beautifully, lifted up its nose as it soared into the sky.

Nwichi executed a smooth take off and took up all flaps as it climbed into its approved flight path.

"Eagle One.. Departing MMA"

"Roger Eagle One" MMA Control responded.

The military emergency Air Traffic Controller. "You are cleared to proceed north-west...flight path 18... Level out at 24,000 feet.

Ten minutes later, at 24,000 feet Air Traffic Control came through the commo lines once again. "Eagle One. This is Murtala Mohammed Airport Emergency Air traffic Control. We have you at 24,000 ft; continue on your current heading. Handing over to Ilorin ATC in five minutes. Over and out."

One hour later, Eagle One was in contact with Sokoto Airport Air Traffic Control.

"Sokoto Control. This is Eagle One requesting permission to land"

"Eagle One. I read you. Altitude. We have you for 24,000.Descend to Level 14..Heading South-East.. You are cleared for landing on runway 02 on direct V approach only. Visibility one mile.. slight harmattan haze. Strong heady winds to your North-East.... about twenty knots,moving to thirty – International traffic to your North-East in Niger Republic."

Nwichi checked his instrument panel and made a visual sweep intermittently.

"Sokoto Control, I have visual contact. Commencing final descent"

"Roger Eagle One. Descent on visual only approach."

Eagle One landed smoothly and taxied down towards Bodinga. With their job of bringing down the plane done, Air Traffic Control perfunctorily scanned through the horizon and asked "Eagle One" to execute ground turnings and park by apron four; where armoured cash trucks were waiting.

Spritely with its three engines on reverse thrust Eagle One glided smoothly towards the Bodinga end of the long runway to execute a turn. But there, concealed in the surrounding foliage, a special taskforce of the Union waited.

"Casbablanca" had monitored all communication traffic between Sokoto AirTtraffic Control and Eagle One and had signalled "Mugabi" as the plane made its final descent.;and taxied down runway 02. As Eagle One swivelled to execute a U-turn towards the Sokoto end of the airport, Mugabi struck. From his concealed ,heavily camouflaged position, he peered through telescopic sights of the AK47 and fired. Five quick shots, in five seconds. The first shot punctured Eagle One's turning front tyres. Two other shots immobilised the main rear tyres. Another two shots shattered the side port-side window and snuffed the life out of Nwichi and Ipaiye instantly.

Briskly, the team raced across the runway and blast open the main doors to the aircraft. Simultaneously, four Land Rovers sped out of hiding unto the tarmac and all commenced off loading Eagle One's cargo into the Land Rovers. Five Minutes. Ten minutes, fifteen minutes. And the emergency Military Air Traffic Control Squadron Leader Lucky Idode peered through binoculars from the control tower at the runway and saw what looked like a normal loading operation. But then he tried to raise Eagle One on radio to no avail.

In panic, he ran down the flight of stairs to alert bewildered bank officials and the Police escort of his discovery. A crash, he thought. That the plane had apparently collided with a vehicle and it appeared skewed with the tyres deflated.

To be fair to the Police escort, the report was unclear. Was it a crash, a collision or a puncture? In any event, it did not appear to be a Police case and a fire fighting truck was sent racing down while all emergency alarms were sounded.

But as the fire engine drew close to the scene of the robbery, it became clear to the fire fighters that all was not well. Four Land Rovers pulled out from the port side of the aircraft and sped through the hedges through bush paths towards Bodinga. The fire fighters were encouraged into an immediate detour with a burst of rifle fire, which shattered the truck's windscreen.

The four Land Rovers sped through the city of Bodinga and headed towards a lonely side road of the Argungu-Bodinga highway. Briskly the Land Rovers were driven into two large fish carrying refrigerated trailers. The trailers, regular sights on Nigerian roads belonged to Union Fisheries a front operation of the Union. With the doors firmly closed, the two trailers pulled out of the side road, linked up with the main Sokoto-Yauri road and headed straight for Sokoto town. As the trucks drove into Sokoto town, fully armed soldiers and members of the National Guard were headed towards Bodinga in pursuit of the robbers.

The trailers drove through Sokoto town and proceeded towards Gusau. At Gusau, the vehicles were fuelled at a Union fuel depot before proceeding to Kaduna. That night in a secret Union warehouse operated by Inua Bako, the heist was stashed away and the Land Rovers were sprayed back to their original Army colours for return to their units.

∞

With the Second World War drawing to a close, what subsequently became the first military hospital in Nigeria was opened in Igbobi, Lagos. The hospital served as a treatment point for all casualty evacuees, most of them from the British 8th Army in the Middle East.

With the end of the war, and with facilities at the hospital easily the best in Nigeria at the time, the institution was opened to the general public and re-designated Government Orthopaedic Hospital and Rehabilitation Centre. Between 1945-50, the Centre became an annexe of the General Hospital Lagos under the management of Dr Tom Lambert. Two batches of paramedical staff under the leadership of Mr P E Ibru, a first class nurse were posted to the Centre from the General Hospital as the nucleus of the health delivery unit; in addition to five Italian prisoners of war, headed by Mr Toloni who provided artificial limb and braces services at the hospital.

It was in 1948 under the Board leadership of Sir Samuel Manuwa as Chief Medical Adviser that a sweeping re-organisation and a re-definition of the hospital's objectives were undertaken. The hospital, which before then offered general surgical, gynaecological and medical treatment to all parts of Nigeria and neighbouring West Africa was restricted to the practices of speciality orthopaedics and rehabilitation. The training of African members of staff also commenced.

In 1954, two Nigerian doctors were posted to the hospital. These were Dr Ademola and Dr Bailey. On completion of specialised training, Dr Ademola became the first Nigerian head of the hospital between 1957 – 1968.

The visit of the British monarch, Queen Elizabeth II, to the hospital in 1956, resulted in a change of its name to "Royal Orthopaedic Hospital, Igbobi." A trauma unit and a casualty block were added to the hospital around this period. Mr M O Kuti, formerly a nurse, had been trained in the United Kingdom in the techniques of prosthetics and orthatics;and upon his return he quickly assumed leadership of the Artificial Limb Workshop in the hospital, where simple braces and other devices were fabricated.

With the creation of twelve states in 1967, the hospital was taken over by the Lagos State Government and the prefix "Royal" was dropped from the name. By this time, the hospital had become very famous nationally and beyond in the provision of its speciality health services. Casualty evacuees from the theatre of war to the hospital during the Nigerian Civil war had stretched the facilities of the hospital.

Emergency extensions were embarked upon and military tents were erected to serve as surgical wards; demand on the hospital had grown beyond what the Lagos State government could cope with. The hospital was consequently taken over by the Federal Government and re-designated "National Orthopaedic Hospital, Igbobi".

With the Federal Government take-over, more funds were poured into the physical development of the hospital. It was upgraded to an ultra-modern hospital with custodial facilities for over a thousand in-patients.

In support of the laudable objectives of the hospital, private funds also poured in to support its physical growth. One of such contributions was the Mobolaji Accident Ward, donated by the Nigerian philanthropist, Sir Mobolaji Bank Anthony. The first phase of the ward was commissioned in 1979.

Before the death of the multi-millionaire philanthropist, he had set up a Foundation to render continuous assistance to the hospital. It was to the credit of the Foundation that extensions to the Accident Ward had been added to the hospital.

On this thursday in August , a multi-million dollar Department of Traumatology, built by the Mobolaji Foundation was being commissioned. The ceremonies started at about mid-day with the arrival of invited guests and World Health Organisation representatives. At about one p.m, with sirens blaring, the Head of the Federal Military Government and Commander-In-Chief of the Armed Forces drove in briskly. And straight on to the business of the day, General Atiku moved on to make a short speech, unveiled the plaque of the new Department; and cut a ceremonial tape to declare the facility open.

And in another ten minutes, the Head of State's motorcade was again blaring away. The motorcade made a turning at the Maryland and Airport Road junction and headed back through Palmgrove, Igbobi and climbed a bridge unto the ever busy Western Avenue, now cleared of all vehicular traffic for the Head of State.

Four hours earlier, Mustapha Alli had arrived at the busy Inyang Ette Transport Service office on the same Western Avenue. He got into line at the adjacent fast food centre, where he bought a burger, a meatpie and a bottle of Maltina. One hour later, he strolled over to the adjacent Granada Hotel and Casino, looking like one of the newly arrived passengers on the Inyang Ette buses. The Granada had been a bustling hotel complex, complete with a night club in the seventies. Then it housed very many military men on courses, duty postings to Lagos and in transit. These were the days when Godwin Omabuwa and The Granadians thrilled audiences to no end at the hotel.

The Granada was strategically located. Situated besides the very central and ever busy Ojuelegba Road/Western Avenue intersection, its six floors shot it high up. And from those upper floors, the kaleidoscopic confusion of the Ojuelegba intersection played out in slow motion daily to occupants of this upper level of the hotel.

The frustration of the traffic bottleneck at this intersection led Fela Anikulapo Kuti into the composition of the song "Go Slow" in the 1970s which painted a graphic picture of the confusion at this junction. Probably in response to Fela's criticisms and to combat the traffic bottleneck, a concrete flyover was built over this intersection by Guffanti, the Italian civil engineering firm, in the mid-seventies. This flyover rose and stood shoulder to shoulder with Granada Hotel. So close, you could almost hold a conversation with a passenger on a passing car on the flyover from the hotel's upper floors.

It was on one of these windows that Mustapha Alli set up his killing machine. A four-barrel automatic swivelling high calibre Gustav Quad

.50. Now neatly assembled, with the four barrels pointed at the fly-over, Mustapha Alli peered through his cross-hairs expectantly. In the magazine of the Gustav were .50 calibre high explosive, armour piecing bullets. Each of those bullets was like a rocket and packed similar punch.

Presently, Geneal Atiku's motorcade drew up on the bridge. Despite the motorcade's speed, there was a brief moment when it had to slow down as it climbed the steep incline unto the fly-over. Mustapha gazed in joy through his crosshairs at the stern face of General Atiku. At that moment, a very grim smile spread across his lips for he knew he had scored. Firmly, he squeezed off... and four .50 calibre high explosive armour-piecing rockets smashed through the narrow side window of the Mercedes 500 Special Edition. The car's high resistant bullet proof glass resisted the initial impact. But the bullet had gone through a particularly vulnerable point. The narrow side glass despite the bullet proof reinforcement could not withstand the rocket's force. The glass exploded into smithereens as another full blast caught General Atiku in the head. Those who saw the body later in hospital said there was no head to the body. This again fuelled the rumour mill later to the effect that a decoy and not General Atiku was hit.

In two seconds, Mustapha emptied a total of forty rounds into the car, hitting the Aid-de-Camp and the driver. At the first explosion, the head of the State Security Services (SSS) detail, riding front seat with the President swivelled backward and grabbed a dismembered General Atiku. He threw General Atiku down on the floor to reduce his target profile; pulled his front seat harness into a reclining position to provide better covering fire for the head of state. Simultaneously, he drew out his throat microphone to raise "Power Station", the SSS Master Control Room in "The Deep" at Awolowo Road. "Power Station.... ",he screamed into the microphone. "This is Brocade Extra... Brocade One is down...I repeat,Brocade One is down... Execute Plan Bravo... I repeat execute Plan Bravo.. Out"

That was the last transmission from "Brocade Extra". For at that moment, the car hurtling down the flyover, smashed into the side railings, somersaulted and smashed into a nearby petrol station, set it ablaze, broke through a concrete wall and came to rest in a second-hand cars showroom on the now panic-stricken Western Avenue.

Within a few minutes, "Plan Bravo" was in shape. A crack team of airborne Presidential Guards men cordoned off the whole area. An air ambulance, a customised Apache mobile clinic, complete with an operating theatre moved in. In less than five minutes, all the casualties were evacuated. The presidential limousine was loaded into a trailer and taken away. With a security net thrown around the neighbourhood, SSS men then commenced a house-to-house search of the whole area. But it was too late. Mustapha with his precious carry-all had quietly strolled out before the net was put in place.

At precisely 2 pm that thursday, the National Radio network suspended its scheduled broadcast to announce to a dazed nation yet another assassination of a head of state. Thereafter, it commenced playing martial music and dirges.

At an emergency meeting of the Supreme Military Council later that evening, the leadership of the country was transferred to General Ahmadu Attah, the erstwhile Chief of Army Staff.

That evening in an all- service nation-wide broadcast, General Attah told a shocked nation that he had assumed the mantle of leadership. He spoke at length about the crises facing the nation and queried why fellow Nigerians would resort to assassination to achieve their objectives. A situation which he described as a grievous and despicable assault on the soul of the nation. He regretted that the political class because of their corruption and naivety had forced the military into civil administration and governance in the first place and that that had inflicted severe professional damage on the military's spirit and morale. General Attah shocked a bewildered nation that evening when he revealed that a vast majority of the Nigerian professional military hated the military's incursion into civil administration and politics and would rather want to remain true professional soldiers.

"The assassination of General Atiku earlier today was the most grievous cut of all" he said "For here was a man who worked tirelessly to bring respect and attainments not only to Nigerians but to the entire black world...I have accepted the challenges of his aspirations and what he stood for and affirm today that from the demise of this great patriot will arise even a greater Nigeria that will be a pride to the entire black race."

Two weeks later, General Attah announced a time-table for the return of the country to civil rule. Parties were to be formed and elections held for a final return to civilian rule in nine months.He also announced the commencement of free,compulsory primary and secondary education;and free education,with free board,tuition and books for all Nigerian university undergraduates.The National Association of Nigerian Students(NUNS) and the Nigerian Labour Congress(NLC) earlier banned by the military government were de-proscribed.

The general response was enthusiastic. General Attah was described variously as a patriot, a nationalist and a messiah. Over twenty political associations sprang up in under one month. After a careful screening however, only four parties were registered. And one of them was the Union Democratic Front (UDF). The revised constitution also provided for independent candidates.

∽

At the next Extra-Ordinary Conclave of the Union attended by its Full Council,which included the Holy One and his Spiritual Adviser, General Attah was honoured by the Full Union Conclave wherein after a few rituals, he symbolically declared for the Union's party – the UDF.

In the dense neighbourhood of Sabon Gari in Kano was s melting pot of culture. Sabon-Gari with its long inter-locking streets was the "new Kano" where "the unbelievers" toiled night and day, with the ever-growing suspicion of the adherents of the faith in Tundun Wada. Here, in Sabon-Gari was the true demonstration of unity in diversity. The ever present Ibo traders, the Yoruba traders and taxi drivers, the Urhobos, Isoko, Ijaws and Bini ethnic groups,most of them itinerant businessmen and traders with middle-class aspirations. There were also The Ibibios and Annangs. And the people from the middle belt, whose women were always so visible and dominant in the social life of the suburb.

In the middle of Sabon-Gari, adjacent to Count-Down Plaza, stood a mysterious brick house. Painted all black with matching black walls. Behind this high black walls and inside a large compound, over two hundred cars were parked this saturday night. It was not an unusual sight. Most saturdays, cars start driving through the fort-like gate of this compound as early as twelve noon; and will be there till the early hours of the next day when they start dispersing.

But this Saturday, out of all the facilities available to the Union in Kano, it had chosen to pick a Presidential Candidate for the Union Democratic Front (UDF) at its Sabon-Gari Compound. Contrary to popular expectations, the secret convention of the Union was really not about ideology or even national politics. Weeks before, the major candidates had traversed the nooks and crannies of Nigeria raising support from the different Houses, Families and Compounds that made up the Union. Thus, the eventual election was not even about competence.

Whereas, the whole country was made to believe that the National Convention for the election of a Presidential Candidate for the UDF was held on a certain sunday at the Eagle Square in Abuja, what happened in Abuja that was beamed to a nation-wide audience on television was a mere formality.

The actual election had taken place two weeks earlier in the mysterious black house in Sabon-Gari, where after highly symbolic fearful rituals, house members were presented with a shortlist of three candidates as prospective presidential flag-bearers.

First to be presented to the Conclave was Professor Ango Usman. A man of high intellect, the Kano conclave was like home-coming for him. For he was a product of the Sabon-Gari melting pot. The son of a Sokoto Kolanut trader who made good his promise to better the lots of his children, he was an intellectual giant whose ideas had enormous influence on the strategic direction of the Union.

Next to be presented was Bob Inene, a shrewd multi-millionaire head of Inene Compound. Now, a man of sixty five, the modern-day wealth of the Union came from his bold entrepreneual forays into what family members call "pharmaceuticals".

And finally, the urbane-looking Inua Bako. Easily, the most visible member of the Union, he represented the Union's more legitimate front office businesses – from entertainment to music promotions and media conglomerates.

The election that followed had nothing to do with personal integrity, morality or even competence. It was about "electability and spiritual blessing". All the candidates were traditional Union people who had paid their dues. They all had tough personal characters, had grown up in poverty, struck wealth by dubious means and were committed Union members. Education was important to the extent that it provided a vista for a clear understanding of events and how they could benefit the Union. It was therefore important to be able to read, write and add sums with a calculator.

They all represented the ultimate dream of the Union. Self made men who had worked their way up and had successfully subverted the system for personal and Union rewards.And above all else,had demonstrated very personal loyalty to the Holy One and his Spiritual Leader.

But although the three candidates shared all great Union ideals, the crucial issue of electability would determine who got the Union's nod at the Special Conclave. Despite their similarities in background, the three men were totally different in their personal attributes. Professor Usman was of high intellect, internationally respected as a scholar, a dedicated academician who got entwined into Union ways because of his ambition to attain the pinnacle of his career. He became an even more dedicated extremist once his rising academic profile provided enhanced opportunities and membership of United Nations,Commonwealth and Africa Union educational committees. His commitment to a leadership position spear-headed by the Union was largely influenced by the unity of purpose that a Union leadership would impose, given its immense grass-roots structures,presence and penetration. He was also a genuine lover of civil society and civil rights with a firm belief that the military's incursion into politics had retarded the overall growth of Nigeria as a nation.

He had a permanent self-restraint and reluctance to trumpet his academic attainments in a society where mediocrity had often triumphed above all else.

Bob Inene on the other hand, lacked high intellect. But that was compensated for by his shrewd organisational skills. All he needed to project at this Special Conclave was his true self. His well-known position on social issues within the Union set him out as a liberal enforcer. He favoured freedom of choice on most national issues – from drug enforcement to gender issues. His liberal broad mindedness-had produced the vision of exploiting emergent niches in habits and technology and through same had built up the single most profitable business within the Union portfolio. Therefore, on the face of documented achievements, he towered above all the other candidates. Additionally, he had a latent mean streak, which had been employed from time to time in his climb in the Union hierarchy. He was a great predatory competitor who never gave up until all opposition was eliminated.

But the focus in this Special Conclave had been on Inua Bako – right from the onset. Neither his promotion agencies nor his high-tech front office operations had been able to make an impact at the Conclave. In this Special Union Conclave, his media technicians were not able to play a part as their technical skills and media manipulations were not allowed into the inner sanctuary deliberations. This was a strict Compound by Compound evaluation and election and Inua was therefore forced to fight on his own, visiting all Union Compounds without the manipulative media tools he was so used to. . After an initial false start, Inua had been tempted by a massive personal urge to fight back and redeem his image. Unfortunately, as Compound after Compound got to know the essential Inua, got to know his real ethnic roots, his lack of strong family structures and support, his ultra flamboyance and perceived arrogance and aloofness, his cross-cultural appeal that was so effective in the mass media had been perceived as a serious obstacle. His fresh re-assessment by all the Compounds had tended to highlight his negatives: Uncommitted, unserious, lacking an ethnic base because of his masked ethnic origins and his cross-cultural romantic forays.Above all,he was perceived by most Compounds to be a "Lagos Boy,"lacking in true Northern Nigeria roots and grassroots appeal.

As it turned out, it became common knowledge, that Inua Bako was not really a muslim despite the frequent addition of the "Alhaji" prefix to his name. Despite his family's long claim to Hausa/Fulani Kano origins, Bako's fore-bears were actually extractions of itinerant Tiv cobblers and pagan heathens from Zuru in Kebbi state,whose pagan progenitors worshipped a marine deity-a crocodile. It was not very clear who circulated these facts about Innua Bako, or whether in his usual frank sartorial arrogance he had volunteered the incriminating evidence. But every Union member at the Conclave had come prepared to vote against him because of his perceived non-electability.

It was therefore no surprise to members when the decision of the Conclave was announced: Bob Inene for President, Professor Usman for Vice President. The Conclave also elected gubernatorial candidates for the regions: Professor Dapo Shobowale of the "Shobowale Plan" for Lagos region, David Ajaini for the Western region and Ashakohleh "Ashako" Imienyi for Eastern region. Also elected were Tofi "Mugabe" Jibo and Joe "Ofege" Ofili for Northern and Mid-west regions respectively.

The presidential ticket was an electable combination: Bob Inene's shrewd dynamism and Professor Usman's intellectual appeal. The ticket also built a solid North-South bridge that was considered unstoppable at the polls; especially Bob Inene's South-South roots,which was widely touted as a panacea to the youth restiveness in the Niger-Delta;and the integration of that region into national mainstream politics and leadership. The National Convention of UDF two weeks later was just a mere formality. But all through the convention, the media,uninformed on the Union's ways and methods put an irrelevant spotlight on Inua Bako. He was the media favourite and his eventual loss was packaged by the mass media to convey a sense of loss that generated immense sympathy from all Nigerians. Political and media commentators were stunned by the result of the Convention and their constant re-appraisal of the outcome put the public on the edge. But all that was required to douse the speculations and resultant tension would have been just a brief nod of support and congratulations from Inua Bako to the Inene/ Usman ticket.

But in the general confusion that prevailed after the Convention, nobody noticed that Inua Bako had slipped away to catch a late flight back to Lagos. This was a cardinal sin as a celebratory Conclave of " Milk and Honey" at which the "Holy One" himself would preside, supported by the unseen hand of the Spiritual Adviser "The Lion" *was scheduled for that night in Abuja.* The Founder, The spiritual Head, The Ageless, The rarely seen "Holy One" does not call for a Special " Milk and Honey" ritual session and he is disobeyed.

The slight was too much. To ignore an invitation from the Holy One! And The Lion! Inua Bako had committed a cardinal sin against The Union!

Chapter 10

PASTOR PATRICK

IT STARTED AS a mild headache, progressing gradually to what the missionary doctor at the nearby Ayangba General Hospital noted was migraine. But the throbbing headache would not go.

The week before, he had travelled with his steward to the Diocesan Conference at the Provincial Headquarters in Oturkpo. There, he stocked for his favourite baked beans, tuna, corned beef and bacon. His meals upon his return from Uturkpo were rich and delicious. So,when he saw the doctor and he complained about excessive fat here and there,he was not surprised. Something about his Body Mass Index being over 30; and the need for him to exercise and trim down. But this throbbing headache?

"Essau" he called out to his steward. For he could never pronounce his steward's real name;and conveniently changed his name to Essau.

"Yes Massa"

"How many times will I have to remind you ... your only "massa" on earth is our Lord Jesus ... Not me ... Not any earthly being ... Call me Patrick ... Pastor Patrick and please get me some cold water ..."

The fellow American Peace Corps Baptist Missionary Doctor at Ayangba put his chills and headaches the next day to stress. The doctor traced it all to the stress of planning for the annual Adult Thanksgiving Harvest. The anxiety and energy-sapping demands of its organisation. Organising the Adult Bazaar in all that scorching heat. He gave Pastor Patrick some analgesics, tranquillisers and multi-vitamins and thought nothing else of it.

It was the period of advent. The church and the whole town wore a festive look. The celebration of the birth of our Lord Jesus was in the offing and the festive mood was pervasive. This would be his second Christmas in Nigeria having served in Makurdi and Gboko previously. But Christmas that year seemed so far away for Pastor Patrick. For three weeks, he had been unable to bring himself to tune his short-wave transistor radio to his favourite Voice of America's News In Special English on the Africa Service to follow developments at the war fronts in Korea and the United Nations efforts in Katanga.

"Essau, more water!"

He often wondered why water cooled in Esua's special earthenware pot, that he keeps in a special dug-out under the mango tree tastes so richly different. So cool and so refreshing. That night the feverish chills came again. And the endless nightmares. Except that that night, it all seemed so real. The dark, tall, bare-chested and very muscular man, who called himself "Hannibal", with the long bristling sword in hot pursuit. As he panted for breath, running away from the hot pursuit of "Hannibal", he was suddenly confronted with the fast-flowing River Niger – and as he contemplated what to do, he heard the loud shrill of "Hannibal" descending on him ... At that moment, Pastor Patrick snapped wide awake in sweat ...

"Massa!"

It was Esau strangely by his bed-side early that morning with his favourite glass of water in hand. Pastor Patrick thankfully accepted the drink, whilst trying to hold back his nervous chills.

At the hospital later that morning, his chills and nightmares were traced to fever. His compatriot, Doctor Chris Hurton said there was nothing to worry about. He made light talk of the issue. In an avuncular manner, he explained that the temperature of the human body is carefully regulated and varies very little under normal circumstances between 98.4 and 98.60 Fahrenheit. That the body summoned all its defence agents when it was attacked by external forces like germs. The elevated temperature and feverish feelings came into play as defence mechanisms to make the body's raised temperature unsuitable for the germs to inhabit; and so that the increased working tempo of the raised body temperature will work more quickly and efficiently to eliminate the external threat. Thereafter, he ran a few tests, took Pastor Patrick's temperature and dispensed quinine, M&B and APC tablets.

But the feverish chills and nightmares continued that night. That night, the nightmares were even more intense. This time he was up in the Plateau, on the Mangu Hills, hanging on to a slight incline. Below, was a wild bottomless forested valley. As he struggled to ensure a firmer grip and climb up to the next landing, he heard the distant roar of a lion. Presently, the lion came into full view; an unusually all black huge beast of a carnivore with fearful scruffy mane and red, blazing eyes.

As the lion roared and lunged wildly towards him, a pretty,busty maiden appeared from nowhere to intercede. In the ensuing struggle, the lion seized upon the well-formed, robustly pointed and sensually provocative left breast of the pretty damsel. In one flash, the lion grabbed and bit off the ripe breast and sauntered off into the mountain; leaving the damsel in agony. Even in her pains, she offered Pastor Patrick a helping hand, and lifted him up from the incline into safety ... Pastor Patrick broke out of the nightmare into consciousness, panting and gasping for breath.

"Massa!" His loyal steward was again thankfully nearby with a glass of water.

Pastor Patrick's health deteriorated steadily in the next few days. The Missionary Hospital was forced to review its diagnosis and came to a new conclusion: suspected meningitis. That a certain membrane which provided cover for the delicate nerves tissue in the brain and the spinal cord was infected and heavily inflamed. That the ensuing cerebro-spinal fevers were responsible for his endless nightmares. He was promptly put on a course of streptomycin, and admitted into the hospital's Intensive Care Unit for close monitoring.

That night, the tall, dark fearsome "Hannibal" continued to chase him in his nightmares. Twice, he made to plunge a spear through his heart ... and twice too was the spear deflected by the now one-breasted damsel. Next, "Hannibal" seized his neck and dragged him into the bank of the great River Niger. As he struggled for breath, "Hannibal" plunged him face-down into the river. For what seemed like forever, Patrick struggled and thrashed aimlessly for air. Even in the throes of death he fought for his life, struggling to get an occasional intake of air. Just when he thought it was all over, he heard a loud shrill, louder than all the thunderous rumbling of the Niger, and the grip around his neck went limp and slipped off. When he came to, the one-breasted damsel was hovering over the dead 'Hannibal'.

All through his stay at the hospital, the nightmares continued. His body temperature shot up and hovered between 104 to 106 degrees. He became markedly emanciated for lack of appetite and sleep. In very hush tunes, hospital authorities started fearing for the worse and commenced medical evacuation plans back to his native Lanham, Maryland, USA.

Two weeks of continuing deterioration even as an in-patient at the hospital was enough. Pastor Patrick was encouraged by his steward "Esau" to be discharged from the hospital against medical advise. He barely scrawled his signature on the self-discharge card and was allowed to go home. Once home, the soothing glass of Esau's water commenced his revival process.

The dwarfed bungalow where Pastor Patrick resided in Ayangba was enveloped in landscaped gardens of coconuts, Mangoes, Oranges, lemon, avocado pears and many more. Upon his self-discharge that evening, Esau unobtrusively, ever- present, took charge of Patrick's medication, with an easy calm. With the scarce communication between them on account of obvious language barrier, Esau nevertheless made himself understood.

First, he plucked fresh coconuts, cut them open and gathered the water in a large bowl. From this bowl, he proceeded to serve glass after glass to Patrick. Much later in life Patrick would come to understand the botanical name to be "cocos nucifera" and the water a veritable source of instant energy, a de-oxidant, a detoxifier and a strong remedy against all toxins. Thus, as he drank the coconut water freely and passed urine frequently, his system was gradually but steadily purged of all toxins.

That evening, Esau put to boil a large earthen pot. In the pot were "all kinds of concoctions" as Patrick put it then. But a sick man that he was, he was ready to do anything. On probing much later after his recovery however, he was to note in his book on his Africa experiences that the steam bath that he undertook and the 'concoction' that he drank consisted of cymbogen actratiors commonly referred to by the indigenes as lemon grass; fresh plantain leaves (musa paradisiacal); psiduin guasava commonly referred to as guava by the indigenes; fresh roots of ginger, fresh leaves of nicotiria tabacum, (tobacco), fresh leaves of mango, with the botanical name of mangifera indica; fresh leaves of paw-paw and neem leaves (locally known as dongoyaro).

Two glasses of this broth taken three times a day and coconut water freely taken became the treatment regimen for Pastor Patrick for the next two weeks: the general purpose cure for malaria, anaemia, typhoid fever and insomnia and general body debility.

A warm bath with this broth first thing in the morning and the last thing at night completed the treatment. One week into his treatment, his appetite had improved markedly. His sleeps were less troubled. In place of the nightmares, he now had regular romantic wet dreams. Every night, he found himself in warm embrace of the damsel, lustily sucking his one surviving breast. And as he sucked, he could feel strength and wellness oozing back into his veins and would wake up from his dreams in fulfilment, with a strong erection and Esau standing by his bed, smiling.

Day by day Pastor Patrick gained in strength and well-being. And with his recovery came a new vigour for life. His libido grew increasingly strong with resultant pronounced erotic dreams dominating his sleep. All the dreams centred around one woman – the pretty, dark-skinned one-breasted damsel. His saviour. For that was what the damsel had come to represent in his life;and that was what she communicated to him in very sensual and reassuring tones in his very frequent wet dreams.

Patrick's residence was one of those very typical Nigerian bungalows built by and for colonial missionaries and District Officers in the fities. A three-bedroom bungalow in front, with an inner so-called Boys Quarters apartment block tucked away in the dense foliage at the distant rear, usually reserved for the servants. The Boy's Quarters or BQ, unit attached to Patrick's bungalow housed Eshugume Agaba (Esau) the pastor's cook/steward and general handyman and Hauwa, Esau's general assistant. Hauwa's daily chores included sweeping the very large courtyard, grass clearing, shopping for foodstuff and house sweeping.

For sometime now, since his recovery, Pastor Patrick had come to long for her daily rounds of sweeping inside and around the bungalow. It was December, with the Lord's birthday festivities now over and a new year was beckoning. It was the period when the North-East trade winds blew very cold winds and dust from across the sahara desert. It was the harmattan season of very cold nights and mornings.

He had woken up with lust and sexual longing that morning. An overnight erection induced by his now nightly encounter with The Saviour just simply refused to come down. That was when Hauwa swept her way into the bedroom. As Patrick came into the bedroom from the en-suite toilet, he saw the rhythmic bounce of Hauwa's well-rounded buttocks as she swept the room. The scanty loin cloth carelessly thrown to cover what excitement lay beyond the gyrating buttocks mocked and dared Patrick. Round and round the bedroom Hauwa swept, with Patrick caught in the sensual movement of her gyrating behind. He gaped; lost in lust as time stood still for him. As his eyes gazed intensely to penetrate beyond the loin cloth, Hauwa swivelled round and caught his darting eyes in lustful fixation.

She blushed, dropped the broom she was holding in shock. Before she could even have her breath back, Patrick darted forward, ostensibly to rush past her to the sitting room. At the same instant, Hauwa made to step aside. A bit of indecision here, poor anticipation there and servile deference on Hauwa's part generally, and they bumped into each other. Before they knew it, they were entangled, in warm embrace. He had physically longed for this moment for as long as he could remember. But always the lulling guilt, imposed by upbringing, suspicion and stark bigotry and racism had stopped him. He had been plagued by loads and loads of negative literatures about the "natives" circulated at the State Department's Orientation Course for Peace Corps volunteers before his posting to Nigeria . Stories about inferiority, disease, witchcraft, ignorance. See who is ignorant now,he thought!

Pastor Patrick ripped the thin fabric that served as Hauwa's underwear apart. She stood still, entrapped in rapture. No fear. Just loving submissiveness as she uttered "Massa, Massa!" to every probing touch of her robust and succulent frontal cleavage. He clutched and clasped her firmly around her buttocks and lifted her in one romantic swing. Hauwa, responded in unison climbing and twinning her legs around him ... so pliable and flexible as she responded to Patrick's every bidding! They groped and staggered and collapsed in loving tango on the bed.

As they landed, he struggled to undo his shorts to unfurl his throbbing manhood long in search of release and liberation. It didn't matter now, what the Peace Corp people thought back in Baltimore. All that self-denial and suppressed emotions. All that hatred of a very loving people just to conform to somebody's script and vision of the World?? Probably written around the corridors of the State Department in DC, Baltimore and such very distant places! Have they ever heard of Ayangba and its enchanting nubile maidens??

A thousand thoughts per second raced through his mind as the intensity of the passion of Hauwa's touch triggered tremors and spasms around his body ... tremors so shocking that they obliterated all the will to obey nurture and supremacist doctrines. He was taken over by a will, an urgent desire for human warmth and comfort and the natural instinct to share a common humanity; not maintenance of expatriate superiority and myths.

He slid his arms around her neck and stroked the now erect mammary apparatus on her chest. When he proceeded to take the nipples into his mouth ... the biblical tales of a land flowing with milk and honey became more vivid. Her lips ... they were sheer high voltage electricity! As the magnetic field expanded, her lips sucked in his own tongue and all in one electrifying tango of shared breath, saliva and flesh. Her supple frame was under his and become entangled from head to toe. He could feel her throbbing heart and the rhythmic vibrations of her breast under his bare chest, as they were grafted together in erotic communion. The birds, many and petched on the surrounding mango trees chirped and serenaded in unison. It was sweet music to the ears, but more to the heart ... as the rhythmic heart beats of the two lovers blended intimately with the music from the birds ... this was heaven! And he wished for no better place.

Unscripted. Not a single word was uttered. No instructions. But a perfect understanding of the non-verbal communication between the two bodies, the throbbing upward thrusts of the breast ... the shared sweaty stomachs as they were bonded in one elastic fold ... the intertwined legs and arms. He took his full head into her hands and commenced a slow, throbbing upward, downward ... upward downward stroking of his manhood against her wet,juicy secret canal in her mid-region.

First, slowly ... then more forcefully with rhythmic regularity ... searching ... not looking ... not seeing ... but searching ... probing for what he knew was there ... waiting for his manhood. He increased the tempo and the strength of his strokes ... yet he did not achieve penetration. Now panting, pleading, he increased his thrust further. Please, please, let me in ... let me in ... am coming in ... please let me in. With her legs thrown wide open ... no obstacle should be on his way ... He raised his waist high and like a pile driver pounded down heavily ... At that instant, a fierce cry of love and agony escaped the lips of Hauwa. She raised herself above the pains and agony of her defilement ... the broken tissues, the broken and bloodied hymen and the searing pains as a long shrill cry escaped her lips as she tightened her embrace around Patrick.

Patrick looked into her eyes as the tears formed around her succulent eyelids. Her legs and arms still firmly clasped around him. As his manhood penetrated, a flood of pleasure never known to him took over his entire body. He could not hold back anymore as he increased the frequency of his thrusts, reaching frightening rhythmic speed that shook even the big bed. What he felt down there was silky velvet; a warmth of hot moisture and throbbing flesh. His mind raced, far away … into a flash of sunshine … torrential rain drops … roaring water falls and martial music in support of the charge of the light brigade … all these, culminating in a brilliant flash of kaleidoscopic colours … as all the brightness and colours faded to black … and then grey … and finally purity of white. "God!! This is the life!" he muttered to himself as he sank into Hauwa's deep embrace and fell into a deep slumber.

With her glazy eyes subdued in fulfilment and enveloped in a calm serenity, despite the searing pains in her loins, Hauwa held tightly to him. This was too good to be true. At twenty, this was her first time of knowing a man. But her strong royal upbringing as a princess of the Attah dynasty in Igalla had prepared her culturally for this day: To bear the pains of the "first time" with pride, honour and dignity; and to be dutiful and ever faithful to the man good enough, bold enough to be deserving of the conquest.

That night, Pastor Patrick slept the sleep of the dead. His wet dreams continued with the pretty African damsel. As he sucked away at the robust breast of the African beauty that night, he made a connection with a black wooden sculpture he had bought in Benin City two years earlier.….

After a two-day travel through provincial colonial Nigeria from Lagos on the Armels Transport lorry, he had arrived Benin City exhausted. He had travelled on the Second Class compartment, a two-row affair, with very little leg-room, passengers sitting and staring unto each others' eyes and a mail box overhead.

The next morning, he was joined at breakfast by the resident British District Officer. After breakfast, he was taken round the city of Benin – the Ring Road, the Oba's Palace, the Benin moat and the craft village. It was at the Craft Village that he saw and was enchanted by the delicate, natural curves of the fine sculptured rendition of the African damsel.Pastor Patrick was immediately attracted to the life-like,human emotions conveyed by the sculpture: Her smile, very frugal and sensual, the small upper lip mole that was so unique. The bright suggestively provocative eyes and full luscious lips full of mystery and elegance ... The full frontal carriage of the breasts, with a belated attempt to cover the fullness with a loin cloth carelessly strapped across the chest to increase the viewer's inquisitiveness. Her slender neck had delicate intricate beauty loops to accentuate her feminine profile; her feminine neckline was distinguished by a deliberate lack of jewellery. He loved the piece of artwork and made to pay for it. But he had no Nigerian currency on him at the time, so the District Officer helped out. He paid three Nigerian Guineas – a princely sum to pay for an artwork in pre-Independence Nigeria.

The artwork had been kept in his trunk box ever since;awaiting his return to Lanham,USA when and where he had planned to unveil it in the family sitting room in all its exquisite beauty as a relic of his African sojourn. Not for lack of interest therefore but more to protect his African Maiden until his final return to the United States;he had had the sculture properly padded and packed awaiting the great unveiling back in his native America.

When he woke up that morning, he went straight to the trunk box to unpack the African Maiden sculpture. As he lifted the artwork out of the insulating foam and old newspapers, he was suddenly shocked into the realisation that his African Maiden and the pretty damsel that had featured regularly in his dreams of late had an uncanny resemblance. But Pastor Patrick's biggest shock that morning was yet to come ...

As he admired the skewed smiles around the lips of the statue... and looked down into her robust full breasts ... the left breast was gone!! In its place, were jagged signs of where the breast had been ... before it was bitten off? He searched fruitlessly for evidence of the left breast having possibly fallen off. But no such sign existed. As he lifted up the artwork in admiration, he involuntarily leaned forward to kiss the remaining breast ... and that was when it happened. Pastor Patrick was suddenly gripped by a violent shudder. As he did, a flow of energy and vitality ran through his body. He stood up confidently, with a new spirit of conquest and strength oozing around him. He went straight to his bedroom and placed the African Maiden on a hallowed pedestal, directly beside his bed. As he positioned it properly ... he turned ... and there, admiring the artwork,with a knowing glint in his eyes and a suspicious smile of understanding... was Esau!

"Massa ... Good. Woman. Good...Powerful woman!"

And that was the beginning of what was to be a nation-wide organisation-The Union. For the next three months and under the quiet nudging and spiritual guidance of his steward,Esau, Pastor Patrick commenced a new unexpected wave of evangelism centred around feminism and Africanism.... a new wave of evangelism centred around the African Maiden as a direct descendant of one of the female followers of the founders of the early church ... With Esau as his interpreter and Hauwa in tow, he traversed the neighbouring towns of Ayangba, Egume, Ankpa, Idah. With every crusade, Patrick performed miracles and healings in the name of the African Maiden, which he now fondly referred to as Our Mother. By the time his new interpretation of the scriptures, liturgy and healings had spread to Oturkpo, Makurdi and beyond, the Baptist Mission was thrown into shock. There were hushed discussions about the need to extradite Patrick immediately before he does irreparable damage to the foundation of Christian Theology and the disciplined image of the State Department's creation-The Peace Corps Scheme.

In April, a special synod of the Baptist Convention in Nigeria was held in Ogbomosho to discuss the specific threat of Pastor Patrick. The synod concluded that it would be unfair to try him in absentia. Patrick was therefore invited to another synod, this time in Lagos. The Church provided a one-way transport to move him and his possessions to Lagos. The plan was to send him back to the United States, as soon as he was found guilty after the "trial".

Pastor Patrick and his entourage arrived Lagos to a tumultuous welcome. Preceded by his fame, the sick, the lame and seekers of salvation besieged his lodgings at the Staff Quarters of the Baptist Academy, Shepherdhill, at Obanikoro in Lagos.

That night, at the pastor's Salvation Crusade, the Elders of the Baptist Convention sneaked into the venue of the crusade to listen to Pastor Patrick's "blasphemy" and take a final decision.

"Praise Our Mother" Patrick shouted, as he commenced his defence before the elders of the church:

"You might as well stop me now … or forever remain silent … For long … you kept these people in the dark." He lampooned the male chauvinists who he said had continued to propagate male domination of the scriptures whilst neglecting the special role of women in the salvation of mankind as contained in the scriptures.

"Women", he said, "have not just been by-standers … they have always been there at the most important moments of our salvation … Jesus, our Lord came to this World through the womb of a woman… through immaculate conception. Take note, there was no coital role for Joseph to lay claim to any paternity…But our Lord was conceived,was carried in the womb of Mary and was given birth to by Mary naturally. And where was the man in all of these? Even the central role of womanhood was in the prophecies at the very beginning in the book of Genesis … and at the end in the Book of Revelation".

The elders of the church remained silent and allowed him to continue:

"But … these chauvinists" … pointing a fierce finger at the Elders "and their foreign collaborators have hidden the good deeds of women in the scriptures from the people.. Why do you continue to stress Eve's Original Sin … why must the original sin be used repeatedly to paint women as evil creatures?"

The small hall was gripped by Pastor Patrick's eloquence. As if transfixed, the elders remained senile,silent and dumb-founded. Anytime they made to challenge Patrick, a wave of hand from him would numb them spiritually and like children, they remained docile.

"Where were all the men in the scriptures, when our Lord went through a painful crucifixion? Where were your disciples? Where were Peter, Paul, and James? Did not Peter deny our Lord three times before the cockcrow at dawn? Did all your male disciples not all scamper into safety at the height of the tribulations of our Lord,Jesus Christ?. But the women!! God bless them.They were all there at the most difficult times..all the way...from the birth of our Lord all the way to the cross!!"

"Turn to the Book of Luke … Blessed is the womb that carried you and the breast at which you were nursed"... and the Book of John "Woman, Behold your son ... and to the disciples: Behold your mother... and in obedience to her mother, the very first miracle our Lord Jesus performed on earth was at the request of his mother. The women were there at the entombment, they took the Lord's body and wrapped it in spice. They were there at the resurrection.......

… After his resurrection, he did not appear to the men, his so-called "disciples", No!. He appeared to Mary Magdalene first, before the apostles. Infact, he sent Mary Magdalene to the apostles. The women collected the stones and loin clothes around the tomb and were central to the establishment of the first ever Christian church. Who were these Women? The two Marys, Joanna and there was a nubile, an African princess, that has been edited out by these hypocrites and racists.Yet, you continue with your male chauvinism,denying women of their rightful places in the Lord's house.You will not let them into the priesthood. They cannot take confessions.They cannot give Holy Communion or say The Mass. Now,I bring you the good news that this African Princess who was there at the beginning with the two Marys and Joanna has revealed herself to me. She has directed me to establish her true church here in Nigeria. This beautiful African Princess is resurrected and is alive with us in Nigeria today. I have met her. She has spoken to me to spread her word. She has brought salvation to her people!The lame walk...The blind see...The sick and the afflicted have been made well again..... Those who desire strength, wealth, longevity, blessings of children, salvation, they must seek first this African Princess – My Mother!! Those who are wise will follow me to discover the rewards in the bosom of My Mother."

After that, he walked through the transfixed hall and disappeared into the night. And that marked the beginning of a cult following as the Nigerian African Union Church which Pastor Patrick established prospered as it wrought miracles across the land. Those who believed, followed him. And they found wealth, power and blessings of the womb.

Ageless, his American roots,family and nationality abandoned, he held sway at the background these days. But his word remained the law as always. The inner workings of the Union remained mysterious. Pervasive. Powerful. No political appointment, no major contract took place without a nod from the Union. Driven underground by orthodoxy, it had attracted all shades of fortune seekers and the original pure and altruistic intentions had come under threat and the very soul of the Union had long been hijacked by criminal elements and ambitious political opportunists.

In no time the Union's standard opening prayer was misconstrued and hijacked by opportunists of all shades:

"My Mother ... look with favour on your anointed children. As we celebrate your journey of sacrifice and salvation, Remember your children. Watch over them Mother ... Guide them Mother... Protect them Mother... Grant Them Peace Mother ... On the day you sacrificed your body for our Protection, you beseeched us ... Take this my one surviving breast ... suck it and be filled with the milk of protection and salvation ... and may the comfort of my breast give you eternal strength and prosperity. Amen"

Chapter 11

DEFIANCE

ALHAJI INUA BAKO flew back into Lagos that evening after the party convention to address a strategy meeting of his very trusted friends. The agenda was to work out his success at the forthcoming national elections as an independent candidate. He assured his strategists that money would not be a hindrance as he had long planned for this scenario. His finances had further been buoyed by the proceeds of the Sokoto airport operation, now held privately in Kano. Two weeks later, he opened a saturated multi-media campaign.

Two months of town-by-town campaigns later, the national poll revealed a Recognition Level of 70% for Inua. His platform of Integrity and Prosperity had scored high nationally. His Preference Rating was 60% whilst his closest rival was at 31%. His preference cut across all the geo-political zones. Assured of victory, he was even beginning to worry about soft issues – who would be First Lady; following the death of Obode five years earlier of breast cancer.

But the stress of all the travellings and the anxiety induced by the many anonymous phone calls, threatening him with a slow,agonising death were beginning to take their toll on Inua . Ten years earlier following burning pains in his abdomen, sleeplessness, heart-burn and belching, he had been admitted into a friend's private hospital in Ikoyi Lagos. There, after a barium meal investigation and a confirmatory endoscopy, a deformed duedenal cap, consistent with peptic ulceration and chronic ulceration and inflamation of the mucous membrane of the stomach were diagnosed.

He was advised to quit smoking, cut down on his alcohol intake, stop tea and coffee consumption and reduce stressors in his life. He was immediately put on H2 blockers to reduce the amount of acid in his stomach, mucousal protective agent to shield the stomach's mucous lining and strict dietary supervision. Although he felt well thereafter, there had been several relapses of the situation since then. At the latest review of his case, his doctor friend had discussed new advances in the treatment of ulcers. He had told him that whether in the duodenum or stomach, the new thinking was that ulcers are ulcers. They are sores caused by a certain specific bacteria, now identified as H.pylori. He had then prescribed additional specific anti-biotics and the ulcers had not recurred since then.

But as he prepared for the television debates that evening, the heart burn, the fullness of the stomach pains he felt were such that he could hardly breathe. He sweated profusely and had to rush out of the studio, halfway into the debate to see his doctor in Ikoyi.

He was rushed through fresh diagnostic procedures; Upper gastro-intestinal investigation, with barium meal; endoscopy and blood, breath and stomach tissue biopsies.

The next morning, his friend of over twenty years, Doctor Adetayo, Consultant surgeon and proprietor of the River View Hospital at Ikoyi ,Lagos reviewed the case personally with Inua.

"Inua ... How are you feeling this morning..."

"Terrible!"

"I know, You see at your age, and with your medical history ... you will need to slow down to reduce stressors in your system." he paused. "The tests have revealed a massive deterioration in the deformation of your duodenal cap and corrosion of your stomach lining ...spreading towards the oesophagus. We also found severe inflammation and many tiny sores in your colon which we intend to probe further in a colonoscopy ... Meanwhile, I am taking personal charge of all your treatment ... Of course, nobody knows you are in this very private room and I have instructed that no records be kept in the hospital's official documentation of your admission here to avoid any unnecessary media interests ... No visitors at all... "

That morning, Doctor Adetayo put Inua on a drug regimen that would serve one purpose: death, for that was his brief from the Union.

That morning, he promptly put Inua on a blood thinning medication for preventing blood clots and stroke- Ximelagatrah, then still experimental and still not approved by the Foods and Drug Administration in Nigeria(NAFDAC) because of concerns about adverse effects. Simultaneously, Inua was put on warferin, a drug used for over forty years in the prevention and treatment of Deep Venous Thrombosis (DVT). These in combination with acetaminophen (Fylenol) over a period of five days was enough to achieve near fatal results. In five days, severe nausea, vomiting, cramping, diarrhoea and very low white blood cell counts had ensued. These drugs immediately induced severe bleeding of the duodenal and stomach ulcers, bleeding from the colon ...even bleeding from his gums when he brushed his teeth ...

As he struggled for life in the palatial private suite in the hospital, he had one source of comfort.

∽

"Allah, be praised" he murmured to himself. A week earlier on his campaign train to Port-Harcourt, he had sneaked away from the media and his personal aides to pay a secret visit to Obode's mother in her quiet Trans Amadi bungalow.Despite the loss of his beloved Obode to cancer of the breast five years earlier,he had maintained his warmth and friendship with the woman he continued to call his "mother in law".The visit to Obode's mother was most revealing.

There, for the first time, he had been told, he was a father. Had been a father for over twenty-seven years. Mama Obode had after the usual exchange of pleasantries gone to the bedroom and returned with a photograph.

"My pikin ...that my pikin Obode ..." She broke down sobbing "e like you well well ... Na love ... abi no be so una de call am? ... I be old mama now ... I dey sick for all my bodi ... that's why I must tell you this secret ... you see ... this boy ... Onini na your pikin! No be my pikin at all-o!! Na Obode born am for London..Na your pikin..you no see-am?",she explained pointing out the resemblance between them in the picture.

Mama Obode went on to explain the circumstances of Onini's birth and why the birth was kept secret ... because Inua had compelled Obode to swear not to have children for him.

On the aircraft back to Lagos, he had read the letter from Onini to his grandmother repeatedly ... Boy Boy! He is a man now and wants to know who his father is!

On his return to Lagos that night, he took time off to write to Onini Ogaga Bako, his son. He told him the story of his life and his latest venture to be President of Nigeria against all odds. Moreso, in defiance of the Union. Ominously, he revealed in the letter that nobody defies the Union and lives! That he had a premonition that disaster was lurking somewhere and that despite the massive electoral gains he had made, he stood no chance against the formidable killing machine of the Union. But at least, he was glad to have known him, seen his picture before getting into this last and delicate phase of his electioneering campaign. He told him in the letter that since the death of his mother,Obode,life had lost its meaning and lustre.That now ,he Onini was his only source of hope and his trusted confidante.

Inua waited for one week for Onini to receive and digest the letter which he had couriered, before making a telephone call to him in England. Talking to each other for the first time, they were on long distance phone for over six hours.

That was a week ago and with his health failing, he made one last desperate call that midnight ... they talked again for over three hours

... and when Inua stopped the conversation abruptly in the middle of his description of the Union leadership, membership and mode of operation, it was the last time anybody would speak to him alive.

The Medical bulletin said, "Alhaji Inua Bako, 65, male was admitted with Oedema occasioned by poor blood circulation, a blood clot and Deep Venous Thrombosis. He was put on ximelagatran and warfarin; but severe blood clots in the lungs occasioned pulmonary embolisis, which caused his death at 03.45."

Chapter 12

ⓒⅅ

ONINI OGAGA BAKO

HE HAD JUST returned from a desertation discussion with Professor John Lambert that evening.Seven years after fleeing Nigeria,he had worked and schooled side-by-side,paying his way through most of the time.he was a fully settled global citizen,who was resident in London;and enjoyed his global,cosmopolitan outlook. With a Bachelors' degree in Business Administration from the University of London, he had opted for an MBA from the prestigious London School of Economics. His discussions with Professor Lambert which centred around the implications of Cross-Cultural Meanings for Global Brands earlier that evening lead him to his computer to search for some sources. In the course of that search, and as he had come to do daily as a habit, he veered to the Google engine for a search for Nigerian newspapers for his daily news update about Nigeria. And that was when he saw it.

On all the newspapers. Front page banner headlines: "Innua Bako Dead!" "The President That Never Was"…"The President Nigeria Never Had Dies". The stories went on and on. His astute business sense, his vast network and social carriage. his enduring love for his late wife,Obode … Single. No child. Was buried according to traditional

Zuru rites in his palatial home in Kano yesterday …

He couldn't continue. The father he really never knew! Just when he had just discovered him!!. And the promised visit to London to see him, when he got out of hospital … visions and vistas of the Presidential Villa … the business empire he had said he would return to manage … oh God! He choked in his own tears, breathless with anxiety.

And for the next two weeks, he was in that state. No lectures. No visits. No visitors. That was when the post man brought the package. Strangely, it was addressed to "Onini Ogaga Bako." He knew who it was from the moment he saw it. Inside were volumes and volumes of documents,photographs and DVDs; some criminal, some treasonable, detailing the modus operandi of the Union and its key functionaries. Of particular note was the document titled 'The Union Manifesto' which detailed the political strategies, tactics and objectives of the Union's "Operation DDT" … details about the criminal disinformati on,destabilisation,termination and take over of the political leadership of Nigeria.The spiritual elements of the Union and the distribution of post-election strategic positions in government to key members of the Union. He read on … and …on. For two weeks. Then he came to the covering note:

"My Dear Son!

Forgive my stubbornness. Forgive me for all the wrongs I did to your mother. How could I have taken a vow of childlessness to promote my vain spiritual and political goals.

It is not by accident that I had to discover you, my own blood at this crucial hour … at a crucial time when I have decided to confront the criminal values and methods I had upheld in all of my adult life. If I do survive the battle with the Union, all well and good. Otherwise, your knowledge of the facts will ensure that I would not have died in vain. Forgive me for all the evil deeds I must have committed in the name of the Union.

I loved your mother dearly; and my love for her truly marked the beginning of my spiritual re-birth. At great personal cost,she painstak-ingly introduced me to the Word and a brand new world of eternal joy and salvation. Now I can transfer all the love I had for your mother to you. I love you.

Do, think of me at my best-always.

Your Father,

Inua Bako"

The letter was signed with a self-assured boisterous flourish.

Total, absolute silence. Then the tears ... first in little drops ... and then in endless streams accompanied by sobs and grunts. He was in this state for two weeks. Two weeks of hibernation when he abandoned his MBA lectures at the LSE to reflect deeply and evaluate his next steps and options.

When he appeared at a certain address at the Canary Wharf three weeks later, he had made up his minds. The door sign read 'Syndicated Logistics' and the brochure he browsed through as he waited in the office lounge said the company provided leasing, freight brokerage and also direct freight movements across the European Union. When he ran into one of the Managing Partners on a tube ride on the London Underground between Victoria and Blackfriars station six months earlier, little did he realise how soon he might be needing his help. Then, he had thought otherwise. His studies were progressing well ... a steady stream of money from his Harrods sales job ... life was good. But he kept the business card all the same.

Presently, he was ushered into the palatial office of Phillips Butcher, Managing Partner and his long time friend from Biafra.

"Nini..." he screamed his pet name, as he limped forward to receive him. The limp and his firm warm embrace took him back ... far away to another time ... when he had had to carry this huge frame on his back for one week......

But the journey actually started in Port-Harcourt when for want of excitement, he had joined the Biafran Port-Harcourt Militia at the height of the Nigerian civil war. He was not Ibo and certainly didn't feel Biafran, but with the civil war raging and all the young men getting into military action, he felt it was the right thing to do then.

Suddenly, what was essentially a Port-Harcourt detachment assumed

Biafra-wide significance following the visit of Colonel Ojukwu to Port-Harcourt and his first-hand observation of the professional drill and manoeuvres of the young Port-Harcourt Militia. Following the fall of Enugu and the very disorderly withdrawal from the erstwhile capital, remnant elements of the 51 and 53 brigades were gripped by total confusion and widespread desertion. It was in the midst of this confusion that Colonel Ojukwu decided to form a Special Squad of young professionally trained, armed, kitted Commandos reporting directly to him for special operations.

When Onini and others in the Port-Harcourt Militia were driven that day to Akagbe, near Awkunanaw to be addressed by Colonel Ojukwu himself, their joy knew no limits. He was to be posted to Alpha Company of the One Battalion of what became variously known as "the mercenary brigade". Or "S brigade;" and was to see action in the temporary recapture of Enugu and Onitsha.

It was after the Enugu battle that he was moved to the dreaded "Delta Squad"- the S. brigade's headquarters reserve company. The company was under the direct command of Major Taffy Wiliams with David Clark as the 2i/c. Phillips Butcher who was a platoon commander in the Company immediately took a liking for Onini and made him his batman

While the battle for the recapture of Onitsha was raging, the "S"brigade Commanding Officer,Colonel Rolf Steiner designed a morale boosting and diversionary attack on the Nigerian rear-guard. A composite company drawn from experienced elements of 'S' brigade was put together under the command of Phillips Butcher. Basically, a Rifle company, the company was complemented by additional reinforcements with a composite support section comprising five RPGs, bazookas, 4 UPMGs, Motars, Communication, food, drinks and sufficient ammo for a one-month patrol.. It was lavishly provisioned and was to operate independently and inflict maximum damage on the Nigerian rear to force them into a retreat from Onitsha.

It was raining heavily when the rear assault squad paddled across the River Niger and veered towards the Asse River. Sections of the

Company had peeled off to attack the Nigerian unit at Asaba-Asse, destroying the Nigerian Army munitions dump. The explosions rocked the skies and travelled over a hundred miles. Another Unit attacked the garrison at Asaba at dawn, unleashing maximum confusion. Yet another squad attacked the Kwale oil fields, captured and held the field for three days, before taking some Agip Oil expatriate workers as prisoners. The stealth of the Biafran advance and the fire-power deployed shook the Nigerian confidence; and forced its military high brass into believing it was a major attack of not less than a brigade in strength.

Capitalising on the ensuing Nigerian rear guard confusion, Captain Phillips Butcher had expanded the mission objectives and made a bold move to enter Asaba. He led the assault personally with a Land-Rover - mounted 105mm gun, drove through the Nigerian rear and into the Nigerian 9 brigade garrison in Asaba; and shot his way randomly into surprised retreating Nigerian soldiers. The element of surprise and the unusual direction of the attack gave the tactical advantage to Philips Butcher. It was a killing field. With the objective achieved, three more Land Rovers were commandeered for the retreat towards Asaba-Asse and Atani.

That was when the two bullets struck. The first bullet ripped through the van's body panel and cut through Captain Butcher's left knee. The second bullet caught his shoulder blade.

Absolute panic and confusion took over, as the Land-Rover shuddered, swerved and went into a ditch. Onini reacted swiftly. First,. he shoved the body of Captain Butcher down to reduce his target profile, got the Land Rover running and broke through the ambush. Fifty miles down the road, with the van out of fuel. Working quickly, he combed the area and commandeered a bicycle. He heaved the large frame of Captain Butcher across a makeshift stretcher on the bicycle and made the over twenty-four hour march to the River Asse rendezvous.

The River Asse rendezvous had been abandoned in the hurried retreat across the River Niger. Thankfully, some of the dug-out canoes were still around. Onini bandaged Captain Butcher's injuries, applied the necessary pressure and tonique and gave him a shot of field morphine. He then laid him gently into the dug-out canoe and paddled stealthily towards Onitsha, avoiding Nigerian patrols all the time.

The medical people were to take over once he got Captain Butcher to the Biafran Tactical HQ at Oraifite. , near Onitsha. Onini was not to see Captain Butcher again until that chance meeting on the London Underground.

Pleasantries over, it was time to discuss serious issues.

"So how are you shaping up, my man ...anybody from the old crowd in London ... You still doing that MBA you told me about ...?" Questions. More questions. When Onini spoke, he could hardly hold back his tears.

"I have just lost a father I hardly knew ... was only beginning to know. Murdered!"

Butcher recoiled in silence.

"Yes. Murdered by a cult ... a group that is bent on taking over the entire Nigerian State ... Can you believe it ... the entire Nigerian government with all that oil money in the hands of a cult, killers, ritualists, evil-doers you may say terrorists!!...".

"Terrible" Butcher managed to mutter.

"I want to stop them and I need your help!"

"You can't. Go back and face your studies. It is a treacherous world out there".

"Well, I believe one man can make a difference, at least in Nigeria – I want to be that man." Onini retorted.

"When last did you fire a gun in anger? When last did you march for twenty-four hours on an empty stomach ...?"

But the look on Onini's face was resolute. Butcher saw that ... remembered again that he was alive today thanks to this young man.

"I can't promise anything. Let's see some time next week and we can take it from there"

Syndicated Logistics, actually a front office for mercenary recruitment for worldwide operations, was not without its intelligence arm. Later that week, Captain Butcher received a detailed intelligence report on the Nigerian situation. When Onini kept his appointment the next week, he had news for him.

"Well, I have the latest reports about your country. What you say is true. Yes, one man under cover, part of the community, systematically striking at the main jugulars of the Union can cripple it for a while. But it is a formidable organisation, who knows, you might be lucky. So what can I do to support you? You are not mentally alert, you are not physically fit and you will need weapons, training all over. You can't get that here. It is risky. I will send you to Kashmir, where we currently have a training operation. When can you leave?"

"Now, if possible" Onini replied beaming with satisfaction.

"That's it then. After that you are strictly on your own."

"Thanks"

The flight to the new Shah International Airport in Bombay was smooth. The Air India Airbus 380 touched down smoothly. Onini cleared customs and immigration and headed into town. His reservation at the Oberoi was confirmed as he checked into the 22nd floor of the hotel.

That evening, he strolled down to the waterfront, near the Taj Mahal Hotel where tourists board boats to see the magnificent sites at the Elephantos Castle. It was there, while looking around that the girl made contact.

"Nigerian Man?"

"No. Lagos Boy."

"Ah ... Lagos Boy ... Fine Boy ... You buy me ice cream."

"Yes ... yes, with all pleasure"

"Welcome to Bombay" She said.

They strolled towards the ice cream stands in a busy courtyard that served as a jetty for all the boats going to the Elephantos. As they did, an Ambassador car pulled up and the girl shoved him inside.

"We go now," the girl commanded once inside the car.

"What about my things at the hotel", he queried.

"Don't worry, we will get them to you."

They drove all night, skipping the major highway most of the time and using back routes. Finally, they arrived at the secret training camp in Kashmir built into the foot of the Himalayan mountain.

For the next one month, he was back to military life. First he had a clean hair cut, disinfected and given shots of tetanus toxoid. The routine was tough: Reveille at five a.m; fifty miles running with haversack daily. Mountain climbing with a sixty pound rucksack on his back, hand-to-hand combat drills, callisthenics. Evenings were in the gym for muscle toning and iron pumping.

Weapons training featured the AK 47, 9mm automatic pistols, the new Russian made RPG-7. Demolition exercises with plastigue cordite and timing fuses which he still remembered from Biafra was reinforced with C4 plastics and claymores. Grenade training, smoke grenades, radio, field medical drills and kits.

He joined a group of young men in their twenties, with glistering biceps as he swung his big frame in rhythm with the drill instruction every morning. No questions asked about his identity and his mission. Gradually, he shed all the excess fat on him. He felt strong, re-vitalised and fresh. The bulge in his mid-section had disappeared;replaced with a bundle of black glistering skin and rippling muscles. He knew, he was ready. Instinctively.

Close-quarter combat exercises completed his re-initiation to military life. Weighed down by 60-pound rucksack and running at a timed pace, he had the RPG-7 slung across his shoulder and the AK 47 on the ready in regulation manner. Running through the range, he was required to fire bursts of the AK47 and the RPG-7 alternately at prescribed man-size silhouetted mannequins. His firing and accuracy was perfect to the point that the other young men of different nationalities on the programme applauded his skills. Now, he knew, he was ready.

Back in Bombay, he put his next scheme into action. He had been promised all he needed, mostly the weapons he had trained with; AK47s RPG-7s, 9m automatic pistols, 9mm Uzis and FN rifles claymore mines, C4 plastics, grenades, rounds and rounds of ammunitions. The snag. Delivery will be in Bombay where he had to arrange shipment to Nigeria.

Colaba Street, Bombay. The four-mile long street was the busiest high street in Bombay. There, major retail and wholesale shops for electronics, clothes, textiles, gift items and many other retail goods were situated. For over thirty years, Nigerian business men and women with a sharp nose for bargain prices had frequented Colaba street. Lately, the focus of visiting Nigerian traders had been on the "Silk George" wrappers, silk linens, tergal, teryline and chinos materials.

For over one week, Onini studied the shops and the shoppers, especially the Nigerian looking types. Then he moved. A young business woman. Obviously well known to a lot of the shop owners, she had been buying a lot of "Silk George" and linen materials. When eventually Onini "bumped" into her by chance in the Dada-West market shopping for trunk boxes, it all looked so natural and accidental.

As they got talking, he found out that she was a graduate of sociology, who after years of fruitless job search decided to join her mother's textile trading business at the Balogun Market in Lagos. The mother, who introduced her to the Colaba market in Bombay had become so frail with time that she had somehow handed over the stressful frequent procurement visits to Bombay to her daughter. Bukola or Bukky as he would come to know her later was warm and very delighted to meet a Nigerian man in Bombay who was not a business man and hustler.

That evening Onini invited her for dinner at the Oberoi. Over dinner, Bukky learnt Onini was an MBA student in England who had come to Bombay for research into the business model of the Tata Corporation. He was hoping to continue that line of research with the Ibru Organisation in Nigeria before returning to London to complete his MBA programme. The mention of the Ibru Organisation naturally shifted the discussion to shipping, the Ibru Jetty at Ibafon, which served as the destination port for goods imported by most traders. Containers, half and full containers, and the economy of group procurement and filling of containers were discussed freely over dinner.

Four dinners after, they were friends enough for Bukky to accept his trunks of "books, personal effects and research materials" in her container. Onini's offer of handsome contribution of five thousand dollars,though initially resisted by Bukky went a long way to settling some of her accumulated bills at the Colaba market.

If the Dean of the Faculty of Business Administration at the University of Lagos, had any misgivings about the MBA application, he did not state it. The candidate had impeccable academic records. The transcripts from both the London School of Economics and the University of London were very good. So good that he would have graduate assistantship teaching offers and scholarships as part of his admission package in most ivy-league universities. But he had opted to come home from England sadly due to stoppage of financial support from home and the need to be close to ageing parents. So,a clear seven years after,Onini was returning to the university that he had to abandon in a hurry to avoid arrest in the past.With a brand new name,an impeccable backgound check and trascript;a brand new look,complete with a large afro hair do, a large beard and moustache,he was very sure that no lecturer from way back could match the two characters.

He resumed for lectures in October and was allocated a single room with all facilities en-suite at the Alumni Post-Graduate Hall. Not unusual for post-graduate students, he bought himself a car, cooking utensils, a refrigerator and other home comforts. With his accommodation settled, he went in search of his convenient heart throb Bukky, that saturday evening.

Adetola Street, by Cele Bus stop. The trim, athletic figure, with a well-cut jacket and smart T-shirt that stepped out of the Honda Accord would have appealed to any lady. Spritely steps, lean angular face, with a bountiful afro hair-cut and a cute moustache, he appeared generally easy on the eye.

Bukky's mother, who was out in the sitting room, recuperating from a nagging flu who received and announced the visitor was very proud of her daughter's choice. Bukky lost a heart beat. But the sight she beheld in the sitting room further confounded her.

"Nini!" was all she could mutter as she slid into his out-stretched arms. He had been a perfect gentle man all that time in Bombay and never once made a move to have her. She had longed for his warmth and affection all the time, but she had to be a lady, had applied the necessary self restaint and did not appear easy and cheap.

But this time, it was different. The embrace was long, intimate and they could both sense their mutual hunger. A night out around town at Murphy's Plaza's Genesis Nite Club, Club Towers, The Vault and Planet 44, climaxed at the Post-Graduate Hall, University of Lagos.

The love making was slow, deliberate and spontaneous. With clasped lips lubricated with shared saliva and entwined tongues, they were joined in this fore-play almost forever. When he gripped her full robust breast and transferred his attention to her erect nipples, she could not hold back any more. She let out a yell as she climaxed and her loins were wet all over. Then, he entered her. First, with slow deliberate thrusts, rising in rhythm and frequency until he attained a virtual locomotive burst in motion. Fast, faster ... even faster ... and cruise control speed. He was on for ages ... and when he came ... a continuous grunt of satisfaction escaped his lips ...

" Bukky ... Bukky ... You are Sweet."

The next day, a sunday was slow. They woke up in each other's arms and remained so as they listened to the birds chirping and singing from the surrounding mango and palm trees. Finally, the pangs of hunger melted their body glue and they separated. He had some groceries in the refrigerator, so she prepared a large breakfast. After breakfast, they resumed their love making. This time, it was a marathon, but run like a relay race, with baton exchange, anchor legs and all!

And that was to be the pattern. Mondays to fridays, for "lectures"(valuable time that Onini had to be alone to do proper recce of his planned targets) and saturday night to sunday evening for Bukky. Except during some of the weekends, when he needed to make "research" visits to the field.

The next weekend was a "research visit" one. A visit to the home town of the Ibrus to establish the cultural and entrepreneural influence of the town on the multi-billionaire's business empire.

Onini drove instead all the way to Kano in his customised Honda Accord with a false bottom, which he had designed and asked a panel beater to construct earlier in far-away Sango-Ota;where such trans-Idi-Iroko border smuggling contraptions were routinely constructed without questions being asked. The panel beater, in Otta, was quite used to such jobs which he regularly undertook for smugglers across the Idi-Iroko border. A large compartment constructed out of the Honda's hollowed-out floor. With a strong metal up-swinging door in place and covered with the usual car upholstery and carpets, the car looked normal. It was into this hollowed out bottom of the car that Onini loaded the content of the trunk box he had collected from Bukky's container the previous night.

Once in Kano, he became conscious of his mission. He was now a changed man. His extra-sensory military training now activated, he drove round the town, making notes of his plans mentally. From Mr Biggs, he bought food and drinks and headed towards Bayero University, Kano. He slid the car into a students hostel car park; which was particularly quite busy with so many male visitors arriving and departing with fun-seeking ladies.

That night, he took the Students Union shuttle bus back to town, dropping off at the Gidan Goldie area. Two hours later, he was at his jump-off position. "This is it," he sighed. He sighed again at the symbolism. The 40th day prayers. The media had been awash with obituary messages. The whole of Kano was filled with pretentious sympathisers from all over Nigeria "Yea" he thought, "They would get a taste of their own medicine. Men, they will know that "Inua" is not dead afterall ..and that he had a son".

Early that morning, he crept into the Union's Worship Centre- The Sanctuary- on Maiduguri Road. Three elderly guards stationed in the outer perimeter were knocked out. To his surprise, security inside the premises had been beefed up possibly because of the Special Conclave planned after the 40th Day Prayers the next day. He crept in stealthily until he got into effective range. That's when he brought out the Stirling from the canvas bag. He fitted a night vision telescope and a silencer and waited. He counted six fully armed MOPOL combat policemen. He noticed there was no particular order to their perfunctory patrol around the premises and decided to take them out one at a time. Six clean shots. He ran to cover the distance, and blew open the main security door.

Once inside, he worked quickly. Planting camouflaged explosives in key areas of the main hall. Next, he blew open a small safe and took out documents; minutes of the Convention conclaves. National Register of Members, their designations ... the strategies of the Union in government and so many more. Next, from the sacred alter; he dismantled the sculptured effigy of the symbol of the Union. He checked all the explosives and set them to synchronise with signals from his cell phone and pulled out. That night, in a solitary patch along the Maiduguri Road, he destroyed and burnt the one-breasted female symbol of the Union . Thereafter, he walked all night, making a long detour of Kano. He made camp at a point on the Zaria Road and waited ...

Later that afternoon, he saw what he was looking for. The soft drinks vending truck had made a routine sales stop when Onini crept in and waited. When the driver and the attendant returned, they were both held up at gunpoint. He asked the driver to move to a secluded point on the Kano Zaria Road and had the two men tied and their mouths taped firmly. Then he took over the wheels of the truck and drove into Kano.

He drove straight to the venue of the 40-Day ceremonies for Inua Bako. Now dressed in a popular soft drinks sales outfit, he loaded crates of soft drinks that he had already prepared with explosives unto a trolley and placed the armed crates around strategic points; even as all the dignitaries trooped into the venue.

One hour later, he was back at the Bayero University car park, where he dumped the vending truck and changed to his Honda Accord.

The crowd at the 40th Day Prayers for Inua Bako was a mammoth one. Politicians, sympathisers, but mostly Union people who had cause to give credibility to the political process that eliminated him, and to douse rumours of foul play around his death. It was this mixed crowd that witnessed the intense explosions around the venue as Onini detonated the explosives from his mobile phone. There was total pandemonium as crates, bottles, tables and limbs flew in all directions. Just when everyone thought it was all over, another round of explosives were detonated. With sirens screaming and ambulances racing towards the scene, Onini slipped out of the scene, calmly in his Honda Accord. Most Union members who survived the attack on the 40th Day prayers assembled at the Maiduguri Road Conclave that night. It was a very sombre gathering that was told of the mysterious dawn raid that eliminated the security men at the compound, the theft of the Union's prized symbol, its central registers of members and other sensitive documents.

That night, with a combined service presided over by the now very aged and senile Pastor Patrick and Esau, the congregation said special prayers to raise the spirit of "Mother". But there was no response. At the third attempt, Pastor Patrick announced to the congregation that his body and spirit were failing him ... that his energy was draining ... that he needed "his mother's" milk of vitality fast. Esau raised the "Mama Nughe" song to galvanise the congregation as he veered into a mysterious cantata, Suddenly ... there was a huge flash, followed by a thunderous ball of lightning as Onini's bombs exploded in relays. a mass of flesh, bones dismembered bowels mixed with concrete, wood and smoke. There were cries of anguish everywhere in the big hall. Another round of explosions. And yet another. Finally, absolute silence descended on the hall.

The Guardian reported the Kano killings the next day as a Harvest of Death. Encouraged in its analysis and reportage by a small note received by the Editor-In-Chief a week earlier about planned reprisals by Inua's loyalists; and a quest to rescue the country from a cabal of secret cult members, the death toll reported by the paper was like a "Who is Who" in Nigeria .

Speculations were rife about the nature of official business that took the Chief of Army Staff and the Inspector-General of Police to the secluded Worship Hall in Kano where they met their untimely death.....

∞

The smart walking doctor in a well cut single-breasted suit walked through the large hall of River View Private Hospital in Ikoyi. With his white over-coat and a stethoscope to match, his confident strides masked his anxiety. Ten minutes earlier, he had phoned into an office in the hospital off an adjoining street on a "Pay-As-You-Go" GSM number he had just purchased with a false name and address and talked to Doctor Adetayo.

"Doctor ...Tunde Phillips here ... Managing Director, Epe LNG" At the mention of Epe LNG, Doctor Adetayo,ever the business man, and conscious of the large employee base of the new start up LNG project that had been dominant in the news of late became very alert.

"Wonderful ... Tunde, have we met ...?"

"Unfortunately ... no. But some of your very close friends." Here he reeled off a long list of Union members.

"Say you are just the Doctor for my case ... especially given the confidentiality I seek ..." Pleasantries over, they had agreed an appointment for seven in the evening.

With on-going expansion that had taken the hospital to fifteen floors and fresh intake of medical personnel, the presence of the young spritely "doctor" was hardly out of place; when he stepped out of the lift on the eleventh floor. With a casual wave to a secretary, he walked into the palatial office of Doctor Adetayo. As he walked in, he locked the door and briskly pulled out the .45 Smith and Wesson, with a blunt silencer attached.

"Doctor ... please this way." he beckoned to a chair away from Adetayo's desk at the centre of the office.

"Are you a doctor here ... what have I done ... what do you want ..."

"Doctor ... don't panic ... you ask too many questions. Yes! I want

225

the case file of one of your recently deceased patients, Inua Bako!!".

At the mention of his friend's name ... the friend who procured the loans and equity contributions for the massive expansion of the hospital, he burst out in cold sweat.

"No ... No ... I didn't kill him ... the records are there ... he died of natural causes ... he ..."

"Shut up !! You bloody ingrate why did you do it!!"

"Who are you Why do you want to kill me ..."?

My name is Onini, Onini Bako ... the son of your friend, Inua Bako ... there is no point, I thought you should know ... because I am going to kill you... "

Doctor Adetayo broke out in more sweat as memories of that phone call that changed everything flooded through him.

"Tayo ... your friend ... our friend and brother Inua has just left me. He is on the way to your hospital. You know the verdict on him ... By the power and instruction of the Unalterable Name ... please do what you have to do!"

"God! He managed to mutter. "But Inua had no child ..."

"Shut up!!"

Doctor Niyi Adetayo recoiled as he was brought back to stark realisation: The face, the bright, fierce eyes ... the dark sharp nasal bridge, the oblong head ... God ... was this one secret Inua hid from him." Just like his one secret that he shared with the mysterious telephone caller, who instructed him to kill his friend?

He was a young medical doctor. Three years out of Lagos University Teaching Hospital (LUTH) and one year into his army Direct Short Service commission. Life was sweet. Commissioned as a Second Lieutenant, into the Nigerian Army Medical Corp he had been posted to 7 Battalion, Jui, Freetown as Medical Officer. It was fun in the rear garrison of the battalion headquarters, with all the parties and all the girls at Fourah Bay College. It was at one of the tombolas at the Headquarters Officers Mess that he met Fatmatu, a second year mathematics student. Three months after, Fatti as he would come to know her was pregnant and refused an abortion. Even all the attempts to induce an abortion in the guise of treating her for malaria proved abortive.

Lt. Niyi Adetayo enjoyed the good time. With the rebel war raging and poverty level very high, there was no shortage of women of easy virtue. He put Fatti out of his mind and moved on with newer "catches". Even when he heard that Fatti was in a prolonged labour for over one week and the surgeons at the Connaught Hospital needed money to perform a caesarean section, he did not budge, and threw Fatti's poor fish seller mother out of his house. By the time the poor fish seller was able to put the money for the surgery together, Fatti had lost so much strength, she died in the course of the caesarean section but the pretty girl, a product of Lt. Adetayo's romance with Fatti survived.

If the loss of her only daughter was just too much to bear, the humiliation in the neighbourhood that Fatti's daughter was a bastard since Lt. Adetayo refused to show up to accept the baby despite all entreaties just simply devastated the fish seller. She took her bitterness and complaints to a powerful Bundu cult in Sewa, near Bo;and right there she swore and cursed Adetayo bitterly. It may have been purely coincidental or psychological. But shortly afterwards, Lt. Adetayo, the young,dashing medical officer went impotent and not all his knowledge of medical science could reverse his condition.

Twenty-two years later, at a flag-off ceremony to launch the maiden flight of the Southern Sun Airline to Freetown, he felt a stirring in his loins when one of the hostesses brushed by him accidentally. Surprised, he followed up and held her hand for a chat ... and he felt not just stirring this time, but a hard throbbing as her touch awakened his long dormant manhood. That's how he met Hidergund or Hilder as he would come to call her fondly after. That's how he would eventually get married at fifty, with a secret only known to the strange telephone caller: that Hilder, his wife was actually his biological daughter, born to him by Fatmatta Conteh through Caesarean section at Connaught

Hospital, Freetown, Sierra Leone!

The mystery unravelled very early in his relationship with Hilder. He could only have an erection with Hilder and no one else. Hildergund was the name the German volunteer doctor at the Children's Ward of the Connaught hospital gave to her; when her grandmother could not breast-feed her after her mother had died during childbirth. That her father reportedly a Nigerian soldier abandoned her.

"What was the profession of this Nigerian soldier?",the German Doctor had asked repeatedly in those days. Whether it was naivette or anger that drove Fatmatta's mother so mad was unclear. But her answers were never helpful.

"He is a Nigerian soldier",she would retort "... do soldiers have any other profession other than killing people.?"she would ask.

Doctor Adetayo's suspicions were confirmed when his trusted friend, the mysterious telephone caller,who ordered the execution of Inua returned from his secret trip to Freetown: Fatti's grand mother, now in her seventies still lived in Freetown. Her grand-daughter, Hilder, worked briefly with Sierra Leone National Airlines (SNA); but now worked for Southern Sun, a Nigerian airline in Lagos Nigeria. The unforgiving grandmother had sworn repeatedly that the Nigerian soldier who put her daughter in the family way and abandoned her to die will never know joy, that he will see joy, but never taste it!

The gloomy report from Freetown was enough to trigger alarm bells in Doctor Adetayo's head. For him to know joy, Hilder must never know the truth and for that to happen, the only living person who can still recognise the successful Doctor Adetayo,the Medical Director of The River View Hospital as one and the same infamous Lt. Niyi of the Nigerian Army,Jui,Sierra Leone had to be eliminated.

That's how Fatti's mother was knocked down on the Kissy-Wellinton Road in Freetown on a quiet sunday on her way back from church. Those who saw the accident said the hit and run car had been parked,the bonnet opened ostensibly for engine repairs on a side street for a while ... But the car had been fixed quickly and suddenly came to life as if possessed when "Mammi Fatti" was crossing the road. The car had hit top speed instantly, swerved menacingly and had knocked "Mammy Fatti", flung her up...and when she hit the hard road with a thud, she was dead.. and the hit and run driver disappeared after that.

Those who attended the burial in Freetown said it was a very lavish affair. Nothing was spared to give "the Mammi" a befitting burial. Hilder's boy friend, a chief Adetayo from Nigeria was everywhere to ensure the success of the burial with the Nigerian High Commissioner and other staff of the Mission providing seamless logistics support. Chief Adetayo danced and "sprayed" money lavishly; the way Nigerians have come to be known in Freetown.

Two months later, they were married in a civil ceremony in Chelsea, London, before a large crowd of friends and well-wishers.

∞

"Please, don't kill me ... Please, I will give you anything you want ... please ..."

He was still begging for his life when the silenced Smith and Wesson coughed three times and snuffed life out of Doctor Adeniyi Adetayo, also known as Lt. Niyi.

The newspapers were full of reports of the murder. They quoted eye witness reports of a young doctor being the last man in Doctor Adetayo's office. The reports said there were no skirmishes or sound of gun shots. Police sources quoted by the newspapers said that just like the Kano killings, cards marked with " Compliments of Inua Bako Jnr" were scattered all over the scene of crime.

∞

The rain poured down ferociously all day. But he marched on. It suited his purpose. The thick army green raincoat covered him all the way. The shoulder-high rucksack, the additional belting of ammo and the slung pouch of K-rations, water, and more ammo. Onini trudged on. He didn't plan it this way, but that is why he was a soldier. Every now and then, he thought of Captain Butcher's advice: "Never stay in hotels. Be flexible and adaptive in your plans. Speed. Move like lightning. Let them think there is a whole Army involved in this … pick your targets … always achieve surprise".

He had returned from Kano and driven straight to Bukky's place in Aguda, where he loaded two more "research trunks" from the container. He drove straight to his mechanic's in Bariga to service and prepare the car for his next trip. That was when it happened.

CD

With all the numerous container- based shops dotting the streets of Lagos, containers had assumed new market values. So when in the last one month, the wife of a Police Sergeant at the Soloki Aguda Police Station had indicated the intention to buy the container, Mama Bukky had asked her to tarry a while. But with the container now left with just one trunk, she decided to move the trunk into Bukky's bedroom and sell the container off.

That was how the lady came with a flat-back, self-loading truck that busy afternoon. Since moving the trunk upstairs was proving difficult, Sergeant Shoyemi and his wife implored the truck's driver to use the truck's Hiab self loading crane to move the trunk from the container to the first-floor balcony. Everything went well … until the wooden trunk snapped open in mid-air and the contents spilled in all directions. Assault rifles, grenades, mortar rounds … Bazookas!! There was absolute silence on the ever busy Adetola Street,following the discovery!

Promptly, the policeman in Sergeant Shoyemi took over. One phone call … and the entire neighbourhood was swarming with anti-crime patrol vehicles in the next ten minutes. One thing led to another … and Bukky was picked from her mother's Balogun Market shop for police interrogation and from the Lion Building police interrogation centre straight to the University of Lagos.

It was the unusual silence around the Post-Graduate Hall that aroused his suspicion. Then the Police Patrol vans … and the heavily armed tactical assault Police teams. He drove straight on to the International School Road, made a left turn and parked the car by the University Sports Centre. Mingling with the crowd of anxious young student-on-lookers, he pieced whatever information they volunteered together. Arrest of a lady suspect ... search for another ... her boyfriend ... student for arms smuggling ... arm possession ... and on and on.

But Onini had stopped listening. Speed. Flexibility. He went back to the Sports Centre and headed out of town, taking the quiet coastal road all the way to Ore. That night, at a mechanic garage near the Nigerian National Petroleum Corporation depot near Ore, the Honda "developed a fault", so he pushed it into the back garage for repairs whilst he continued his journey to Ife.

That night he disappeared into the thick rain forest and had been marching since then. As he fled from Lagos, driving at normal speed without panic, Onini had worked out an outline plan in his head. Without maps, compass and GPS, he had decided to use the NNPC pipeline route as a beacon.

∞

Since the first crude oil finds in Araromi, near Lagos by the German Bitumen Corporation in 1908, Nigeria had come a long way. With the Anglo-Dutch consortium Shell D'arcy, later shell BP opening up the Niger-Delta of Nigeria for oil, came the need to build refineries in Port-Harcourt, Warri and Kaduna and an ambitious integrated nation-wide distribution through a network of underground pipelines.

The feedstock for the refineries all came from the Niger-Delta, where numerous Quality Control flow stations sifted water and associated gas from the crude, before pumping on to the export terminals and the refineries. From the refineries, the end products were again distributed through this network of pipelines across Nigeria. Onini therefore reasoned, that once you could get into the network of pipelines, surely you could march your way with a clear beacon to any location of your choice and under the cover of foliage.

He marched, mostly at night for cover, camping and resting in the day time. By now, he realised that an All Point Bulletin would have been issued by the Police to track him down. Six nights of arduous march and he hit the outskirts of Benin. That night, he reconnoitred the Benin Retreat of the Union. Not surprisingly, it was all quiet. Onini knew from his notes that the Union Retreat held saturday nights. The next night a friday, he went back. If his intelligence and all that he had gathered from Doctor Adetayo were right, a big Union meeting of sorts was planned for this big monastery-like fortress on the outskirts of Benin, one hour south as the crow flies from the popular Palm Royal Motel.

The element of surprise. That was crucial, he thought as he crept into the compound that morning. Since the meeting was scheduled for the next night, a saturday night, security around the Retreat was lax that night. The few guards on duty were asleep at the security post. Very far away from the Retreat Hall. No break-in. No tell-tale signs. Maintain the initiative. Surprise! He kept thinking back to his tactical training at the Himalayan foothills. He worked through the night, planting high velocity bombs into the hedge plants around the Retreat Hall and disappeared into the thick rain forest at dawn.

He slept and rested all through the day. Around midnight, when he set out it started raining. Slowly at first, then it burst out in torrents. There was an incline and an anthill that he had identified the previous night. He climbed it to gain a vantage view. From there, when he checked his cross-hairs through his night vision goggles, he looked straight into the double massonia doors that led into the Retreat Hall. At precisely 2 am, he lined the RPG on the two doors and waited for the detonation triggered by his mobile phone. The huge explosion and ball of fire were muffled by the heavy rainfall … but the next round of explosions tore the whole house and the adjoining car park apart. Then Onini fired the RPG at the doors … one second, the doors were there … and the next, they had disappeared in a ball of fire. He fired another six RPG rounds into the Retreat Hall … and disappeared into the jungle.

Confusion. Pandemonium. The whole place, swarming with police and military special forces was thrown into confusion as they were caught between saving lives and establishing the nature and direction of the attack. The fire and explosions raged on as the cars in the car park and their fuel tanks were singed by the intense heat and exploded randomly to add to the confusion.

Onini marched throughout the night briskly in a south-easterly direction. He made camp at dawn, but could not rest as the rains poured down even more ferociously this time. It rained the whole day and the next night.

∽

It was a shocked nation that received the news of the Benin attack the next day. The casualty figure was as high as they were high profile. Esau, alias The Lion, the all-powerful, all knowing Ritual Head of the Union, now in his nineties looking every inch frail and senile ... Pastor Patrick, who had renounced his American citizenship for a Nigerian one ... the highly respected founder and head of the Union ... whose word was law ... who hand-picked Presidents, Governors, political and Industrial Leaders ... and more! They were all caught in this flash of thunder, steel, fire, mangled flesh and shattered bones. The newspapers had pictures too gory to be looked at. There were stories across the media ... and emotional editorials on the lives and times of these great men. One newspaper reported that the reason it rained for seven days and seven nights after the Benin attack was the symbolic mourning and the tears shed in heaven itself! That death could only have come to the two famous spiritual men because of the destruction of the Union's spiritual Headquarters in Kano and the theft and destruction of its universal source and symbol of strength. That the health of the duo had been failing since the unfortunate developments in Kano and the loss of the source of the milk of vitality,strength and longevity from "Mama".

One national newspaper in a front page lead story blamed the Union for the rot in the Nigerian society with the cult's manipulation of political appointments and decisions; that a radical cell within the military had sworn to uprooting the evil in all its ramifications; and was probably behind these attacks.

The long tabbing from Ore all the way to Benin and the incessant rainfall had started to take its toll on Onini. He was now drenched all over, with his dungaree boots all flooded with rain water. His situation was exacerbated the previous night when he had to make a long detour away from all the military and Police check-points on all the roads leading out of Benin City. He had marched all the way through Ekenwan Village, by-passing the traditional town of Ughoton to the right before forging through River Osa. After marching for another two nights, he was now confronted with two quick rivers to forge – the Ugbenu Plymouth River and the mighty River Ethiope.

But he was beginning to feel feverish. It started from his sore, cold feet and had gradually been playing up on his mind. A feeling of heaviness and numbness around his joints, restlessness and delirium. The previous night, he could not sleep. He was all the time conscious of the malaria threat. Having been out of the tropics for so many years, he had packed ample prophylactics to protect and stimulate his body to produce long-lasting protective anti-bodies. He had taken jabs against cholera, typhoid and cerebrospinal meningitis at the training camp in Kashmir.

But still, he felt pains all over. His throat was parched and he could hardly swallow. Throbbing headache, painful rashes, a throbbing noise in his ears. Palpitations, a debilitating flu and painful inflammation of connecting nasal tissue.

Despite his pains, he dared not seek medical attention. He knew he had to move on to get help but with all the media reports about his fugitive status; and with every security personnel on his trail, he could not afford to slip.

He crossed the River Ethiope that night and marched groggily all night. With his destination now fixed, he was more assured in his tabbing. He was delirium and convulsive even as he continued the next night. But very early that morning, he arrived at the farm. He heaved a sigh of relief as the breaking dawn announced the farm and the adjoining rubber plantation that his grand-mother had frequently brought him to in his adolescence . He had always come to associate her grand-mother with the farm. Not for want of food to eat. Not for money. But more like a social and spiritual duty. To work. To till the land. Even in her old age, "Nene" which was everybody's pet name for her kept a daily appointment with the farm, since relocating back from Port-Harcourt.

Early that morning, when she saw her beloved grand son in the farm house with signs of delirium, convulsion and vomiting, she broke down in tears and shock. She quickly mobilised, plucking a few leaves here and there to prepare a hot steam bath. Then she prepared a native broth of "pepper soup". The next morning, she came with even more food, blankets and clothes and native medicines. One week of nursing after, Onini was well again; and the grand-mother could now ask all the nagging questions:

"When did you come back from London, what have you done? ... Lately, the security people have been scouring everywhere in the village... are they looking for you? Why are they harassing the entire village?"

For the first time, Onini learnt that the search for him had led all manner of security operatives to the village. They had searched the entire village house by house. When nothing incriminating was found, they had established heavily fortified police check-points at all the six entry/exit roads to the village. They were still there waiting for their prey whilst Onini nestled in the warmth of her grand-mother.

He explained in hush jungle tone – for he had learnt from child-hood that you never talk loudly in the farm for fear of arousing evil spirits – the "discovery" of his real father ... all the intimate secrets that he shared with him, the plot to kill him, the evil men and the cult.!

"They should be hunting down those evil cult members ... instead of preying on me ... Nene ... can't they see I am a crusader fighting for a just, clean society?"

"I know ... my son... I told those policemen who came that we are not thieves in our family ... but we have a rich history of fighting for justice ..."

The policemen who came with her to the farm the next morning had been instructed to keep her under full surveillance so when "Nene" set out for the farm, they followed. But if 'Nene' had any apprehensions, she didn't show it. It was unnecessary anyway as there was no sign of Onini when they got to the farm. Nothing. Everything cleaned out, and the farm house swept clean. Onini had travelled all night, a short march to Effurun from the farm in Kokori. From his concealed cover, he watched the Petroleum Tanker Garage on the new expressway to the Delta Ports all day, taking in all the details. Presently, he focused on the tanker closest to the exit gate, already cleared and parked by the road side, ready to move at dawn. It was one of those double cabin types.

When he crept in very early that morning, he had hidden under the back cabin, when the driver and his assistant came in. There was no resistance as he knocked them out, taped their mouth and feet and dumped them in the back cabin. Then he took over the steering and drove all the way through the check-points from Warri,Sapele,Benin,Ore and Ijebu-Ode to the depot in Ejigbo.

That night, he freshened up at the Petroleum Tanker Garage Rest Rooms at Ejigbo and went into town. He bought for himself a nice suit, shirts, ties and shoes to match and had a fresh,low hair cut. He also went into a cyber café ostensibly to browse. There he booked a double room on the 20th floor of the Hyatt Ikoyi Hotel. He paid online using one of his numerous aliases – Victor Smith, British Citizen and an employee of British Telecoms.

Looking resplendent in his suit and his tools of trade now neatly packed in a new suit case, he checked into the Ikoyi Hotel early that morning. With his assumed British accent, and a tired receptionist who had done an overnight shift, he slipped into the 20th floor without notice.

He set to work as soon as he checked in. With his high –powered binoculars, he scanned the palatial waterfront home of Chief Inene, head of the most successful branch of the Union, Presidential candidate of the Union Party – the UDF at the forthcoming General Elections.

All through the day, he noted movements in and out of the large compound. He studied the security details, their strength, deportment and weaponry. By 6 pm, a convoy of cars drove in and Onini knew that his wait was over. As the security man struggled to clear a path for the occupants of the big Hummer Jeep, two gentlemen in well-starched flowing traditional "Agbada" robes stepped out. Chief Inene, tired from his long campaign tour of the West stepped unto the shaded drive-way, followed immediately by Professor Usman. They made small talk as they walked in followed by hordes of aides.

Quickly, Onini called the hotel reception for a car hire; and as they drove towards Lekki, he finalised his outline attack plan.

The car dropped him in a quiet Lekki Phase I residential neighbour-hood. He paid the driver off at the gate of one of the houses and made to knock on one of the gates as the driver of the car sped off. Promptly, he crossed the street to the water front at the opposite end of the road as soon as the taxi was out of sight; and made for a thick foliage that he had identified from his earlier scanning from the hotel. Quickly, he changed into his military fatigue and packed all he would require for the operation into his haversack.

Down the lagoon waterfront where professional sand diggers make their living during the day, the night had descended on the now de-serted beach. There, he stole and boarded a dug-out canoe and pad-dled stealthily across the Lagoon to a plot next to the palatial home of Chief Inene. Chief Inene's neighbour, the expatriate Technical Director of Quest, a Unilever company was out that night at a Board Dinner. When Onini bore his way through into his compound, it was all quiet. The security guard, unarmed, was at the front of the house watching a TV programme.

Onini picked a mid-way point on the separating wall with Inene, Sprayed a special chemical on the base of the wall, in a circular fash-ion and the section disintegrated without a noise. Onini moved in and darted towards the kitchen. A shocked steward, had a pistol stuck into his ribs and was asked to lead Onini to the library where Inene and Professor Usman were having very private discussions.

When the door swung open to reveal the snub-nosed silenced pistol, the veteran in Chief Inene knew it was all over. Still, he darted forward to reach a concealed weapon in a drawer …

"Stop!" The voice was so harsh, he was stupefied. "Well … I think you should know … I am Onini … Onini Innua Bako! I know you are a criminal, a cult member … a dangerous combination that will hijack the Nigerian State, muzzle her citizens … and put the wealth of this great nation into the coffers of the Union … into private pockets. The citizens of this country deserve better. Quality education, good shelter, roads, electricity, water,social welfare benefits,welfare pecks for senior citizens and employment for the teeming youths of this country … Is that too much to ask for? That's why I must stop you! I weep for Nigeria, my country …that cannot feed and employ her youths … that has forced the youths of this country into a new wave of the trans-Atlantic slave trade … Except that this time, our youths steal, borrow, mortgage their souls to buy tickets and visas to get across the Atlantic and go into slavery in Europe and America … Can you change that …?

"Yes … Yes…" it was Professor Usman … trying to offer a plea, and as Onini's gaze was diverted, Chief Inene reached for the gun in the drawer … the .45 Browning, with the snub-nosed silencer fired two shots each at Chief Inene and Professor Usman … and it was all over.

All the newspapers received the sealed envelope the previous night and they all struggled to beat each other to the scoop: The Union Manifesto. The Tactics and Strategies of the Union how they planned to take over the political leadership of Nigeria, membership, their secret meeting places, their various front offices … the secret minutes of the Union Conclave in Kano for the UDF Party convention.

Amid reports of riots and protests across the country demanding for the prosecution of the members of the Union, many cases of suicide and hurried flights out of Nigeria were reported.

That night, it was a stunned country that received the special announcement by Captain Dan Ningi. That following the untimely death of the Head of State, General Attah earlier that evening, the Supreme Military Council had been dissolved. The announcement said all political parties and party activities had been banned; membership of secret cults was outlawed, all previous memberships to be investigated and criminals in their midst brought to justice.All identified members of secret cults found within the military and security services were dismissed and were to be dealt with most severely under the terms of the Manual of Military Law. Planned elections were cancelled and a new time-table for the return of the country to a true all-inclusive multi-party democratic government was announced;with general elections organised and supervised by the United Nations,The Commonwealth and the European Union to be held in six months .

Mr "Victor Smith" slept throughout the night on the Air France flight from Cotonou en-route Paris.

He was going through the Transfer Desk for a connecting flight to London the next morning when he saw the reports on the Coup d'etat and the other cleansing measures in Nigeria on the CNN.

EPILOGUE

Seed of man,

How like a full-grown river you are.

Torch of man

How like a clouded sky you look,

Journey of man,

How vast and overcast you are

With twilight yonder was the seed planted …

This blissful ecstasy in the elastic basin

They were brilliant,swimmimng rhythms ,

More like starch droplets

Meandering their way into the lake.

The cheerful moan.

The jittery jerk

The rhythmic ennobling shiver …

O, the joy is higher than life

Yet, even now a new life is planted.

The scattering tearaway,

The rhythmically marshalled outburst of strong muscular thrusts through the aperture …

O, now the light shines

And probes through the opening,

And now the pellets, one thrown, led to the target

By the moist and elastic channel

"Stop!" "What for? I can't"

The fishes, starchy slick and aided by the puzzle of nature swim the juicy tide aided by little hidden rivulets.

At last!

The clogs are pushed aside,

And the pinnacle of bliss bursts like a torrential besiege spontaneously... U-uh ... The seed is planted.

Seed of man,

Vague and Indefinite

Seed of man

Little and naive at inception,

Seed of man,

Unwary visitor pregnant with resolves

How famished and fanatical you plunge ...

Even as a hellish enclave eagerly waits.

Twice in its gallant struggle in the juicy abode was it made to shift and bungle clumsily – first up and next down ... a wonderful sign of things to come.

Now, a distant cry announced his arrival,

Head first and later to be disregarded.

This frail and innocent stranger stares at;

Without seeing the unwholesome convictions around, of nature and nurture

A stripling with unsymmetrical tomorrows.

To be run down the rungs in uncivil trivialities..."

"Wretch", Dost thou remind the old man of his crime? To steal under the shadows of darkness and gallantly ride the mount, without a passing query? And you, you to come in blood and tissue like a vigilant knell constantly tolling the bell for justice? Did you anticipate a grin for a diliquent act covertly laid – and now brought to the scrutiny of justice?

To be dealt fatally by this nappied bundled rebellion....

In a deception of calm and serenity and the occasional musical whinning?

O, Seed of man, how tyrannical and famish they try you so!

Journey of man, how you plummet and swindle so? Pilgrimage of man, what matchless labour to decipher ...

Voyage of man how unsymmetrical and yet encroaching you try so.

This spell bursts in rapture with traction in every direction, plotted and yet unplotted.

The travels charted with premeditation above. To concoct and rehearse every scene with thespian vigour ...A Proper Script Well Rehearsed...

To fix every preposterous riddle with unbridled calm ...

To rig arrogant and masterly panacea to every clog ... And to lubricate with Masterful Strokes, the ups and the downs of the voyage – even as several cauldrons boil under.

To flood the gate of many with abundance and the milky – honey place not afar – and whet the appetite for utopias.

A taste for money bags and a lap and bosom filled with warmth from eve's own aura.

A fancy for opiatic gulps and dwell in the abode of delight.

A place on the Throne high up on the ladder – then cut off the Rungs.

Do you desire to climb now – You? Aspirant with Lusts, Desires and Drives for Residence at the Top?

Even now that the Rungs have been Cut Off?

Now to comprehend the shifty pilgrimage and the meek philosophy in Want and Abundance … Man and Darkness are One when One is the Other … Man and the Ravaged, the Ravenous and the Rag Tag are one in Light and in Darkness if the plot of Pilgrimage Dictates.

Does it now matter with Silver and Dust, Riches and Penury if man chooses to be One with One?

So too is the Moon one with the Sun …

And Man one with them all – when Light is crucial and the subject is Vision.

Yes…there has to be One who has Aplenty;

And the other One who Lacks Abjectly;and Desires Abundantly,

Then, Only then will Plenty receive Acknowledgement.. Good Enough to Whiten a Dark Pigmentation…..

And Bold Enough to Bestride The Firmament..

"… Voyage of man, inexplicable and conclusive in judgement.

Voyage of man, Now here you come over cataracts, waterfalls, sand-bars and strong tides.

Voyage of man, now with resilient currents do you rush into the blue expanse.

The flustered and perturbed curves of your current betrays your depth of experience. Under toil have you steered and cruised leaflets, droplets, pallets – all to this destination. What carnage you testified to and the butchery slaughter of close tributaries! Now mellow and full grown, the testament of your toil are yet to be chronicled. What torment and pestilence! What badger and pester! What brute force saw you through the gauntlet? So now have you pawned all the meek and serene fragrance of juvenile times for this relic of ancient struggle?

River of life, what violent gale troubles you so!

Yes, the puzzle, the puzzle of the seed matured and manly in the tree. The puzzle of the exit through the aperture – first with the cranium. O' what puzzle! Did the eye ever testify to the ascent of a tree via the leaves or the growth of a seed first without germination? What tiny lot, its hour of arrival come round at last ever came first with its legs stretched akimbo and hoped to survive?

So too did the seed welcome the stem. And the stem eagerly called the foliage … All held in the subterranean build by giant fibrous muscles. But will the foliage call in fresh seeds? It was one stem that bred new branches which held the leaves. Yet, veined and serrated as they all are, their apexes point not to one direction. And the same nutrition it was that grew the giant umbrella Iroko and the stunted cane. Now must it be difficult to hazard a guess which leave will kiss the dust first under this violent combination of harmattan and gale.